Cellini's Revenge

THE MYSTERY OF THE SILVER CUPS

BOOK 2

What People Are Saying About
Cellini's Revenge, Book 2

"Wow! Wendy Bartlett has done really beautifully here. I read *Book 2* all in 24 hours and I was really intrigued. This book stands well. I enjoyed the whole book thoroughly, and I have to say, I think Wendy Bartlett used the therapist well. After all, Peter would have blamed Jeannie for what was wrong in his relationship."
—Terry Sheldon, UK resident

"For those lucky enough to have read Book 1 of *Cellini's Revenge: The Mystery of the Silver Cups,* Bartlett's first book of this trilogy, they will find old friends between the pages, as well as some new characters. For those who are jumping straight into Cellini's adventures with this second book, *Cellini's Revenge: Book 2,* you will be caught up in a whirlwind of characters and events that span many years and continents.

"A good mystery keeps the reader on their toes, and always has at least one major twist. This second book of this trilogy does not disappoint. *Cellini's Revenge: Book 2,* is a mystery wrapped in several mysteries. Two are solved by the end of this book. The other, which is the theme of the trilogy, is yet to be unwrapped in *Book 3.*"
—Helen Cameron, Ph.D, Higher Education Administration

"In *Cellini's Revenge, Book 2,* a centuries old curse continues to bring struggle and tragedy to this likable cast of characters. Wendy Bartlett's beautiful prose is so smooth that it's easy to forget you're holding a book and reading. Mood is embedded in each scene, drawing the reader deeper into the story and making the physicality of the characters and their trials a reality. The creative ability of the author kept this reader in awe. High tension and a talented storyteller makes this a hard-to-put-down novel."
—Jane Glendinning lives in Oakland and is one of the featured writers in Donna Kozik's *365 Days of Gratitude,* which will be released in November 2020

A fascinating and ambitious mystery that unfolds over several centuries. It is an enjoyable and engaging story–highly recommended!
—Joe Miller, writer, editor and award-winning banjo and guitar player

"When you have eliminated the impossible, whatever remains, however improbable, must be the truth."

—Sherlock Holmes

Cellini's Revenge

THE MYSTERY OF THE SILVER CUPS

BOOK 2

WENDY BARTLETT
San Francisco Writers Conference Award Winner

Kensington Hill Books
Berkeley, California

Kensington Hill Books
Berkeley, California

kensingtonhillbooks.com

Cellini's Revenge: The Mystery of the Silver Cups—Book 2
/ Wendy Bartlett
ISBN 978-1-944907-14-3 print
ISBN 978-1-944907-15-0 ebook
Library of Congress Control Number: 2020923312

This book is dedicated to my two grandsons,
Leo and Charlie

ACKNOWLEDGMENTS

First and foremost I would like to thank Laurie McLean for choosing me as the runner-up for the Fiction category in the 2007 San Francisco Writers Conference Writing Contest, which was started by two amazing, hard-working agents: Elizabeth Pomada and Michael Larsen.

I would like to acknowledge the following people for their very kind help and advice throughout the writing of *Cellini's Revenge, Book 2*: Joe Miller, the first editor of *Cellini's Revenge, Book 2* and Stefanie Reich-Silber for her sensitive editing from a British point of view. I especially want to thank Terri Sheldon for his historical British input, Leonard Pitt for his editing of the Paris chapter; Tom Gilb, Lindsey Brodie, Dean Curtis, Paul Lynch, Jane Glendinning and Beverly Tisdale for their varied and valuable input. I would especially like to thank Tyra Gilb for her excellent, sensitive artistic feedback on the colors for the three covers.

I would like to thank my writers' group for listening endlessly to this book and all my writing over many years: Dean Curtis, Joyce Scott, Marilynn Rowland, Sarita Berg, and Ruth Hanham. I would also like to thank Lindsey Brodie for her great suggestions.

I would like to thank Elizabeth Stark for her endless input along the way (and also for her suggestions regarding my blouse for my author photo), and her help with the great photographer, Angie Powers, whom I admire and thank so much for taking such an excellent and professional author photo of me and my dog, Timmy.

Last but not least, I want to thank and acknowledge the publishing guru, Ruth Schwartz, who has been a wonderful friend to work with, and who is working to finish the publication of *Cellini's Revenge, Book 3*.

CELLINI: 1512 A.D.

It was the day of their first trip to Venice when Cellini's father rowed him across the water to an island just half an hour from Venice. Here was where the gold and silversmiths worked. As a lad of twelve, he saw what he was meant to be and do in his life. In fact, he remembered his uncle casting his horoscope, predicting this enlightened moment for this very day.

Cellini's eyes pierced into the silver as the smithy magically turned it into a cross with the figure of Jesus in all his suffering. It looked laborious, but with all Cellini's bursting energy, he would relish setting his mind to this trade.

Back at home in Florence, he announced his future. Some people patted him on the back. Some laughed. But he knew.

"You'll see!" the young boy said and skipped out into the street to watch the lamplighter finishing his rounds. Cellini looked up at the silvery moon and vowed to be the best goldsmith in the whole town. Perhaps he would one day go back and become an apprentice right there on that island near Venice.

Cellini remembered how, that night, he had pulled the cover over his chest, held his young hands to his face, and imagined a small cup that he would one day cast. He thought of his horoscope for the day: Scorpio.

Then he thought of all the astrological signs and decided, just as he drifted off to sleep, that one day when he was older, he would make twelve silver cups, each one with the astrological sign and a nice little drawing of a crab or a balance or half-horse, half-man.

One morning, years later when Cellini was a young man and living in Rome, before the rooster crowed, he woke up with a feeling of a bright candle's light flashing behind his eyes. His new idea lunged into his brain again: he was ready to create his twelve, small silver cups, each with its astrological sign engraved on it. They would be an amazing gift for the wealthy d'Este family. All other tentative designs he had held in his mind fell away as this new idea opened its bud and invited the sun and the stars.

Cellini raced to his table and began sketching with his chalk: a Scorpion for Scorpio, and half-horse, half-man for Sagittarius. Lines flowed from his chalk: a lion's face, perfect for Leo, and his burnt sienna chalk flew on in order to get the idea down before his mistress woke up. Small! They would be small and portable. They would be unique in the whole world. He had never seen or heard of anything like them. He stamped his feet and laughed out loud as he stepped back from these first sketches of his new masterpiece.

"Come back to bed," mumbled his young mistress.

"I can't, my love. I have created a wonderful new design."

Cellini added one more stroke, slung his chalk across the room, dived on top of his mistress, and forgot everything else. But soon enough, his mind churned over his cups as his lips teased her, and he lunged and groaned as the birth pains of his silver, shiny cups took on a life in his mind that emboldened him with his own power and ecstasy.

"I love you, my love," he said, as the cups flew into the air, sparkling in the sunlight and landing around the young woman's head like a crown. They lay together, exhausted and calmed.

Cellini kissed the lips that seemed to be waiting for one more passionate sign of his love.

"I love you. I love everybody!" Cellini shouted as he jumped up and pulled on his pantaloons and shirt. Cellini added shading to the cups with a dark line to enliven the volume.

"They will fit into the palm of a lady's small, refined hand, these majestic cups!" He laughed from somewhere deep inside himself where he hadn't been in years and raced outdoors and peed against a tree right in plain view of anybody who might walk by!

CARUSO BINDS THE CUPS: 1527 A.D.

Cellini, as a young man, spent three years making the twelve silver cups. The final engravings of the astrological signs were the most difficult to design. After all, he was a goldsmith first and a draughtsman second. He remembered how he had scribbled from the time he could hold a feather quill pen, but he always imagined objects as something he could put his hands around, not flat like the paper he was given. As he grew, he took the paper and twisted and cut it until his drawings had become objects to hold, then he worked on it in clay.

One morning, when the cups were finally completed and before the sun had peeked over the mountains, Cellini swept into his studio and shook his helper, Caruso, awake.

"Up, man: if you're going to make it in time for your ship, you'd better get those cups bound into this box."

Cellini placed the box and the cups on the large, wooden table near the bales of hay that Caruso used for his bed.

"I really can't see much," said Caruso, yawning and blinking his eyes while he tried to widen them.

Cellini lit a candle and put it with its flickering light down on the table next to the shiny box. The silver cups sparkled next to it. Cellini, so young, so proud of his extraordinary cups, was not amazed, as were others, as to how he, himself, lived so many lives each day, yet managed to turn out these treasures even while carving his other projects.

Caruso, a quiet man, best with his hands, looked at this energetic man who hired him between voyages and could see the pride in his eyes even in the early morning darkness.

"A fine set of cups, sir!" Caruso said, leaping up from the straw. "Finest in all of Italy." The real puzzle bothering Caruso had been how he would bind Cellini's box.

"Finest ever made," bellowed Cellini, not a man of false modesty.

Caruso's wife, laboring as the sun rose on the distant farm with his young son alongside, would now be humming hymns. Caruso stood at the table and turned the cups around, peering at their unique astrological carvings. He didn't know much about astrology, but he could appreciate the delicacy needed, which only Cellini could carve out, to do the subject justice as the morning light now threw its grace upon the tiny figures of the astrological signs.

Caruso placed the cups, one inside the other, as Cellini stood by, sideways, hands on his hips, admiring his gift for the d'Este family. Caruso placed the twelve cups into the long, rectangular box, almost exactly as they had planned, and closed the lid, glancing momentarily at Cellini's face. Caruso then pulled the small, sturdy chain around the box and fastened it with the lock improvised the day before by Cellini.

Caruso had lain in his bed of straw that previous night, imagining this final christening of the cups. He didn't realize that Cellini would be standing there in a ceremonial way, watching his every move. But when it was done, Caruso held the box out to Cellini's strong, brown, rough, waiting hands, and Cellini smiled at his triumph.

Caruso tied the precious treasure securely onto the saddle of Cellini's waiting horse.

"Get away with you, man," Cellini said to Caruso as Caruso lifted his bag, slung it over his shoulder, and began his long walk to the Tiber River to hitch a boat ride to the port, beginning his second voyage crewing on an Italian galleon.

"You're always welcome here, you know that," shouted Cellini. "With all the upheavals on the horizon, I hope my studio will last. But find me whenever you return. There is always extra work to be done."

PETER, THE BOY

Storms at night brought young Peter out of their house in Rotting-dean. He had stepped outside to think about his mysterious father, from a dark, murky past where his mother, Angela Evans, hid her secrets. He always went out the back door and over the hills with a grand view of the sea in the direction of distant Brighton. The rain tapped against his umbrella as he leaned into the wind and pushed on. It was muddy, but with his tall wellies, it was just fine. It was adventure; it was freedom; it was a boy against the elements. His blue eyes penetrated the white beach cliffs and the tumbling sea.

As he trudged up along his familiar path, Peter yearned for a father he could only just imagine. He didn't require much: a hint even, a detail, the color of his hair and eyes, how he smiled, or if he had a temper. He was a ghost Peter had hunted without knowing it. Peter's father was a spark in the grocer's eyes that hit a part of Peter's stomach and knocked him sideways. It was the swagger of a dockhand, then the straightening of a pair of glasses on a proud nose, or perhaps the suit of a businessman, rushing to catch the bus into Brighton. As he made his way over the hill and through the tall grass, he remembered endlessly searching the faces of neighbors, especially the fair-haired ones with curly beards.

His mother's silence over questions about his father informed Peter that he should not ask them. Peter turned back as the rain grew heavier. His umbrella blew inside out as he made his way back down towards the house, his face dripping wet.

Safe at home from his blustery adventure, Peter lay on his bed listening to the crashing rain against the windowpane and made up his own answers. His yearning to find out about his father seemed only to deepen in the void that surrounded the subject. He turned over and fell into a deep sleep.

THE SEARCH

One day in 1960, when Peter was ten years old, he decided that he would go back to London alone to search for his father. He made a small sandwich and put it into his satchel and yelled, "'Bye, Mum!" to Mrs. Evans, who was still half asleep.

"'Bye, love. Mind the traffic!" she said quietly like she did every school morning.

Peter slung his blue school cap onto his blond hair, straightened his yellow and blue striped tie, buttoned his blazer once, grabbed his long blue and gold scarf from the coat rack, and made off down the hill. He walked down toward the sea, the bus stop, and the police hut.

"Good morning, Peter," said the policeman, Harold, as he rode by on his thick-wheeled black bike.

"Good morning, sir," Peter mumbled and nodded. He was walking the wrong direction for school. Would Harold notice? Peter dodged behind a red brick wall and peeked out to see if Harold had turned around. Harold had gone on and was just turning the corner in the distance. Peter hustled along a few more blocks toward the sound of the waves that were his daily background music. He saw Simon approaching, so he nipped behind a stone wall to hide. Simon whistled past.

The reality of his search began to penetrate his plans. He'd never been to London alone. It was much bigger than Brighton, so where should he start: walking from Victoria Station, or a bus or a tube to somewhere?

But then Peter remembered the most important fact of all: his mother and he had only moved to Rottingdean in 1957, three years previously. They had lived in Hampstead before that. His father must be from London. Peter and his mother had lived there for all his young years since he was born.

Peter sat down on the bus going towards the Brighton train station and pulled his money out of his pocket. He remembered that the nearest underground station was Belsize Park, the stop just before Hampstead. A return trip from Victoria Station to Belsize Park would be possible—just. He would go quickly by underground so he could walk around and get back home before his mother realized he had not gone to school.

He took the train from Brighton without mishap. When the train pulled into the station in London, Peter got off and followed a grey-suited, fair-haired man down the platform. There was a sense of flurry about Peter, and the noise around the hurrying crowd was much louder than at Brighton Station. Peter found himself scuttling along at the crowd's pace until he filed through the gate and was confronted with a throng of tall, short, white, brown, and black people bustling along, walking busily in all directions. Peter finally spotted the sign saying *Underground,* and he walked and wove his body through the crowd towards it. He went up to the ticket window.

"Return to Belsize Park, please," he said.

The ticket was exchanged for cash, and the bald man behind the counter delivered some coins. "Cheers, then," he said, pointing out the direction to Peter.

Peter stood on the wide escalator down into the bowels of the earth. People bumped him, said a brief, "Sorry," and sped along, not really seeming to care. Some people didn't even say, "Sorry." He got a seat on the Tube and began studying the other passengers. There were Africans, West Indians, and dark-haired people, maybe Irish, bundled in together, never looking at anybody else in the eye, standing in a way that best prevented their touching anybody, but hardly acknowledging it if they did. Everybody seemed occupied—mostly reading *The Daily Mail* or *The Times* or a novel–anything, it seemed, to keep from making eye contact. But Peter stared and searched for a fair-haired man and found it quite puzzling and difficult now.

As he studied the Tube map above the seats, Peter checked that, after he changed at Charing Cross, he was on the Northern Line going towards Belsize Park. He was thankful that his teacher had made them all study the London Underground map for homework a few months back. After Camden Town, he stood up, watched people flood off and on, and then checked the map. The next stop was Chalk Farm, and then finally Belsize Park. He had been on the train half an hour when he alighted and joined the flow of people towards the lift.

"Mind the gap," said a muffled, recorded voice as he got off the train. People hurried along to squeeze into the large cage that lifted them all endlessly up to the top of the station.

Once at the top of the station at street level, Peter copied the other passengers, slinging his ticket at the vacant booth. He found himself outside where he saw the usual little shops up and down the street: a corner bank, a large town hall, a flower stall. He was only seven the last time he was here, and he only remembered the cinema and the bus stops, though there was a memory inside him of the cold and damp, in spite of this sunny day.

Peter felt a bit of a fool. He saw so many men here who could have been his father that it became clear he had no chance of finding him this way. He would have to think of some other way. He went to a nearby tearoom next to the Belsize Park Tube Station and bought a small pot of tea and put far too much sugar into his cup. A woman wearing a dark blue headscarf sat nearby reading a book. Two men perched themselves at their table, sipping tea. Peter noticed the clock and sighed.

After Peter had finished two cups of tea, he got up and left the café, making his way up Haverstock Hill. Belsize Park and neighboring Hampstead were places that clearly Peter had few memories of–not a book, not a flower, not a street sign, not a crack in the pavement, until, at last, he saw the postman walking by on his first round down Pond Street. Peter remembered him. He remembered how this very postman used to greet him when Peter opened their door. The mail would hardly be entering the door's mail slot when young Peter would run and open it wide to see the man's dark beard and hear his crusty Irish accent.

"Top of the morning to you," the postman had said every time. Or, in the afternoon, if Peter were back home, he'd swing open the door to hear the smiling postman saying, "Afternoon, young man!" He had said it exactly like that.

Memories swarmed back, but the name of his street was still a blur. Peter put his cap on his head and dashed outside towards the postman and stood right in front of him.

At first, as Peter stood there with his knowing smile, the postman didn't seem to notice. And then, the postman said, "Top of the morning to you, young man!" and Peter puffed up like a balloon, so pleased to be remembered even though he wasn't standing at his door and even though he was inches taller and had lost his pudgy cheeks.

"'Scuse, please, sir," Peter began. "We've moved to Rottingdean, and I can't remember my old address. Could you remember it for me? Evans is our name."

"Ah, yes. 27 Pond Street, down on the right, there, past the George pub, and down the path," said the postman, pointing, then scratching his fuzzy chin. "What brings you here on a school day?" he asked with a broad wink.

"I'm going to see my father," he lied.

The postman worked his fingers along his beard; his eyes turned upwards. "Good luck, then; must be getting along. Sorry." He walked on, and Peter watched him go up the hill towards Pond Street.

As Peter walked along, he began to whistle an aria from one of his mother's records. It had no name, but Peter knew every note precisely. He kept it so quiet that he wouldn't bother people nearby. It gave him a lift as he headed up the gentle slope towards the George pub and his old home. Would he remember it? He turned the corner only to see a man coming up the path towards him dressed in a pressed suit who seemed to be in a great hurry. Peter stopped whistling and bumped the wrought iron fence around the huge Gothic church to the left, observing the preoccupied man closely.

As he passed him, Peter wanted to ask if he was his father, but the words wouldn't come. It was like there was a scent in the air that Peter could smell, so familiar and yet undecipherable, so hinting of a very old memory, but from where, he didn't have any notion—before he could speak—just a sense of a moment from the cradle or even from his birth. Peter's breath quickened. He turned and ran after that man who was checking his watch.

"'Scuse me, please, sir."

"Yes?" said the well-dressed stranger.

"Are you my . . . I mean, do you have the time?"

"Certainly," said the man. "It's 10:30 exactly. Sorry, I must dash."

"Thank you ever so," Peter said, slurping in the smell and the eyes and the sense of style that Peter hardly ever saw in Rottingdean.

Peter stood and watched as the man sped off, but as he turned the corner, he looked back at Peter for a long moment, as if he wondered again why Peter was not in school.

A memory flashed of the old police station up Haverstock Hill. Peter feared momentarily that the man was a headmaster and was going to turn back and take him by the ear to the police station for truancy.

Peter turned and quickened his pace until he stood before the tall brick house he now remembered so well. He felt the cold, painted white brick post upon which hung the iron gate. He remembered it as being very high. And now it was perfect. The gate looked stuck and unused. Peter stepped up on the one smooth step he had tripped over when he was five and then up four more steps. The crack in the bricks at his feet was still there, just as it had been when he played there with his toy trucks. The mail slot in the door was different, a shiny golden announcement of a better sort of tenant or owner now living there. Peter crept up the cement steps and admired a feeling of stability this new tenant had given the front entrance, with a Chinese umbrella stand tucked into the right-hand corner by the door, and a door knocker shaped like a lion.

"Hello?" said a gruff voice behind him.

The policeman, with his tall hat, and his hands behind his back, was standing still. Peter leapt down all five stairs and ran through the iron gate. He ran across the street, turned up the path with a last glance backwards, raced up the hill, and turned left down towards the Belsize Park Tube Station. Puffing up to the entrance, he pulled out his return ticket, showed it to the ticket collector, then went down the very long lift ride into the center of the earth, just making it onto the train platform as the train was about to depart. He kept his eyes focused on the floor for most of the ride back to Victoria Station.

Peter didn't ask anybody else if he were his father. Yet he felt as if he had accomplished his first mission in some strange way.

PETER RETURNS

"Hello, Mum," he said, puffing hard as he entered their house.

"We've been worried about you, Peter," scolded Angela, Peter's mother. "The police are out questioning the neighbors. The school is alarmed. Where have you been?"

Angela was a levelheaded person, not easily miffed. But Peter could see she might have been crying.

"I played truant today, Mum."

"Oh, Peter, how could you do that?" she said and carried on without an answer. "Right then, where did you go?"

At this point, a lie had to be told. He didn't want to worry her more than she had already been.

"I went to Brighton and hung out in all the bookshops," he said, coughing.

"Well, that sounds like you, Peter, but, whatever for? Why not go there on the weekend? And why not tell your poor, worried Mum where you're going?"

"I can't explain it. It was only on a whim. I'm looking for something. I can't find the books I want in the school library, so I thought I'd do the rounds in Brighton."

"What could be so important that you'd skip a day of school?"

For a brief second, Peter thought he would dare to tell her. But her silence on the subject for his whole life intruded and sealed his lips.

"I'm looking up some facts for our history project on Sherlock Holmes."

"What did you discover?" she asked and seemed genuinely quite interested.

"Not a lot, Mum. But I had a good day, anyway."

"I am going to forgive you this one time, Peter, but never again. It is too upsetting for everybody. Now, go have your tea and do your homework. I'll let Harold know that you're safe at home."

The following day, the sky darkened, the clouds slid across the sun, shadows evaporated, red flowers disappeared, and seagulls sat facing the ocean.

As he looked out his bedroom window, Peter wrote down a list of the people he'd seen. He stood up and looked in the small mirror on the wall. He felt his smooth chin and inspected the fuzz hardly there above his upper lip. He remembered how, as he had skimmed the stones along the ocean beyond the small ripples on the shore, he wished for a real mirror of his coming manhood and yearned for someone older than his schoolmates who might run with him on the beach–someone to inspect the colorful stones he found there, someone with deep, throaty laughter who might praise him.

Peter went to the school library during the noon break and hunted for a Sherlock Holmes novel. The librarian handed him *The Hound of the Baskervilles,* and he blushed. His mother would see it and know he had lied. But he took it out anyway and stuffed it in his satchel. When he got back home, soaking from the sudden downpour, he shed his clothes and got into his old pants, shirt, and cardigan, curled up in the armchair and began to read.

"Mum, was Sherlock Holmes a real person or just made up by Sir Arthur Conan Doyle?"

"I don't really know, Peter. I would guess it is just a story: fiction. But maybe he knew a man like that who wasn't really a detective and just made up a good story using him for a hero."

"Strange sort of hero," Peter mumbled. But in another way, Peter liked his strangeness. It made him feel better about his own questioning behavior in London. After all, a real detective has to ask thoughtful questions. Peter decided the only way to be normal was to become a detective like Sherlock Holmes, even if he never found his father.

"What's that about now, Peter?"

"Just a detective story, Mum. I'm only just starting it–seems good enough for my book report."

"Well, keep warm after all that soaking. Tomorrow, take a *brolly*. I heard it's going to rain like this for days."

Peter looked out the window at the endless grey ocean, the wind blowing the dark clouds, and the sheets of rain pounding down upon their old, wooden back deck. Then he pushed his nose into the detective story and was lost for two hours.

The next day he had a terrible cold, and his mother insisted he stay home for the day. He was thrilled. His book beckoned. In his mind, he became Sherlock: he smoked a pipe and wore the same peaked cap and dashing cape. He got to suspect liars, take fingerprints, follow people, and take notes about all of it. He got to have mysterious adventures like Peter had had only yesterday.

SHERLOCK HOLMES

Peter had the sense to see that his behavior was outside of normal expectations. Talking to perfect strangers was several notches worse than talking to their dogs! But asking personal questions without first referencing the day's weather was rude beyond imagination. Peter could hear how his mother would express her consternation if she ever found out.

"Peter," Angela said, a few days later, in a voice emitting a whole paragraph. Something was coming at him, he knew. He backed up slightly and looked out of the window. The pause between gave him a view of a seagull and the rolling clouds above the ocean. He noted that the day had turned out fine and that probably there would be showers later on when he was asleep. He turned to his mother, straight-faced.

"Yes, Mum?"

"I heard a rumor that you have been talking to strangers in a forward fashion. Is that true?"

Peter thought quickly. He didn't like to lie to his mum again. She had taught him well. And yet, here it was. His newly acquired interest in Sherlock Holmes bolstered him as he replied.

"Mum, I've been reading Sherlock Holmes again. Well, you know I have." He hesitated. It was a good beginning. He had decided that a lie had to have a lot of truth in it to be a really believable lie.

"I'm only asking them to tell me the time, and then I comment on the weather," he said. In response to his mother's look of shock, and before her inevitable question about, 'Why in the world would you do that?' Peter smiled and said he was studying accents for his school project on Sherlock Holmes.

"I've now heard Irish responses which, Mum, I find very musical. I've heard our pure Cockney, which is poetic. I've heard French." Here he glanced at this mother. He had heard French, but it had been in London.

She put her hand on her hip. "Peter, I feel you are leaving some important ingredient out. I'll never understand you. In any case, how does a French accent sound?"

Peter turned red and tried to remember the words he'd heard on the bus.

"Well," he began, "When they say, 'may I help you,' they say 'elp' without the 'h.'" Angela's silence, combined with the now crossed arms opposite him, ruffled his composure.

"Actually, I saw that at the cinema in that film I went to with John and Terry. But it's true!"

"I hope you aren't being intrusive with these people, Peter. It's the worst thing anyone can do. I don't want to hear of it again."

"My project is almost finished. I have to finish *The Hound of the Baskervilles* and review it, and then I'm finished. But I have to say, Mum, I'd like to be a detective when I grow up."

"Why's that, Peter, my love?"

"Because I'm nosy!" he laughed. She gave him a serious look, chuckled along with him, and then the subject was dropped.

Peter sat in the armchair before the window while nursing his cold and opened *The Adventures of Sherlock Holmes.* Then he put that book aside and opened *The Hound of the Baskervilles,* which he had finished. He thought of the local moors in their part of the country where he had spent hours wandering over the hills, hiding in the long grass, throwing stones over the sheep, and hiking to see expansive views of the rolling hills and the horizon at the ocean. But now that the hound was in the picture, now in his dreams, Peter hovered close to home and only ventured out to find out if there were truly hounds that big with paws like a giant and teeth like a combine harvester. His mum brought him a cup of tea. He smiled and said, "Ta, Mum," and pretended to be reading while he sorted out truth from fiction in his own life.

ANGELA

Privacy was like an old king in Rottingdean, respected not only for his age and wisdom but for the eternity of agelessness and royalty—it was an absolute. Yet gossip and whispers went with a pint or two. The village kept quiet at Angela's appearance and left her alone, but probably imagined her loneliness in quietly bringing up Peter, managing it well, not like some who ended up drinking the children's food away until the pubs closed.

Angela spread her quilts out on the sitting room floor. The flower patterns of the old war dresses were to her historical evidence of the poverty they had all shared during those lean times when cake was only something Marie Antoinette ate, where fresh food was what people who had departed to live with relatives safe in the countryside could eat.

Angela cut up a new find, a grey dress with tiny hopeful flowers that some charwoman had finally tossed away. Most of it was faded, but there were just enough squares of solid color that it was worth using. She would be holding her class again this very night and telling her enthusiastic women quilters the stories she felt were contained in each square.

Each stitch gave Angela a new feeling of peace. Each stitch erased the war that frightened her so much that every noise was a catastrophe of tension that shattered her mind. Each stitch was a journey to sanity and hope; she knew it but never spoke of it, yet gave it to the group. Their stitches brought out war stories, sadness, heroic stories, and death stories, brought out the depth of loss, poverty, despair, and hope for peace, as three stitches were overlapped in the same conclusive spot. By the end of their evening, the women wiped their tears away, rolled up their work, and trudged home in the rain, a little softer in their souls.

Despite her anxiety at taking over her legal husband, David's, house in Rottingdean, not that long after he died there, Angela found herself ready enough to move there and start a new life. She loved looking at the clouds racing across the sky. It was a spacious view, and it was freeing in some way. Even in the storms, it calmed her.

Angela had kept all the furniture–she loved the easy chair. She had added her beloved watercolors of Hampstead Heath and Hampstead High Street that she had bought at the Whitestone Pond Fair years before. She moved some of David's pictures and put her watercolors in the hallway so they would not become sun-bleached.

She missed Hampstead. She missed its anonymity, the feeling that nobody cared where or who Peter's father was. She was just one of many shopping at each shop, saying the familiar pleasantries, commenting upon the weather.

"Thank you very much," she said. "Lovely day, isn't it?" she continued.

"Bit of a drizzle today."

"Might clear up."

"Bit windy today."

"Hello, love."

"'Bye, then."

"Thank you very much."

"Thank you very much."

Here in Rottingdean, it was all the pleasantries but multiplied by the necessity of seeing more familiar faces in the same greengrocer, the same pubs, and the same haberdashery. If Angela kept to herself, it was to protect her heart from the bored nosy parkers who never quite mentioned her husband. After all, a lot of them had husbands who had died in the war. They didn't pry, but they had a small town's right to be a little friendlier. Their faces weren't strangers' faces like in Hampstead. They even said, "Hello," which opened up the possibility of further conversation, and Angela would step back an inch to subtly let them know they had come too close.

The teacher and headmaster at Peter's school thought they knew that Peter's father had died some years back, and they were observant of the silence that necessitated their further protection of Peter.

The well of loneliness that accompanied Angela was hers to protect. The words that kept her social bored her. Her secretiveness made her cry. Yet it was the only thing for it. Even when the women came to knit and quilt, they never brought it up. They were kind like that, and Angela was grateful. No one asked how she got the house. Perhaps she rented it. Perhaps she inherited it. But the murder hung like a cloud over the house—a cloud of silence.

How Long

Cricket was now Peter's favorite sport. He didn't mind waiting out in the field for the occasional ball. He enjoyed the expanse of the field, the birds flying above, the sense of movement, watching the clouds. He was frequently accused of being a daydreamer. He didn't mind. It was a fine pastime except for that time the ball hit him on the shin. At the moment it hit, he had been feeling particularly angry with Angela for avoiding the subject about who his father was. He didn't realize that he was angry until his shin stung, and he heard the laughter of some of the players, and then, "You all right, mate?" from kinder chaps.

As a thirteen-year-old, Peter had become moody, his voice crackling so badly he swore he wouldn't talk until this "stage" of growing had come and gone. At least Angela had sworn to him it would go, and he'd have a fine, pure voice an octave lower. It was interminable, and it made him angry. The only compensation was that his classmates all had the same problem. He thought he'd invent a new club called *The Crackling Voice, Red-faced, Lanky, Pimply, Short and Tall Club*. But he never did.

Peter's angry moments happened again and again. Angela got the verbal brunt of them, but Peter noticed she didn't even seem to care about it: just went about her sewing and cooking and teaching quilting, and worst of all, just saying, "Peter, go to your room and calm down a bit."

29

He preferred his own company anyway, so it was hardly a reprimand. He took up listening to Irish and English folk songs on an old radio. It was so old it crackled a lot, but it gave his nervous energy something to hold onto, and once in a while he would hum along. He liked lyrics. He liked a sad story. He liked a slightly political slant against war and for peace. World War II was constantly on the lips of people in the shops who had seen it all. A song or two drifted onto the radio even about the First World War. He listened to the news in-between the music. It was 1963. The President of the United States had been shot.

There was a song Peter loved called "Mrs. McGrath." It had a nice stomping beat. He'd heard his mum sing it once or twice. Perhaps he would take up the pennywhistle. But how stupid he would feel compared to Elvis Presley, with his soupy knees and gyrating hips. So he never asked Angela for one. A guitar was out of the question while their money was eked out on bread and milk. He dared not even ask. Once he thought he was so worthless, he felt if he died, nobody would even notice except Angela. He knew she loved him, but he thought he was also such a burden. Peter was shy and hardly had a true friend he felt he could confide in. He didn't know what to do with himself, except daydream and be helpful with the rubbish.

"Peter, come and lay the table," said Angela.

"Done it," he replied.

"Well done. You *are* growing up, Peter, aren't you?"

"Mum, how long do I have to wait to hear the truth about my father?"

"Peter, bring in the laundry from the line. There's a dear."

Peter made a face behind her back and picked up the wicker basket and went out like a robot and took down the laundry, one item at a time, each time with an angry explicative that he knew would shock his mother.

THE SILVER CUPS–
MICHAEL AND DAVID

As Michael made his way towards the underground and the bus stop, he felt jarred at talking to that young boy. In an unguarded moment, he mused that it might have been his nephew, Peter. But, of course, Peter was at school in Rottingdean, so it couldn't have been. And yet, he certainly looked like him, just a year older. It bothered Michael the whole day and more.

On his bus ride to Camden Town on the way to Holloway Prison, Michael remembered how, way back in 1956, he had gone to Rottingdean to visit his brother, David, and how when he got to the door, he saw that David had his usual self-protective stance. David obviously knew what Michael wanted to talk about. Within minutes they were at it, even before Michael was invited into David's house.

"Those are my cups!" Michael had raised his voice to David.

"Sorry, Michael, they are mine, always were," David replied calmly but sternly.

"Bloody hell, I found them!"

"*We* found them: but I saw what they were; you just pulled them out of the bag!"

"Wrong again. *I* saw what they were. I tossed the rest back. You only held the box," Michael said.

"Pathetic memory you have, always had!" David said harshly.

"*I* spotted those cups," Michael insisted.

"Sorry, mate," David was just short of yelling. "*I* was the one who saw them first. Remember, I picked up that huge bag and poked inside it and came up with the box of cups. Once I looked inside it, I remember that I could see as clear as day that they were silver."

"What a bloody awful memory you have!" Michael puffed. "I was the one who picked them up and saw that they were valuable. You were just looking at the junk in there with them. *I* said to the rag-and-bone man that he could keep all the rest."

"Not a chance. I spotted them first, and that is that! You can lie all you like, but the truth is the truth. Now be off with you and just let it be, Michael."

There was a pause that always came at this point in the argument. Realizing that David would not budge, Michael stepped back for a quick think and then stepped forward again with a change in his attitude.

"All right, then, here we are again at a stalemate. Why don't we split them, six each, until we know more?" Michael said.

"You know they won't be half as valuable if we do that. They are a set of twelve, for the twelve astrological signs."

"So we should sell them and split the money," suggested Michael. "That's fair. We've always done that–why not now?"

There was a long silence while the brothers stared at each other.

"All right . . . " David said, his face tense, ". . . for now, you take half, and I'll hold the other half until we can decide what to do. That way, neither will be foolish enough to sell them until we can find out more about them and their value. Fair enough?"

Michael nodded, his face not happy. They both walked into the kitchen, and David handed Michael a cloth bag from a kitchen shelf, lifted six of the small cups out of the box, put them in the cloth bag, and kept the box with the six remaining cups in it for himself.

"Right, then," said Michael holding the bag to his chest. "See you later."

David closed the box, and as he watched Michael walk down the hall-way and out of the house, he wondered where he could hide the cups so that Michael wouldn't find them.

The next day when David's wife, Catherine, wasn't at home, David went outside with a shovel to dig a deep hole under the back deck so he could place his box of six silver cups in it and bury them.

Deep in these memories, Michael almost forgot to get off the bus in time to go to the prison. He rang the bell and hopped off the back of the bus just before it pulled away.

AUTUMN 1956

That day, the ocean crashed headlong on a surge of waves rolling into the land, rollicking, slithering, landing–ending, while David dug deep into the earth under the deck. There was headroom even for a man his height. Michael would never guess David would actually bury them in the earth. David had had a dream, and in the dream, the cups were supposed to be buried in the earth. Here was the only earth he could be sure of. One day he would tell Michael, and one day he would tell Catherine. But right now, the cups needed to be alone in the earth where nobody could have them or use them or own them or sell them or give them away or put them up for the highest bidder. They had a right to just be.

David dug until sweat poured off his brow, until the sun was setting. He hurried. Catherine would be home soon–too soon. He wrapped the box in plastic, then lowered it into the damp ground and covered it with newspaper, then shoveled the dirt back on top of it, saying, "Farewell, my lovely treasure," as he grunted and filled in the hole, then stamped hard on top of it. He pulled clumps of weeds nearby and planted them into the dirt. It was a place nobody ever came to, so time would cover it all up nicely.

After David buried the silver cups under the deck, he went back into the house and drew a small map marked with an *X*. Then he hid the map along with some of his writings in a folder which he placed into a basket, climbed up into the attic and stored them in a far corner. That would keep Michael's hands off them. David then went into the bathroom and took a quick, hot bath, after which he made a pot of tea and set out the cups, saucers, biscuits, and jam.

"Hello, dear!" Catherine called as she always did when she entered the house and hung up her coat on the coat rack by the wide front door.

"Hello, my love," David answered. "It's going to rain soon. It's been a while. Things are drying up! Unusual for this time of year."

David thought of the ground getting wet. He wondered if the cups would settle, and the earth would sink like some graves at the cemetery did over time and when the weather shifted.

As far as Catherine knew, it was a normal afternoon and evening, this day when he'd buried the cups. Catherine sewed, then read while he wrote an article for the next day's *Daily Mail*. He read all five of his newspapers–his homework, he called it.

David continued his investigations about Benvenuto Cellini. He suspected that the Italian silver master might have had something to do with the cups. He read and wrote constantly now, typing daily on his Cellini manuscript. His trip to Italy years before had come in very handy. Soon enough, he and Catherine would be going back for their holiday, and he could find out the very last details to finish his writing. He smiled to himself, sitting in the kitchen, while he read over his manuscript once again.

THE THEFT

Benvenuto Cellini kissed his box of silver cups, checking the excellent handiwork as Caruso strapped the box onto the back of Cellini's favorite horse. These cups were such a treasure that Cellini didn't trust anybody else to deliver them. The very wealthy family d'Este was expecting him in a few days. Cellini dressed in his very best traveling finery and wore his sword, mostly to look fierce and scare the beggars away. It was all part of the grandeur and showed respect for the family, and was evidence of the value of the gift he was bringing to them personally.

Cellini kissed the young lady that lived with him at the studio, took a swig of wine, stuffed a bread loaf in each of his ample coat pockets, and mounted his fastest horse. He patted his horse's neck and guided her around in a circle, and then they galloped off for a very long journey towards the d'Este mansion and the completion of Cellini's amazing gift and its delivery.

After a while, Cellini slowed down as he rode into a small village to let his wonderful horse recover from the frantic gallop that Cellini had commanded of her in his excitement.

Suddenly, out of the bushes jumped a spry man with a sword. In one swoop, he slashed the bindings on the box of cups and, grasping it to his chest, ran back to his horse. Cellini bellowed, turning towards the man.

The thief's horse, it seemed, took fright at the noise, and the man help-lessly watched it run away, leaving him to try to outrun Cellini's horse.

Cellini galloped after the thief, gaining on the man like a lion chasing its prey, then leapt from his horse. The thief swore at his disappearing horse, tossed the bundle down, turned back, and drew his sword.

Cellini's eyes pierced into the man whose face gave his fate away: he was going to die. Their swords clanged and clashed, while sweat poured down Cellini's face. The blades struck each other like destiny had called them to do their duty. Some villagers ran away, yelling and tripping over each other.

It was just then that a little urchin picked up the box and disappeared through the yelling crowd, climbing onto his father's horse-drawn wagon. Nobody noticed them. They lumbered away as fast as they could without causing suspicion. The cups were gone from Cellini forever, as his sword now pierced the thief through the neck.

The thief was dying and bleeding, his throat gushing blood, a streak drawing the line along the direction that he was being pulled by two vil-lagers. Cellini wiped his sword across his britches, slid it into its silver sheath, and whistled for his horse.

Cellini's eyes traced the ground for the cups. They were nowhere to be seen.

"You there! Where are my cups?" he shouted at the people watching if they had seen where the cups had landed, but nobody could remember anything except the exciting fight, and they were still watching as the bloody body was being dragged away.

His horse arrived, Cellini mounted her and then charged the crowd, his eyes sharply devouring the spaces between their feet for his box of cups. He squinted as he searched the arms of the scattering people. His head twisted like a tornado, his horse prancing with its knees high as Cellini turned it first one way, then the other. Cellini galloped around and around in larger circles, inspecting every child or woman with her arms full. He re-drew his bloody sword, wiped it off again on his saddle-bag, then held it high while the remaining people shielded their heads and ran away screaming.

But Cellini saw nothing, and if he saw that old horse and cart moving towards the wharf far into the distance, it didn't occur to him that some little urchin had swept up the box and tossed it into his father's cart, that it might be in there, moving away from him as he swore at the crowd and the dying thief.

Cellini's miserable face overflowed with shock, surprise, and anger. Then, with the full realization of the loss of the masterpiece of his life, his angry face turned to fury. His cups were gone! All the years of intense work and study to get them perfect was wasted! It was a catastrophe!

Cellini kept riding around in circles like a madman. He could have cried if everybody had looked away, but they were still running from his approaching horse and flashing sword, looking back at him as if he were a wild man ready to slice off someone's head, the horse's eyes bulging to match Cellini's.

CARUSO, THE WITNESS

Cellini charged the crowd again. The labor that Cellini had put into his twelve cups wasn't just the years of their execution. His fury was not only because they had been stolen. It wasn't that he was incensed at his own natural fighting reactions that enabled someone to slither away with his prized cups. It was the originality of the idea of the twelve astrological signs on his cups that was stolen; his extraordinary conception from his own dreaming as a twelve-year-old that had now disappeared, vanished and had almost broken his heart!

"I'll make you pay," he yelled, "not only with your lives but for generations ahead—way into the future. I curse your family now and into...." Cellini made a grim face. He imagined those twelve cups, and now he could imagine not only killing the thief but also cursing him and anyone who owned the cups for generations to come. He kept chasing the people running from him, his sword in the air, yelling and screaming and swearing an oath of death to all of the thief's offspring and everyone who touched the cups until they were returned to him.

The villagers ran towards the safety of their thatch-roofed huts, watching as Cellini and his horse galloped off towards the port, the sea, and the likely merchants who might at this very moment be trading something for his treasures.

The villagers gathered in small groups by the water spigot and horse trough in the center of their tiny town and whispered. Those artists were all mad! Look at the murderer racing away on that poor, exhausted horse! They returned to see the other villagers around the dying thief who had been slain by Cellini. The thief would never rise to steal again.

The boy in the cart and his father were long gone until they heard the pounding of an exhausted, galloping horse. They hunched down and steered their horse towards the edge of the narrow, dirt road. They could see the ship in the distance. Cellini rode past them, not knowing how near his treasures were, not noticing how fast the horse was made to lumber beyond its natural capacity, not considering that there might be a reason for this poor horse's unusual hurry.

As Cellini galloped past, the father and son slowed their cart and horse. Cellini momentarily looked over his shoulder at them while his horse sped on down towards the quay, the ship, the culprit.

The old horse began pulling the cart faster again. The boy covered the box with another blanket and shifted more hay across it. The cart moved towards the galleon. Ahead was but a cloud of dirt and dust, kicked up by a maniac on a horse who cursed the world.

Cellini searched the docks and asked everybody if they had seen anybody offering a box of silver for sale. Everybody looked dull and disinterested. Nobody had been seen that looked suspicious. A galleon up ahead was preparing to depart. Cellini rode up to the ship's captain.

"No, never seen anything like that," the captain said, scratching his curly beard, with a sideways eye on his ship.

Cellini rode away as fast as he'd come while the old horse lumbered closer, pulling the old cart along the quay to that very ship's captain, who said with a smile: "Did you get them?" It was as if there had been a plan— a conspiracy.

"I did, indeed. But John might well have been slain. I want me pay now. Time we hid for a while."

The box was handed over, the contents quickly inspected, and coins were passed from one clean palm to one crusty hand.

Caruso sat astonished in the crow's nest high above this transaction. His face had a look of surprise and disbelief that he could not conceal, that people had said that nobody had seen it. And, in fact, apart from him, no one really had.

CELLINI'S PROMISE

After yelling at the busy seamen with only grunts for a response, Cellini, who had not seen what Caruso had seen, left in disgust.

Now, Cellini didn't know which way to turn—go home or go on to the d'Este family in Rivoli. Cellini knew he had to face the truth. He guided his horse in the direction of the d'Este mansion, wondering what he could possibly say to the noble d'Este family? He was exhausted. All he wanted was the glory of recognition at his immensely creative effort, and now his hands were empty, and all he could do was offer his profound apologies. Of course, he had never apologized before in his whole life!

The following day, Cellini arrived at the beautiful d'Este mansion. He dismounted, and a servant took his horse. Cellini was shown to the massive wooden and iron door. Another servant opened it, and Cellini was immediately escorted into the mansion, into a large washing room down the hallway at one side of the house. A servant took his sword, another one took his shirt, and while he waited, they were brushed and cleaned for him. He donned his shirt and placed the now clean, gleaming sword into his scabbard. He was led upstairs to the vast gilded entry hall and escorted into a large, maroon-curtained room where he waited impatiently while the master was informed of Cellini's presence.

As he walked forward to meet d'Este himself, Cellini lifted his chin and thought, after all, his cups were more like a gift, so d'Este could be disappointed, of course, but Cellini's reputation would still be saved. They greeted each other and offered pleasantries.

"Signor, I beg your pardon," Cellini reluctantly began, "I am so very sorry to say that on my way here, the twelve silver cups that I created for you were sliced away from my horse's saddle, and they have disappeared. I am utterly devastated, and so very sorry. They took so long for me to make. I am not sure I will ever have the time to try to make them again." Cellini bowed and backed away half a step.

"Ah, my friend!" d'Estes said, "I am so very sorry to hear that. Of course, you must know that I do appreciate your efforts immensely, Benvenuto Cellini, and I am most terribly sorry that now I won't be able to see your final work. I imagine it was astounding!"

"Indeed, many said the cups were astounding, Signore," replied Cellini, bowing in gratitude. "But, if I may, I would like to try to make one special silver cup for you, perhaps somewhat larger. It will take a while, as there are so many pressing orders now, but that would bring some consolation to us both, at least."

"Ah, how delightful! That would be a very treasured masterpiece, indeed. Our family thanks you with great appreciation and anticipation."

After a further brief visit, with the usual pleasantries about the weather, Cellini left and went back outside, mounted his rested horse and galloped home, still burning with anger, but also hardly able to breathe, his throat was so pinched. He had given his very soul to each small astrological sign. He had studied the books and drawings of the signs for years, it seemed, and had sculpted them perfectly. He knew he could do it again, but for now, he didn't have the will. Some things could only be done once, and that was the sad story of his cups and his devastation at their theft. He could only hope that somebody would find them and bring them back to him. Nobody else could have made them, so they would have to be delivered to him if they were ever found.

CELLINI'S CURSE

When Cellini got home, his mistress threw her arms around him to console him. But it seemed that for days Cellini had then marched around his studio in a temper and a fury that no amount of warm arms would diminish. He threw tools across the room, knocked over treasured items in progress. He swore at everybody who came within earshot.

At last, when he calmed down, he walked around to Francisco's house and told his friend that he had spoken with a wise woman: perhaps a witch. She had told him that he could make a wish that would come true, as he had been so wronged. He confided that he had already wished that whoever harbored the cups should have a tragedy in their lives that would avenge that horrible theft. The witch bit her lip, he recounted, as if to say, that is a hard punishment for some innocent person who might be given those cups or find them. So she made him think about it a little further. He told her that only the people who received them and didn't move them along to the rightful owner would befall a tragedy. She seemed to feel that was a more just vengeance that she could put into the mix.

Francisco put his arm around Cellini's shoulders and invited him to have a drink, and off they went down the road in between the scurrying townsfolk. Cellini felt avenged by this promise and his ability to get his revenge forever.

The bustle of the townsfolk was more electric than usual. There were meetings, people shouting, and galloping horses. Cellini knew he might have to leave his studio in Rome if all this disruption from the invaders kept up. He sighed and started to design his new cup in his head.

ONE CUP

Not long after the theft, the rumblings in Rome were of a nature that Cellini knew he could not stay on and stay alive. He had his assistants pack up all his models and half-finished sculptures, along with all of his tools and clay, wrapped well in wet cloth, putting everything into round barrels. He had all his furniture stacked high on two huge carts pulled by his horses, alongside many other people, all leaving on carts. Cellini was on his way towards Florence, where his father lived. The idea of making even one cup was something Cellini had to forget for the time being. Escape was the only thing to do for now.

His father had found a suitable studio for rent in Florence, not far from his own house. Cellini had his assistants unload everything and find temporary places for it all while he decided exactly where everything should be placed. His mistress came with him and helped sort everything out, making decisions about where the pots and pans would go. Everything was a mess, and it was hard to weave in and out of the items that were so necessary to Cellini's existence before they found their proper corners. Every day they all sorted and stacked and shelved. At last, it was in such a settled state that Cellini declared he might be able to start work again.

The twelve silver cups receded into a far distant place in his mind and didn't resurface until early in 1543 a.d. when he found he had a little time and much inclination to make one delightful cup for the d'Este family.

By then, Cellini was quite renowned, and one cup was as valuable a gift as all twelve were before he became so well-known and admired.

CELLINI'S BIRTHDAY

On November 3, 1956, the 456th anniversary of Cellini's birth, Michael Evans decided to find his brother, David, when Michael knew he was at home alone in Rottingdean. Once again, Michael would try to convince David to give him the other matching six silver cups.

Michael made his way by train south to Rottingdean, then watched from a distance as Catherine wandered along Rottingdean High Street buying groceries. The weather was shifting from warm to dark and stormy, and Michael knew he had to get this over and done with before Catherine got home. He trudged up the hill and knocked at the front door. David opened it.

"Hello, mate," Michael said, standing squarely in front of his brother, David.

"What are you doing here, Michael? I told you never to come here."

"Sorry, David. I made sure Catherine wasn't here."

"Snooping again, are we?"

"Please let me come in for a minute, that's all."

"Come on in then—but no tea. Just let me know why you are here when I have told you to stay away? What's wrong with meeting in the pub?"

51

"I need those cups now, and I figure they are still here someplace, David. So, why not just hand them over. You know they're mine."

"Not true," David said sternly. "You can say that all you want, but it doesn't make it true. Leave me alone. I have things to do. I am keeping those cups until I can find out exactly where they come from."

"You know they are from Italy–probably sixteenth century," continued Michael, his voice getting louder. "They look like Cellini's, but as far as we know, he never made twelve cups. So now you know. I can do research as well as you."

"You are on the right track, Michael," David said, eyeing Michael through narrowed eyes, "but it will take a lot more work to sort this thing out. I'm the one to do it, so go away and leave me be."

Michael's face was reddening. Enough of this! David was too high and mighty about all this. He needed a lesson. Michael jumped up and swung at David as David was chopping up the apples for a pie. Then David pretended to come at Michael with the knife–perhaps just to scare him, like when they were children–to get him off his back and change the subject.

But as he lunged towards Michael, David slipped on an apple peel on the floor and lost his balance and fell hard down to the floor, right onto the sharp knife. Michael didn't see the blade at first. But he was alarmed to see that David had a strange look of agony on his face, and then dark blood was oozing from under David's side.

"Oh, my God! Horrible! Horrible! David!" Michael yelled, backing away, avoiding touching him and not touching the knife. It must have punctured something vital, for David's agonized look and wide eyes made it clear that he was dying right before Michael's eyes, and then he seemed to be dead within minutes.

Michael saw the future all too well: someone would come in and think he had murdered David. He bit his lip and took one more last excruciating look, then dashed to the back door, closing it gently, guarding his fingerprints with his shirttail. He ran down the street on the other side of the hill, where it flowed downwards towards the ocean and the bus stop to the Brighton train station.

Michael was shaking as he fumbled for the change to pay the driver. He sat in the very back of the bus, agonizing over and over what had just happened. When he got to the Brighton train station, Michael jumped on the train that was just about to pull out of the station to London. He paid the collector on the train, then sat in a slump, not reading a newspaper as were all the other people, but just sitting, half-mad, staring out the window and trying not to weep.

CATHERINE ON TELEVISION

When Michael finally arrived back home in Hampstead, he tried to settle himself into looking and acting as he usually did. He walked quickly to his house, took a big breath, wiped his feet, and sauntered inside.

His wife, Janet, her multiple sclerosis pulling her body and mind down hard, was trying to get up to turn the television to the other channel. She usually left it on all day long on the BBC, but she would try to assert her own powers once in a while. She fell onto the floor as she was shaking and reaching out. Michael ran to her, picked her up gently and said, "Now, my love, you know you can't do that anymore. Please don't try it again. Pretty soon you won't be able to be left alone for very long at all; I can see that. Here you go, love, sit down, and I'll change it for you."

"I like to do it myself, Michael," she stammered.

"I know you do, my love, but look what happens when you do. Now just sit there and enjoy the programs. They're all quite good. We agreed about that. Please stop frightening me!"

"Where were you, Michael? Rosie went home an hour ago. Did you see your friend in Camden Town?"

Michael slunk back and forth across the sitting room and mulled over the day, remembering how he and David had fought as children. It was part of being brothers. It was usual, but not wielding a knife as well. Why was he even holding a knife? What did it matter?

He thought of David, lying there now, dead, and perhaps discovered by now. He turned the channel to the news on ITV, and there it was. He opened the newspaper to hide his feelings from Janet.

"But what's this?" he mumbled to himself, reading the afternoon *Evening Standard*. It was already in print! Catherine was being accused of David's murder? "No! That cannot be. That cannot happen!" he shouted.

"What's wrong," Janet looked up and asked him.

"Oh, just my horoscope again," he answered.

There it was—and there was Catherine on the television, being hustled out of the police van and into the jail.

"Oh, no!" Michael moaned.

"What, love?"

"Oh, just something silly on the telly." He switched it back to the BBC as Janet pulled up her ever-heavier head.

Michael heard a rustling at the front door and leapt up to open it. There stood his son, Geoffrey, almost seven now, with his big smile and his arms wide for a hug. His babysitter handed Geoffrey's rucksack to Michael as Michael held him firmly and then took his hand and brought him inside.

"Must be off, Michael," she said. "He's been a good boy, such a love!" and off she huddled in the drizzle.

Michael guided Geoffrey over to the settee and put him next to his mum. The two of them hugged each other as their eyes slowly steadied onto Michael's face.

"I'll just go and make our tea," Michael said, as he went into the kitchen, put the kettle on, and pulled out the bread and butter.

Michael now knew that Catherine must be in a lot of trouble. Otherwise, why would they take her away? He looked back at his son with his Down syndrome and Janet with her M.S. There was no way he could risk telling the police what had happened. If he got blamed and was sent to prison, who would look after Janet and Geoffrey? What would happen to his son and his wife? It was unthinkable. He wanted to forget it all, but he couldn't forget David lying there, and he couldn't forget what he'd just seen on television.

Michael felt sick to his stomach. The idea of eating repulsed him, but he had to go on, make their tea, and pretend that nothing had happened.

The police would come and ask him questions. He knew he had not touched the knife and had opened the back door with his cardigan sleeve and shirttail. David had opened the front door, so that was all right. His mind went round and round, going over the last possible detail he could think of. Had he leaned on the table? No, he didn't think so. What had he touched? Nothing: he wasn't there that long, and only in the kitchen. It could have been a lot worse. He wouldn't get the blame unless somebody had seen him leave by the back door. He hadn't seen anybody there. It was an accident. Catherine couldn't be blamed for that. She wasn't even there when it happened. But who knew that?

Michael walked back and forth in his sitting room, pacing like a caged lion, keeping a close eye on the news, constantly listening to the radio to follow the horrible story that was developing about Catherine. His stomach began to grind, and he ran into the bathroom and vomited.

MICHAEL, THE TALKER

Michael could hardly eat anything at all. Losing David was devastating to him, but with Catherine getting the blame, his body became uncontrollable. He kept thinking of going to the police and telling them the truth. He would get up and go to the door. After all, the police station was only a short walk away. He went by it every week, but he could never quite go up the wide stairs and walk in. Then the vision of Janet stuck in his mind, having so much trouble walking, and only getting worse every day, and then Geoffrey with his sweet smile, so helpless. It was too much. He had to think of them.

Catherine had been put in jail, but she could survive. But Janet and Geoffrey would not–could not. He knew that in his bones. He wished he were religious so he could go and be forgiven, or he wished he could even just sit in a church and pray. That was not an option. He decided he and Janet would instead visit Catherine in jail. Catherine wouldn't know who they were, as David had kept Michael a secret, but at least Catherine would know that somebody cared in a strange way and was a witness to her possible upcoming dreary, endless existence. It might give her hope. It was all he could think of to do.

Michael was a talker. He could entertain people for hours with his ability to come up with a million things to say. But in this case, he knew he could not even say one word to Catherine, or he would start up like an engine and tell her everything. Then, she would push him to confess to the authorities so she could be freed, and he couldn't do that. He just could not do that!

GRACIE

Michael felt his heart was spread thin, what with the increasing demands of his new lover, Gracie. That first time in her arms was the moment he drew the courage to continue his miserable life. It was Gracie, an ex-con herself, who strongly suggested that it was time to go back again and visit Catherine.

"I remember so well," she'd said to him, "that loneliness, that constant feeling of emptiness, knowing that nobody cared or knew what went on in that prison. A visitor would make life worth living; give a ray of 'ope. Now, you go there and give her that ray, love."

"Right, then, Gracie, I will. I'll first check my horoscope to find out the best day." He rustled through all the papers and studied his sign.

"Says here, *'Scorpio, this is the week to mend bridges. It won't be easy. You won't know they are mended. But the time is now. Do not hesitate.'* That's it then, isn't it?"

"You go there, love. I have a lot to do now, so don't you fret. Put on your best clothes. Make her feel better than a worm. Make her know she's not invisible. She may not like what you did, but one day when she's free, she'll remember your visits and might be able to forgive you some."

Peter put his clothes on as he gazed at Gracie's round hips.

"Go on, me love. It'll do you good to get out and walk, like the fine gentleman you are."

Michael looked at the woman who had saved him, surrounded by her version of antiques, and blew her a kiss.

Gracie was an anchor in many ways, giving him a shoulder and an occasional bed and not expecting much in return, except a newly purchased antique now and then and a few bills paid quietly. Of course, there was probably his story of those silver cups, which she, most likely, probably kept tidily in the back of her mind. Perhaps she mused that one day those other six cups would turn up and that one day Catherine might return to hunt for them. It had been four years now. Meanwhile, Michael knew that Gracie knew there was money to be made at Portobello Road with her sharp eye and her way of bringing an ancient-looking piece home to let him appraise it when he had the chance to visit.

MICHAEL, IN DEBT

For a long time, Michael pushed on with his regular search for antique treasures. His stash of the six silver cups haunted him. Nobody else knew of them. Janet sat in her armchair quivering, her head now bent permanently. She might remember Michael's silver cups, but she remained somewhere in her head and never mentioned them nor much else either. Her main hobby was watching television, which drove Michael out of the house at the slightest excuse.

"Going out to get pork chops, dear," he said, knowing full well there were two pork chops in the small freezer section of the fridge.

"I'm fine, Michael," she said, as usual. But he knew she was not at all fine.

Michael put on his coat, hat, and scarf and closed the door softly, admiring his new gold plated letterbox slot in the door. Perhaps he'd take the bus to Camden Town and search out his favorite antique shops.

Alighting near the Grand Union Canal and walking up the bridge's slight slant, Michael stopped to lean on the cement wall and admire the long, red and blue canal boats and the people who seemed content enough to live this slow, watery existence.

"Hello, mate!" said a voice behind him.

"Hello, then, Robert," Michael replied, trying to remember if he still owed Robert any money.

They discussed the canal boats: the bookshops, the tourists, and the weather. Finally, Robert said, "Don't suppose you have the rest of the lolly, then?"

Michael immediately dug into his pockets and produced five pounds. Robert took it with hardly a "Ta, mate," and then Michael slowly produced the final five pounds. Robert's mouth formed a contented smile.

"Hated to ask you, but the business has been a tad sluggish lately."

"No worries," Michael lied. His fortunes were falling. He was holding those six cups like his hands were soapy. If things didn't improve, he'd be forced to sell them. Without all twelve, he would incur a considerable loss. It was time to visit David's legal wife, Angela, who had inherited David's old house in Rottingdean. He could hint at it, or he could just come out and say it. They must be somewhere in her house, but where?

He took out his cigarettes and offered Robert one. "Ta, mate." They lit up and contemplated the dirty canal.

"Needs cleaning up," Robert said.

"Does, indeed." They lingered and smoked, and then, Michael said, "I'm off now. See you, mate."

Michael sauntered along the road. He needed to cover his time away from home for his trip to Rottingdean, so he wandered over to Richard's house nearby. His wife, Rosie, was always willing and available to look after Geoffrey and Janet.

"Hello, love," Rosie said.

"Hello, Rosie, love, I need to go on a day trip tomorrow—business. Could you help out again?"

"No trouble. Eight o'clock then?"

"I'd be most grateful to you. The whole day, including supper?"

"The usual, then, love."

"There are chops in the fridge."

"That'll do nicely. Cheerio, then."

"Cheerio," Michael said, "I'm very grateful to you."

Michael smiled. He had to smile anyway at this kind, elderly lady who gave him the freedom to visit Catherine upon occasion, letting Catherine know there was a witness to her incarcerated existence. He wished for a witness to his incarceration, but his wife and son had no concept of his caring. He was furniture: loved, accepted, but he felt he was not understood or appreciated.

He'd visit Catherine at Holloway Prison, as well as Peter's mum, Angela, in Rottingdean on the same day. Pity Angela had made him keep it quiet from Catherine about her moving into Catherine's own house. But he knew that no words to Catherine were the best words.

Michael glanced at his brogues, shiny and hardly worn since his grandfather's death: same size as his grandfather's. He reached down and picked one shoe up, quite tempted to cradle it like an old friend. He had fought with David over these shoes, but Michael fit them perfectly while David's feet were slightly larger, so Michael got the treasures.

Michael sat down, slipped each shoe on, tied the laces, and admired his shiny black brogues. A feeling of calm entered his body; a warm, secure feeling that came from the soles upwards, reminding him of his solid grandfather who had taken him up on his knee, telling him stories of Kublai Kahn and Marco Polo, that undoubtedly inspired the awakening Michael felt at a young age for antiques. From those tales, Michael particularly loved the stories about Chinese gold and silver from all those hundreds of years ago. Portobello Road became his haunt and his life and his good luck at finding treasures.

Michael kissed Janet goodbye and strode out the door.

Along the road towards Belsize Park Tube Station, not too far in the distance, Michael saw a schoolboy heading towards him. The boy's gait was familiar, but it couldn't be Peter, as Peter was in Rottingdean at school.

As they neared each other, the boy searched Michael's face. Michael looked down, feigning disinterest. The boy would never recognize him. But he was obviously going to ask Michael a question.

MICHAEL SEES PETER

On his way to Holloway Prison to visit Catherine, Michael walked past the Belsize Park Town Hall, past the cinema, the greengrocers, and the bank; past the bus stop and the wide pavement with people walking up and down the street, posting their letters in the round, red pillar box; the road glittering from the recent drizzle; people hurrying by in case of another drizzle, gripping their umbrellas. He wandered across the street, looked into the Belsize Bookshop window, and saw mystery books, romances, history, and political books. He walked in and browsed as he had done hundreds of times. But this time he hovered in the mystery section. He pulled out *The Hound of Baskervilles* and flipped through it, then went to the cashier and bought it. He would leave it for Peter, but anonymously.

Michael missed his nephew, Peter. He'd hardly recognized the boy. It had been too long since he had seen him, now that Angela and Peter lived in Rottingdean. Angela had her reasons for not wanting him to see Peter or visit them, but there was a yearning deep inside Michael's soul that made him spy on Peter when Peter was a boy, watching him grow up without a word of recognition from Michael. He longed to tell Peter all the stories of Peter's father, David, and Michael and David's young years together. But Angela's wishes were paramount, so he reluctantly kept his life private and quiet, granting Angela her wish.

Michael spied on Peter infrequently, maybe once a year, yearning again to tell David of his knowledge of the growing lad—but the silence of David's death was loud, louder than any fight, or punch in the eye, louder than any look of fury or growl or avarice between them. Nothing could be said, not in anger, not in sorrow, not in apologies. It was as it was—the end of a conversation between brothers; the end of a relationship, now only set in stone by the mural of their past lives together.

Over the next several days, Michael fell into a deep depression. The sight of that boy who looked like Peter right on the very street near where Michael lived shattered his composure after he had exchanged those few words, then taken that furtive glance back at the boy and walked briskly towards the underground to go to Holloway Prison.

It was nearly four years now since Catherine had gone to prison; four years of guilt pulling Michael's face down, lining it at an early age, his mouth severely held with a true "stiff upper lip."

The shock of seeing that boy close up, who might have been Peter, all these years later, haunted that bus ride to visit Catherine in jail so that tears flooded Michael's eyes right in public. If Catherine only knew the story about how David really died, and that Michael had been there and had not come forward to save her, she might die right there in prison. Silence was his only retreat. He would continue his visits, but he was afraid of his own honesty and inability to bite his tongue should he chance to glance into her eyes.

When he arrived at Holloway Prison and was shown in to see Catherine, he remembered how he stared into the mirror that morning after shaving and chosen Old Spice for his aftershave, patting his cheeks into roses that faded before he'd left the bathroom. Janet loved the scent of his shaving lotion, so he had kissed her goodbye and lingered for her slight sniff, clearly a bright moment in her day. Rosie had arrived and commented, "I do love that smell, Mr. Evans. Reminds me that the war is long over, and the little niceties of life have returned."

Michael sat before Catherine in the visiting room, his secrets about why she was there, pulling his shoulders down, crunching his lungs with remorse and guilt. He held them like that unconsciously as long as he had to remain silent with her.

PETER: PUBERTY

Walking with his usual determination, Peter pushed up the hill alongside the sparse traffic. It was late winter, and the tourists had not yet appeared. The village of Rottingdean remained sleepy and stuck in its patterns with two cups of tea in the morning and two pints of beer at night. But the rumble of voices from London almost seeped into the blood of the locals. Their incomes would increase as the volume of people arrived at the seaside, and the days grew long and light.

But today the village slumbered, just its eyes showing slightly over the covers like a baby kangaroo peeking over his pouch, to check the clouds and feel the surge of spring creeping into its veins, adding a desire to throw the blankets back and leap out of bed, but not actually doing it.

However, Peter managed to leap out of bed anyway, even though it was a Saturday, and he had stayed up late, reading Sherlock well into the Friday night before. At fourteen, Peter had a sense of freedom that he loved. He loved that Angela stayed later in bed, especially on the weekend mornings, and he could leave the house before she invented more chores for him to do. Sometimes he rode his bike. Today he walked. His voice was now breaking on the high notes as he sang to himself up the hill; pimples annoyed his chin; hair was growing in places it had never been.

Peter still felt a deep yearning to know who his father really was. Perhaps he wouldn't have cared if Angela had just come out with it. But all her secrecy made him nervous. Perhaps there was something dreadful about his father that Angela was protecting Peter from. Perhaps his father was in prison for murder. Perhaps he was a married man living in the north with a huge family who didn't want to remember a lad without a father.

All of his proper English upbringing told him to keep secrets behind closed doors, not to embarrass people with leading questions no matter how politely asked.

Peter made his way up the hill with his hands clasped behind his back. He couldn't shake it. It was like a stream of discolored blood running through his body. There was no way to hide it from himself. But there was nobody to talk to about it. He wouldn't dare tell it to his friend John or John's father, Terry. For now, Terry would be a substitute father. But down to his very bones, Peter had to know this missing part of his identity.

Peter moved away from the road over to the right to his favorite spot at the cliff. From here, he could look out over the English Channel and imagine all the ships that had arrived on their shores, warships from France hundreds of years before; ships carrying strange colorful cargo from Italy and Greece and India. It seemed from here there was another world, another possibility, another way to live even. But it stopped where his boots stood in the wet, green grass–for now–perhaps just like his father. His father must exist, must be out there somewhere: if not London, why not Italy or France? Up here in the chilly wind, anything was possible. He loved the expanse of sea stretching out before him. He felt like Sherlock, pondering his fate, his existence, and his own father, who he had sworn to himself that he would find one day.

Again, he was determined to be a detective. He turned and ran down the hill with his strong legs and full lungs and his windblown, fair hair.

PETER: A YOUNG MAN

Instead of climbing up the hill, Peter, now in his late teens, kept on walking away from the ocean. He had a definite feeling that someone was following him, and he figured if he circled around, the culprit would find himself going the wrong way. He dared not turn around: that would be rude. In any case, Peter felt he might have been mistaken and would be severely embarrassed if he turned around, and the man was just talking to someone he was following who was just behind Peter.

The clouds were forming into one of those dark, lively windswept afternoons when one ought to have been sitting by the fire and having tea. Perhaps he should turn back and get home in time for tea. Going this way, he would be late, and his mum might worry. He talked himself into turning around, cleverly looking at the ground at first so that no eye contact could be made with the person following him. When he casually looked ahead, he only saw a disappearing heel dipping into the corner pub. He walked by the pub and hesitated, then pushed the door open and looked in. It was quite empty. It had hardly opened up again in the afternoon, so that was not surprising. And yet, where had that person gone?

It began to rain, so Peter retreated, ran towards Nevill Road, and turned the corner up towards his house.

People started rushing here and there, trying to beat the downpour. He slung his scarf around his mouth, pulled his cap down over his eyes, and ran up the hill. He loved the feel of his leg muscles as they pushed him so easily upwards—it gave him a feeling of power. He could run away from anybody. He almost sprinted the whole way up the steep hill and into his front yard, but before closing the wooden gate behind him, he took a quick look back down the street and saw a man just standing there at the corner looking up the street at him—he was definitely looking right at him. Peter felt a shiver all over his body. He dashed into the house and slammed the door.

"Peter, don't slam the door! How many times do I have to tell you?"

"Sorry, Mum. Someone was following me." True, that someone was a long block away and down the hill.

"Come and have your tea and tell me all about it."

"It's started raining. I have to wash my face in hot water. Hang on." Peter went to the bathroom and ran the water for a while, then splashed the hot water around his face. It felt good and warm and clean. He noticed his new fuzzy beard begging to be shaved. He would talk to his mum about it. It was past time.

"All right, now, Peter. Who was following you?"

"I don't know, Mum; a well-dressed man, like a Londoner."

Angela stopped short. She stared at Peter. Peter studied her face.

"Probably just someone chasing butterflies, nothing to fret over, Peter. Now, have your tea and get on with your homework. Not to worry."

TEA WITH ANGELA

Meanwhile, Michael went back out into the rain. He knew he could not follow Peter all the way up to the house, and he knew he really ought to get back home. He walked quickly into the pub. A few more people had arrived as he made the call home.

"Hello?" Rosie said haltingly into the phone.

"Hello, Rosie. I am afraid I won't be able to get back tonight."

"Not tonight, then?"

"No, sorry. I was hoping you might be able to stay the night with Mrs. Evans and Geoffrey once again?"

"I daresay I could do that, love."

"I am so relieved. Thank you very much."

"All right, then, Michael. Goodbye."

"Goodbye, Rosie, and thank you again."

That accomplished, he asked the pub owner if he had a room to rent for the night. He did. All was set. In the morning, he would pop round and visit Angela. She would be upset, but he would go anyway and take the consequences.

The next morning Michael went downstairs and paid for his hotel room. He bought the morning paper from the newspaper stand, then went across the street to the workingman's café, and sat down for a hot pot of tea and a full breakfast of two eggs, bacon with little fat, two thick sausages, broiled tomatoes cut in half, toast and marmalade.

Michael loved his newspapers. They were part of his day. They were the oil that greased his engine and made the rest of the day make sense. It reminded him of David and how he devoured the papers, all of them, every morning, even reading an Italian newspaper with his Italian-English dictionary when he could find one. It certainly warmed Michael on this blustery day. He sat for a full hour and read everything he could, particularly his horoscope.

It brought back fond memories of their youth. Why did things have to change? Why did they start fighting, even as men? Alone, each one was calm and collected. Yet together, they became competitive, with a little bragging just to see who found the best antiques and got the most money from selling them.

The silver cups were the very best thing they had ever found. And now Michael only had six of them. The day he ran away from David as David bled to death on the kitchen floor, Michael still wanted to yell, "Where are they?" But he knew he had to leave very quickly. He knew he could never guess where they were; he could never understand David, really, or where he might decide to hide those other six cups.

The rain had diminished to a slight drizzle. Michael felt it was late enough that Angela would be up and dressed. He folded his newspaper under his arm, slung his scarf around his neck, and began the climb. There was no way Michael could have run up that hill at this point in his life. But it was good enough exercise for a brisk walk. When he finally got to the top, he went into Angela's nice, flat yard and walked up to the front door.

He knocked and waited. When he glanced at the side window, there she was, peeking out at him. This proved to him that Peter had seen him. She was clearly already on the defensive. Never mind. He knocked again, this time louder.

"All right, Michael," she said as she opened the door. "You are so incorrigible. I'm hardly awake! Come in out of the weather, then."

Michael wiped his shoes on the mat and walked into the familiar house.

"I was just making my tea, so you might as well have a cup," she said in a grumpy voice.

"Thank you. It'll take the cold off me." He went over to the soft chair and sat on it. Soon his tea was sitting on the coffee table in front of him.

"So, what do I have the pleasure of seeing you for now, Michael? I thought we agreed you wouldn't be stopping by anymore? We did agree, didn't we?"

"That was a long time ago. Things always change."

"Do they? What things? I didn't say you could come back, did I? And yet, here you are. I didn't change, Michael."

"Yes, but I did. I need to see you more. Things are getting really sad at home. Janet can hardly get out and about anymore. I feel like an animal in a cage. It's so difficult. Nobody else would understand. They think I just have to grin and bear it. But I need company, real people to talk to; intelligent people who have something to say."

"And that is me, or is it Peter?"

"Well, you know it's you." Michael flinched, thinking of Gracie.

"I don't know, Michael. Times are hard. Peter isn't a child anymore. He's got a girlfriend now. He wouldn't be interested in talking to you anyway, even if I said you could, and I have definitely said you cannot."

"Angela, I wish you could change just a little. I am Peter's uncle, after all. People are not the same as they once were. Rules are changing. People are more free these days and less judgmental."

"That may well be in London, Michael," said Angela, "but we still live in a small town where people gossip and judge just as they always have. You've got to realize that when you come round here. People still like to see what a single woman is up to. I can hear them right now with their gossip."

"Couldn't you come up to London now and again, Angela? Come and meet me for a drink and we could go to the cinema. You never do that down here. I know that. You live such a quiet life. You need to get out more, just as I do. How about that?"

Angela looked at Michael and sighed. Michael knew what she was thinking. But clearly, life went on, that was all. She did what she had to do to survive. She said her classes and her monthly check were what kept her alive. She didn't need to go to the cinema. She didn't care. She just needed to get Peter off to a good start. He was a good boy, almost a man, did all his homework, and had ambitions to be a detective. Meeting Michael, she said, would just make it too confusing for Peter, not to mention for her.

JEANNIE

Why they got the sixth-form girls together with the boys' school was beyond Peter. He had seen this beautiful girl around the village of Rottingdean over the years and had always watched her. She seemed to pretend that she hadn't noticed him.

This time their meeting was inevitable. They had been given lessons at his boys' school on how to act with these girls. Peter heard that the girls also had strict instructions on how to act with the boys. But it is one thing to learn it in a class full of boys and quite another when Peter could not help staring at one girl like his eyes were stuck.

The music in the hall was dance music: a waltz. Nobody was dancing. The girls hovered on one side of the hall while the boys laughed too much at their own jokes on the opposite side while sneaking glances to see if the girls might be watching.

Jeannie was standing there with her friends while the teacher announced the dances and tried to get the boys and girls dancing together. Finally, the Headmaster of the boys' school was dancing with the P.E. teacher of the girls' school. Peter thought they danced well together. It was a good idea. Everybody watched them—their smooth steps, their parallel shoulders—and their subtle smiles.

At last, Jeannie looked back at him. He took a big breath and headed across the hall in her direction. Her friends started giggling. In no uncertain terms, he offered his hand towards her, his face as serious as a man proposing, and she and he joined the physical education teacher and the Headmaster in the waltz they had all practiced for so long to prepare for this frightening day.

Soon, Peter whispered in Jeannie's ear. "My name is Peter."

"Mine's Jeannie," she answered softly.

The warmth of her body was comforting when they touched, but it wasn't often, and it wasn't a lot. It was only a hint of possibilities: a hint of a kiss, a hint of a full hug. This was being a grown-up. This was a gift from one school to the other. This was the recognition of the inevitability of things to come, families to make, children to have. But Peter only felt the heat of her breath on his neck and caught himself humming in her ear.

The Pub Garden

Even with the war years behind them, the hunger and camaraderie they all shared then remained. Peter could never buy a sweet and not offer it to friends first. No matter if there were even the smallest bite left for him, he was last to eat it. Angela had drummed it into him from before he could remember. A man in their pub never rolled a cigarette without first asking everybody there if they wanted one, and he would calmly roll as many as were needed before he finally got to his own.

In the pub's garden in the summertime, Peter learned how the men would order a round. It was unheard of to order one's own beer. When the Americans started visiting Rottingdean, they, of course, felt no remorse at ordering only for themselves. It would take a lot of gentle hints to change their ways, but the other men always included them in their own rounds. One day, possibly heavy with guilt, the American might order a round for people who had included him, and after a while, he had got the message.

Peter eyed Jeannie across the pub's garden. She was so pretty, with her brown hair in plaits and her lovely dark eyes. Her parents didn't know Peter's mother, and Peter was there with his friend, John, so Peter and Jeannie only glanced at each other with a casual flicker that no one else would notice.

Peter yearned to say something to Jeannie. There was an electrical current zapping between them while the noise of the jolly boozers clanged around them, the weather predictions, the teasing, the sports banter, the gossip, the laughter.

There was a way Jeannie brushed her fringe aside too often, almost as if she had the fringe that length just so she could spend all her time calling attention to her face. She would raise her hand to her face, alerting Peter immediately, bringing his eyes to her face, ready to read the sign language she was using. She gestured, and he resumed his normal self. She meant no harm. He was safe from the necessity to speak or respond. But she did it again. He was unnerved. He had to look at her pretty face again to see her serious look, not at him, but down somewhere, at her glass of cider or her fingers.

For Peter, this gesture meant she was a little eccentric, and he liked that. He felt he was, after all, a quiet eccentric himself. Another eccentric might forgive him for his snoopy tendencies. He'd read a paragraph or two of Freud by then, and he tried to analyze his own self. If he understood himself and his motives, how much greater a detective he would become, as he could then better understand the motives of others. At seventeen, these were his thoughts. Life was to be taken seriously. It was not all about cricket, after all. Peter wanted to delve deeper; penetrate the unknown. Here was a girl, or young woman, who was sufficiently neurotic (how he loved that term) to be of interest. By the third time she'd brushed her fringe aside, he was at attention, waiting for the moment to re-introduce himself. The expanse of garden tables and umbrellas from where he stood, holding his beer mug to his chest, feeling very adult, and where she stood, so far and yet so near, was an expanse of ocean to be challenged.

Peter nodded and stepped away from his jostling young compatriots, gripping the handle of his half-drunk pint, and moved as if swimming towards his beautiful fantasy. Did she glance at his distant approach as he tossed the sharks aside? Did she brush her hair away once again so she could see the winner and give him a medal? He took another swig of that dark bitter drink that had changed him from a boy into a man, pacing his landing, slowing as he arrived, standing beside her friend, awaiting acknowledgment, scuffing his shoes, and looking down. Finally, he looked up. Just then, as her hand gestured around the back of her head, their eyes met.

"Hello again," he said. "Still dancing?" His smile was wide enough to show his slightly bucked teeth, enough to let her know he was safe and friendly and welcoming of her positive response.

"Oh, hello," she answered with an equally amiable smile. "Peter, wasn't it?"

If words were divine, she had just said them.

THE ACCIDENT

One day Peter saw Jeannie riding her bike back towards her house. He was standing alongside his bike just ahead. She glanced at him as she rode by–past the café, the Olde Black Horse, and the greengrocer. She looked down at the cobbled road, worn smooth over the centuries.

As Jeannie neared Peter, who stood quite still, never altering his gaze, Jeannie took her eyes away from the stones under her bike's wheels, their eyes met, and she couldn't avoid a pothole in the street. Her bike shot sideways. Jeannie was tossed into the swirl of fall leaves and rolled into the oncoming traffic.

Peter threw his bike towards the stone wall and dashed to her rescue. He stopped the traffic. The blind man held up his white cane. Peter knelt and took her head in his lap and yelled at another man standing by him, "Get a doctor!"

The doctor's office was only a block away. The man turned and ran like he was in a race. Within six minutes, the doctor was puffing towards the backed-up traffic and the little crowd of people offering Peter advice.

"Move along, move along," said the doctor, his bag crashing to the ground, one hand upon her head, the other pulling out his stethoscope.

"Is she your sister?" he asked Peter.

"No, but she's my friend." Peter didn't want to be one of the people he might tell to move along.

Two people came running along with a brownish-green army stretcher, and the doctor and Peter lifted her slowly onto it and carried her to the doctor's office. She was unconscious. Peter helped the secretary telephone Jeannie's parents.

Kind people put the two bikes against the wall, and they stayed there until Peter took care of them, limping Jeannie's bike back to her house first. They let her go home in a few days. By then, Peter knew he was in love with her.

MICHAEL

Michael didn't like the idea of returning home without evidence of also making money. He cursed his brother, his mother, and his father. To be left out of the will was preposterous, but the will was foolproof: he could not fight what her clever lawyer had written down for her. David was always the favorite, always did everything the right way, always smiling, earning money, and helping the right people out. Michael knew he was just as clever as David, but he also knew that their mother loved David's father more than his own long-disappeared father.

It was true: Michael's father had been unfaithful to Michael's mum on a regular basis. It had nothing to do with Michael, though. His mother was bright enough to figure that out, but she still preferred David and David's father, and that was just that.

Michael felt that some things in life were just not fair–look at poor Peter. If Peter could only know Michael, Peter would at least have a role model for a father figure. But Angela still wondered aloud right in Michael's presence if he had actually killed David. She knew of David and Michael's animosity on certain matters, and it seemed that she always questioned if it were really an accident.

The day that Michael felt in his bones that he had met Peter passing him near Pond Street in Hampstead was the worst pain Michael ever had in his heart. To be that close to David's son and not be able to say, "Hey, young fellow, I'm your uncle. Let me take you to the café round the corner. I will tell you all about your father. He was my brother, and his name was David."

Peter would then have looked up to Michael as if he were a hero, and he would have listened with rapt attention as Michael explained how he and David would play together as young boys and how they went antique hunting from such a young age. And Michael would have taught Peter all about antiques and taken him to *The Daily Mail* offices and shown him where David had worked.

Angela most likely had not thought about that with her deep-seated secrecy about David. One day Michael promised himself that he would do all of these things for Peter.

"Hello, love," Michael said to his son, Geoffrey, giving him a hug, and then he gave Janet a kiss on her fragile cheeks.

"Hello, then," Janet said, her arm around their smiling child, just a few months older than Peter, yet years behind him mentally.

Michael thought of the chance of fate in all of this. If Janet hadn't become pregnant, he might have been married to somebody else, and he might have saved a bit of money first and been able to buy even a larger flat. As it was, it was hand-to-mouth ever since they got married, and it was only getting harder for him. The antique business was waning, and no matter how he searched and tried to sell his new acquisitions, it was getting more difficult. He had to work many more hours on a sale than he used to. The silver cups were always in the back of his mind: one day, he would have all twelve, and he could just retire, and that would be that. But David had hidden six of them somewhere in his Rottingdean house, but where, Michael could not fathom, no matter how he wondered and tried to think like he thought David would have thought.

Michael brought the tea out to the sitting room and put the sandwiches onto their plates and felt sad at the lack of decent food he was able to put on the table.

"Here, my loves, have an egg sandwich then," he said, as he always did to both Janet and Geoffrey.

They would look at it like they loved egg sandwiches–every day. Every so often, Michael produced spam or tuna fish, but the old standby was eggs, sometimes with Cheddar cheese.

Michael tastefully laid the table every time, using his antique plates and cups and saucers, and making a little food appear like it was a small party. He washed the serviettes every other day, along with all the other laundry. He ironed his trousers with a fine crease. He ironed his shirts, making sure he presented himself as a successful person. Geoffrey was turned out as if he had a mother there who could take care of him.

"There you are, my love," he said to Janet, pouring her a cup of tea. She was having more and more trouble lifting the teapot, so Michael gradually and gently took over.

And a few hours of television, Michael helped her up and to the toilet. He helped her wash her face and hands, then put her into her own bed, covered her up and kissed her forehead. Michael had left her bed long before when his snoring and her sleeplessness combined to make this compromise a necessity. And then he would hold Geoffrey's hand, take him to the toilet and wash his face and hands, give him a hug, tuck him in, read him a story, give him a kiss on his forehead, and look lovingly at his smiling little face.

Michael would then sit by the television and wonder what had happened to his life, night after night. He desperately wanted to talk to David, but he couldn't ever do that again. Some nights he drank a little too much wine and found himself asleep on the settee at two in the morning, still dressed. He would put himself to bed in the spare room, taking care of his clothes the next day once he had got Geoffrey off to school, and Rosie came to sit with Janet. Janet had not come with him to Holloway Prison to visit Catherine for a long time now. But he could still tell Janet about his visits. They were boring, as he and Catherine didn't talk, but he could tell her how Catherine looked: older and sadder.

ANGELA

Everybody in Rottingdean knew when a stranger was in their village. Somebody would be peeking out the window, checking to see where the stranger might be going. Michael had gone there that once and had risked being noticed. Although Angela had always told Michael not to visit her at her house, Michael knew she could hardly turn him away at the door without even a cup of tea.

"Hello, Michael. I thought we'd agreed not to meet here?" She opened the door wide enough and gestured his entrance.

Michael took off his hat and stepped in. He glanced at his brogues. Back at Holloway Prison, he knew that Catherine couldn't really see them while he sat there observing her drawn face. He had left her two hours before in a sorry state.

"She's worse," he said to Angela, moving into the sitting room and gazing out the window at the sea.

Angela Evans brought the tea in on an old English tea tray, poured a dash of milk into the bottom, and poured two cups of dark, black tea. She put two sugars into Michael's cup and one in her own. They sat quietly and thoughtfully.

"She's thin now, and her eyes are hollow. I wonder if she gives all her food away or exchanges it for something. Maybe it's stolen from her.

Those other prisoners look a right lot." Michael settled back in the one big comfortable chair and lit a cigarette.

"One of these days I'll stop smoking–I've cut right down–bad for my running. But it's hard to let go of. Mostly it makes Janet cough, so I try to keep it to the outside. She's in a wheelchair now."

"Sorry to hear that. Does Janet remember where you go?" Angela asked.

"Not really, or else she could fool me. No, she's got too many worries to think about where I go when her caregiver comes. Sad, really."

" Michael, I think you really can't come round anymore. This is such a small town. You're a married man!"

"And you're a married woman, in a manner of speaking!"

"Both pretty miserable about those circumstances, too. But let's not dwell on that. Peter's growing up into a tall young man. He has an inquisitive nature. He loves Sherlock Holmes, he says. Been acting strange lately."

Michael finished his second cup of tea, then stood up and walked over to the window.

"You never found any small silver cups in David's things, did you?"

"Silver cups? No. Why?"

"He was keeping them for me," Michael lied.

Angela squinted at Michael like she had heard him lie before, and perhaps she sensed a lie now. She seemed to let it drift as he walked to the door and lifted up his hat and umbrella.

"Well, Angela, always lovely to see you. Let me know if those silver cups turn up, now, won't you?"

"I will, Michael. Meanwhile, please keep to London for now."

Michael drifted away through the gate and down the hill and disappeared over the edge of the stone wall.

1968

On the way to Holloway Prison on his next visit, Michael sat in the bus yet again and admired his brogues. He remembered his old grandfather, who had given the shoes to him and had said they would bring him luck. The old man was not a superstitious type, but in this case, the few times he'd worn the shoes had brought him good fortune, and he jokingly passed it along. The shoes were hardly worn and looked quite new. Michael only wore them when he needed better luck than the day promised. Here were shoes that never went out of style.

Michael flipped through the *Daily Mail* and gnawed on his fingernails. He knew Catherine was finally being let out of prison this very day. He had remained silent for so long when visiting her that the thought of meeting her when she was free and finally speaking was impossible.

He alighted from the bus and found the brick wall across the road and opposite the front door of Holloway prison. Here he would hover and watch her exit into freedom. He would see how she looked at the sky, how she coped with all the new traffic, and how she managed her first steps into freedom. He hated himself for this behavior, but he had to witness her first moments of freedom and for his own reasons, knowing his own freedom was colored with the guilt of knowing he might have saved her if he had come forward and been less encumbered by his wife and son.

One day he would somehow help her. He had that thought firmly in his mind, but this day could not be that day. She needed time to readjust to life and find her place in the world.

Michael had found out by discrete inquiries with people in the prison who had come to know him over the years that she was to exit the prison at about two. It was almost two o'clock now. Sweat poured across his brow as he shifted in those shoes, trying to look like he wasn't particularly hiding. He checked his watch. He traced the clouds racing across the sky and leaned on his umbrella. He checked his fingernails. He nodded at a woman walking by with her sniffing, short-legged dog.

The doors opened. Out she stepped. Michael leaned back behind the brick post to the church's pathway. Did she look capable of this leap into the world? He squinted. She stepped up to the curb, watching the traffic. Was she surprised? She ran across between the packs of fighting little cars into the gaps between them, through the fresh air, away from guards and bars, into the world of choice, and over to the bus stop.

Michael took out his handkerchief and blew his nose. She was only fifteen yards from him. He kept the handkerchief over his nose and watched how she fingered the coins, creased her brow, wiped her nose with a handkerchief, shifting her weight from one foot to the other. As she began to step onto the back of the bus platform, Michael stepped out into view and paced towards the bus. He came up behind her and went up the circular back stairs of the red double-decker bus. He wanted to watch from above as she changed buses in Camden Town, but then he would carry on, remaining on the bus, and let her go. He would try to let her go. For now, he might try to let her go.

Catherine alighted after ten minutes of bumping along past the two-story brick houses. Michael turned around, a deck above her, and watched her nervous steps and her apparent bewilderment. Where would she go? He had to let her go, further and further away, as the bus pulled into the center of the one-way street and on towards central London.

Michael turned back in his seat and held his handkerchief delicately to his eyes.

Peter–Eighteen at Last

Peter was excited. Turning eighteen was special. Angela had once said that she wanted to tell him who his father was on his eighteenth birthday. Only one more day to go. It had been years since she had said it. She hadn't mentioned it at all since then, but he would ask her on the very morning right when she brought in his cup of tea before she went back to bed for a few more minutes of dreaming.

He woke up earlier than usual, and instead of waiting for his tea, he jumped up and made her a cup and brought it to her as a surprise.

"Wake up, Mum! Here's your tea."

"Oh, my love, Peter. What a lamb you are! What a surprise! You must be growing up! You must be all of eighteen now!"

She sat up, covered her shoulders with her faded pink knitted shawl, and put the tray onto her lap.

"Many happy returns of the day, Peter! Eighteen!" she said and toasted him, then drank her first sip.

After a decent interval, Peter started in.

"Mum, do you remember you were going to tell me about my father when I turned eighteen? Well, I've waited patiently, and here I am, eighteen!"

Angela's smile evaporated, and there was a heavy silence for a long minute.

"What, Mum?"

"It's nothing, Peter. I thought you might have forgotten. Why not wait until teatime?"

"Mum, I can't wait another minute. Can you imagine how it has been all these years just waiting for the moment I turned eighteen? I have been very patient; you have to grant me that!"

Angela sighed and motioned for him to take the tea tray. She got up and put her robe on, then sat back down on her bed.

"Peter, you may not like what I am going to tell you, but yes, I said I would tell you."

Peter put the tray down and sat on the armchair near her window. He folded his hands.

"Peter, I know you have always wondered who your father is. It's time for you to know, but it isn't a happy chapter in my life."

Peter sat forward slightly, hands still folded.

"His name was David…"

"Was?"

"Was—I'm afraid—he isn't alive anymore. You won't ever be able to meet him."

"Why didn't you tell me sooner so I would have been able to meet him, Mum?"

"You were almost seven years old when he died, and he and I had previously agreed to keep him a secret until you were eighteen. We didn't know he wouldn't be around at that time. I am sorry you never got to meet him."

"Who was he, Mum? You can tell me that."

"His name was David Evans." She paused to see if Peter noticed his surname.

"Evans, Mum. Of course, you were you married to him."

"Yes, I was formally married to him, but we never lived together. We agreed to live apart, and he married me to give you legitimacy, his name…"

"And to you!"

"And me."

"How did he die, then?"

"He had…a heart attack," Angela lied.

Peter sighed and lowered his head.

"I was almost seven. Was that why we moved here then?"

"This was where he and Catherine lived, Peter, but I inherited the house because I was his legal wife and his other wife was...thought to be dead."

"Here? This very house? Right here, my father lived and died?"

"I am afraid so, love. The solicitor came here with me and told me that it would be my house quite soon. That is why we have a roof over our heads and not much to worry about."

"This very house?" said Peter. "You mean I was this close to knowing something about him, and I never even knew it? You should have told me before this, Mum. It isn't fair to learn this now. Think of all the time I spent dreaming of him and who he was and meeting him one day and playing cricket with him and...."

Peter ran out of the room and up into his bedroom and slammed the door very hard. He flopped onto his bed and cried hoarsely into the bedclothes. He pounded the bed, rolled over, and stared at the ceiling. All his silly Sherlock Holmes stories he had made up to himself were so far off the mark that he was even embarrassed to think he could ever become a detective. He didn't think he would ever erase his vision of his father as a cricketer. He would eventually have to ask his mum. Maybe David played cricket anyway. And what did he do for work? Was Peter anything like his father? Did he have fair hair? Did they walk alike? Did Angela notice if their voices were similar? How could she keep it a secret from him? He hated her for this. His mind churned with dozens of questions.

What was she thinking, leaving him to try to figure it all out with so little information? That wasn't a mother's love. Not that he cared. He didn't care one wit about her now. Not a wit. She didn't care about him, obviously. He was going to stop talking to her altogether. He would go out of the house every day and leave his cup of tea cold and full. That would let her know what she had done. They say a mother loves her children. His mum evidently didn't love him, keeping all this from him. There he was, living in the very house his father had lived in and died in, and she didn't even tell him or hint to him about any of it.

Maybe even Jeannie even knew it. He truly hated everybody. They all knew about his father. How could they not? And they didn't tell him or ask him? He hated everybody.

The house was a silent as death for three whole days.

DAREDEVIL JEANNIE

Peter lumbered down the street, head down, shuffling, kicking up pebbles, and tripping on a curb. It barely three days before, as he turned eighteen, when he knew he had missed the plane, the boat, the flying machine, the giant bird, the right way, the wrong way, anyway. He just felt like a bewildered duck, waddling down the street, averting his eyes, knowing he looked ugly, not caring, caring too much. He would have spit in the street, only his mother's voice would be too loud in his head, so he imagined it, not very rebellious, no matter what he was feeling right now.

The sun just would not come out. The shadows hid. The grayness of the whole town pressed into his arms and feet. He was afraid of his own self. He felt betrayed by his mother. He felt like killing himself. Everybody was looking at him. They could tell. He tramped up and down the street, not wanting to go home, not wanting to believe life could be made tender with a nice hot cup of tea. He put his hands behind his back, looked behind him, and winced. There she was—Jeannie.

"Damn," he said, despite his mother's warnings. 'No swearing, son!'

He stole another glance. She was walking towards him. Should he hasten his step? He didn't want her to see him so glum. He wanted her to think him a hero. Fine hero! Not he! He looked up the street to the top. If he just reached it before she caught up, he could escape her gaze. She was pushing her bike, a little mist escaping her beautiful lips. This road was too steep, always slippery, moving towards winter, cobblestones matching every wall: small stones, like his heart, a heart of stone, small, round, smooth–impenetrable. Fog escaped his mouth as he trudged higher up the hill and even towards the sky. A patch of blue opened up right at the top of the road. With it came his smile, his breath–his happiness. Now he could look right at her. With that welcoming blue sky, his dour mood evaporated. He felt it strange that just with a little blue in the sky, and slightly more light on this windy day, life was now good. He stopped and waited. She came on up the hill.

"Hello," he ventured and even cracked a slight smile.

"Hello, then," she puffed, then stopped and glanced at the blue hole in the sky.

"Maybe no rain after all," he said, feeling stupid but following her eyes.

"Maybe no."

"Yes, well. Bit cold. Autumn is coming on too soon."

"Yes," she said, her beautiful, round lips widening to show her fine, white teeth. With that smile, he felt himself stand taller, almost like a soldier, at attention, amazed at the energy in such a momentary pull of muscles around her mouth. He would like to kiss her mouth. He would like to hold his hand against the back of her head and pull her face towards him and gently lay his own bursting mouth over hers and then pull her towards him, and....

"Cheerio," she said as she passed him.

He turned marginally and watched her puffing further up the street. Then she turned around, mounted her bike, and sped past him with a huge smile, too big to kiss, wide open now, too big to touch with his fingers, to stroke, to line his being with. And she was gone, smaller and smaller, down the hill. What daring! He would never have done that. She must have such courage, such inner strength. He wondered how he might get that, too. He turned away as her brakes made a horrible squeal, and she turned the corner.

When he reached his house, he parked his bike against the wall. It was his turn, so he dropped his rucksack and wheeled his bike back out to the top of the bumpy road. It was too steep. How could she have done that? How could she do it if he could not? He placed his foot on the pedal and pushed off. His throat was tight. His mouth wasn't open and smiling but rather grim and tense. His lips burned together while his head hunkered down as the hill shot up at him and his feet pushed on the brakes harder and harder, yet hardly stopping the frightening momentum. How did she do this? He pressed on. He could, and he would. And then he froze and broke out in a sweat. He jammed on his brakes again, jumped off, and saw the cascading bike churn away from him as it skidded, slipped, and cartwheeled around, crashing down another dozen feet.

Jeannie came running from around the corner; her mouth was open, but not in a smile. She looked horrified. She looked at his bike and looked up at him as he hopped away on one foot and gained his composure. His bike had survived! He ran down the rest of the hill, picked up his bike, leapt on it, and kept going.

When Peter looked up, she was gone. He was all right, and after all, that was what mattered. He didn't need a cup of tea. He might have liked sympathy, but indeed, it was better that she had left him alone to sort out how she had done it, and he could not. Perhaps it was the make of bicycle: hers was newer; everybody's was newer. She was lighter. He had to face it: she just had more courage, or was it more daredevil in her?

THE CLIFF

Peter smiled. He loved Jeannie even more and would try to ride down the hill again–but maybe not today. He wheeled his bike around the corner, and there she was. Her back was to him as she was mounting her bike, with her groceries in the basket on the front of it. He wheeled his bike around the pedestrians and followed her down the street and around the corner. Jeannie's house was up the other side. He knew exactly where she lived. His mother would not appreciate his rude behavior, but he couldn't help it. He followed at a decent gap, looking away once when she turned around. He wondered what she might be thinking, and he wondered about those lips; that smile, that daring. Maybe he just might be in love. Then there was a burning in his loins that made him turn away and ride in the other direction. He needed to ponder, but more, he needed to ride furiously. He stole around the other corner and headed out on the road towards the sea.

It felt like the bike rode him. The wind and the waves crashed against each other as he peddled, harder and harder, breathing like a dragon, like a horse with huge nostrils, like a hunted man, like a rocket to the moon. The rain began. He didn't mind. His bike would never slip again. He would never jump off it again. He would wear a crown. He would go faster than any boy ever had. He would let the whole world see a champion. All the men he rode past would see him, his muscles, his jaw, his balance, his exactitude, his absolute drive, his determination, his forward momentum–impossible to beat–impossible.

Peter reached the top of the cliff and then began his descent. As he sped down, faster and faster, his bike fell sideways and skidded under him on a muddy patch, losing its traction, falling, disappearing like a frightened dog, down the hill towards the cliff, while Peter saw the cliff shooting ominously towards him.

"No!" he yelled. But nobody was there. The rain had chased people home or into the pub. As Peter slid, terrified, to the very edge, he grabbed the tall grass in a huge clump, and it somehow held his body from flying over the cliff. He watched as his bike flew over the cliff, and he heard it crash on the rocks far below.

"Good!" he yelled. "Very good! Well, done, Peter! What a man!" he laughed. "I needed a new bike anyway," he added to the seagull above his head.

Peter looked over the cliff: the bike was broken in two–like he might have been. Ha! Muscles, daring, gritted teeth, manhood. Ha! Broken, escaping, grasping a chunk of grass. Mum would be...never mind.

He was alive. He had conquered something: fear, his love and hate for Jeannie, that daring girl who checked to see if he was all right. Of course, he was all right! Just like now. He stood up and brushed off his bloody hands. What a thrill!–a thrill that he could never have done without that energy, that amazing energy, almost to show somebody he had it–to show somebody–somebody.

"Mum," he said, dashing into the house from the rain. "Mum?" he yelled. "Mum!" he tried once more.

In the kitchen, he found a note: unusual. She hardly ever left notes. He knew she would leave his tea. Her quilting was scattered around as if she had been interrupted and had left in a hurry. But his tea was not prepared. The kettle was not even warm. He looked out the window at the storm and the gray clouds doing their best to cover the land with tears. Peter plopped down into his chair. He wouldn't mind a cup of tea; he wouldn't mind a sandwich. He looked over at the cupboard and the door of the pantry. It was open. Mum never left it open. He got up and went over to close it.

"Mum!" he yelled. He bent down and pulled her out of the pantry. "Mum," he said, his hand against her cheek, her eyes closed. "Mum?"

He pulled her up to sitting and settled her dress down over her knees. He didn't know what to do, so he patted her back quite hard. She coughed. A big breath pulled into her lungs, and she coughed like she wanted to get something out. She choked and spluttered. He patted harder. She didn't stop him. She nodded. He pounded. She choked and coughed. He hit her really hard. Out came a thimble.

"Mum!" Peter said, picking up the wet thimble.

"Sorry, love. I could hear you coming in, but I couldn't say anything. I must have just swallowed it a minute ago just after I wrote the note. I was just getting your tea...."

"Never mind my tea, Mum. Come and sit down. I will make you a cuppa."

He helped her into her chair and went to put the kettle on.

"Don't know what happened. I had the silly thimble in my mouth, and I think I hiccuped or something, and the next thing I knew, it was blocking my throat. Good thing you got home when you did, or I'd be dead by now."

She looked at his hands. "What happened to you, then, Peter? All bloody hands and such?"

"Oh, Mum, I had a little crash with my bike. I'm afraid it went over the cliff. It's broken in half."

"Oh, Peter! Poor love," she said, clearing her throat. "It's time for a new one, somehow. Glad you only have a little blood. I'd rather have a bloody son than a perfect bike, not to worry, son! And thank you for saving my life!"

PETER,
THE YOUNG DETECTIVE

Rottingdean was a quiet town with hardly any thieves remaining after they closed the tunnels used by the smuggling seafarers. Everybody went to live in London and get a proper job in an office, out of the wind and waves. Peter felt a longing so deep to find out the truth of any matter that he could not imagine sitting in an office sorting through letters and telephone messages. No, he would be the one they said, "Peter, go to Mayfair at 1 a.m. and follow a man with a checked jacket out of the Brown's Hotel. See where he goes and write it all down in your notebook, not forgetting the address and the way he walks and dresses." Now that was a job!

But it didn't work out like that in real life—not in Rottingdean at any rate. Eighteen-year-old Peter would hang out at the tiny police headquarters, such as they were, like a box standing on the street at the foot of all the roads, across from the warm pub. He would wait and wait. Meanwhile, his imagination would be spotting all sorts of people who might just do harm to someone else. Only they hardly ever did. People in Rottingdean sat indoors, reading or writing books. They read to their children on stormy nights by the fire. They mended gates, fed their cats, shopped at the butchers, nodded to their neighbors.

Being a young detective wasn't quite what Peter had imagined it would be. But his nosy tendencies could still be used on a daily basis, even though it was rather cold, and he couldn't really wear a cloak like Sherlock Holmes. But, he argued, it would get more exciting if he just stuck it out. Most of the time, he found himself yawning while waiting for something exciting to happen: women out for walks with corgis or men picking up wives from the office. It was all quite boring for him. He needed to run after a thief or charge after a murderer.

Really, if he thought about it at all, Peter might have preferred that possibility in London. It was only for six weeks' summer holiday, though, and his mum would be lonely without him coming home for tea and telling her his tales for the day. She was a pleasant audience. She didn't mind at all that he had no murders to report. In fact, she seemed quite relieved.

"What did you discover today, Peter?" she asked one rainy day right in the middle of the summer holidays.

"Not much, Mum. I learned that the chief himself drinks a lot at the pub when he's off duty. His wife left him years ago because she hated his smoking. He flirts with a married woman, but it isn't serious."

"Nice job you've got there. I dare say, though, you could use bits of that information someday in some way you would not be able to imagine right now."

Peter wondered what in the world that information would do to brighten his existence, except to keep him from being quite bored that particular day. There would have to be juicy information from other quarters the next day to keep him from falling asleep.

The next day a woman came into the small office complaining that her daughter had not come home from school as yet. Yes, she was riding her bicycle. Her name? Jeannie Worthington!

At this, Peter leapt up and went straight up to Jeannie's mother. He could smell alcohol on her breath and even had to back off slightly to be able to stand politely near her. He listened to her talking to the policeman.

"I'll find her!" he blurted.

Jeannie's mum looked at Peter. "You're her friend, aren't you?"

"Yes, I am, but it doesn't mean I can't find her. I mean, even though I know her, I could do a good job trying to find out where she's disappeared to."

The policeman wrote some things down, and Jeannie's mother signed a paper. Then Peter was told he had the assignment. He should look for her for two hours. If he didn't find any clues, he was to phone or come back and tell them what he did find. They told her mum they would find her in her pub and let her know of Peter's progress.

Peter had a smile on his face as he bundled up against the unusually chilly summer day. He was worried about Jeannie, of course–very worried. But he was also the right 'man' to go out and brave the elements and find her.

"Cheerio, sir," he said to the policeman.

"Let us know immediately if you find any information whatsoever. I know she's your age, and you are more likely to be able to find her than just about anybody. Off you go! This is a serious assignment, Peter!"

Peter couldn't help it. He saluted the policeman who gave him a wonderful smile. He wasn't Peter's father, but his smile was almost like a father's.

Peter got on his bike and started making the usual rounds and enquiries with the locals. He stopped by some school friends' houses. Nobody had seen her that day. He climbed the stairs to the top of the hill where he stood under the clouds and scanned the whole village and even down to the sea. He biked along the top of the hills on his trusty new bike, along dirt roads with fences on one side, and on pebbled roads that made his jaw chatter. He called, "Jeannie!" just in case. He biked down the hill and back to the police hut and then to the left up the hill and round to the top of the cliff. He was just turning away when he saw a red scarf in the long grass. Jeannie had a red scarf. He tossed his bike down and ran to it. Nearby, there she lay, quite still.

"Jeannie!" he yelled at her. She didn't respond. "Jeannie, wake up!" he yelled. She still didn't wake up. She was breathing. He pulled her up into his arms.

"Jeannie, my love, wake up!"

Jeannie's eyes opened slightly, then closed. Peter suddenly realized he was working and should not have been holding her like he loved her.

But nobody was looking. At least, Jeannie saw him, but nobody else did. He pulled her close to him and hugged her and cried.

"I found you! You're alive!"

Jeannie opened her eyes again.

"Of course, I'm alive. What did you think?"

"You've been missing the whole day," he spluttered, gently disengaging from her, "and everybody is ever so worried about you."

"Oh, that's fair enough. My parents were drunk since this morning, and I just spent the day away from them. I just fell asleep up here after riding all over the cliffs for miles."

Peter backed off but offered her his hands and pulled her up to a standing position. She brushed off her coat.

"Thanks for finding me, Peter. I always thought you were a special sort of person. Now I know!"

"It's my summer job. I am a detective. Well, assistant detective. But I would have looked for you forever until I found you even if I were not paid to do it."

Jeannie gave Peter a big smile and leaned down to pick up her bike. The two rode back towards the town side-by-side, ending up at the police hut to tell them she was fine.

" Don't tell my parents where I was. They don't deserve to know!" she said to the policeman. "Just say I came by."

"I have to make a report, Jeannie," he replied. "But they don't need to see it. Please don't be running off like that again. If you have trouble, go to the library if it's open and read a good mystery!"

"If it's raining, I will!"

Peter asked if he could accompany her home. The policeman said she should go right over to the pub and just let her mum know she was fine. And yes, Peter could go there with her.

They went outside, leaned their bikes against the wall, then crossed the street and went into the pub.

"Hello, Mum," she said.

"Jeannie, me love, you gave us such a fright! Where were you?"

"Not far, Mum. I just needed to get out of the house. You know why."

"All right, Jeannie. But you have to tell somebody. I don't care who it is. We need to know!"

Jeannie smiled and gave her now rather drunk mother a kiss on the cheek. Her father sat there and just grunted.

It was the end of a long day for Peter. He said goodbye to Jeannie and went home to tea to tell his mum about his exciting day.

"Well, my love," said Angela. "That was enough to keep you in the trade, wasn't it?" Angela sat stitching her quilt, which was getting to be big enough to think about stopping. It had a life of its own, though, and it would let Angela know when it was finished.

"Mum, it was so exciting! It was like in all the stories! I had to go to the top of the hill, search the cliffs, wondering if she was dead, and then I found her. What a triumph!"

"Well! Good for you, Peter. Now there's your tea waiting. You can go to Brighton tomorrow if you'd like. Just let me know, so I won't worry."

Peter thought of Jeannie. He would ask her to the cinema the next day.

PETER, THE MAN

The music blared into Peter's dream; classical, as always: violins, cellos, staccato, repeating and repeating; high notes, low notes; confidence in the stroke of the bow, all together, the baton keeping them together.

Peter struggled out of bed, his head hurting. The night before, after he gathered himself together, he had gone to the pub and tried some beer in the garden. He got it from John's father, Terry. John was there. Peter and John were both men now, weren't they? It was a bonding moment with John, his father, and Peter. Peter drank too much in spite of himself. He jumped out of bed and dashed down the hallway into the bathroom, where he vomited into the sink.

Peter moaned and wiped his chin. He didn't regret a moment of that bonding. Terry was like a father figure to Peter, and if it meant vomiting in the morning, he would do it: for a while, at least. The idea of beer right now was sickening to Peter. He wouldn't do it again tonight; that was definite. It was Saturday, and he could get away with it this time. This night he would invite Jeannie to the cinema. He didn't know what was playing, but he figured he wouldn't see much of whatever it was anyway. He went round to her house when he felt better later on in the day.

"Come in, Peter! Have a cup of tea," Jeannie's mother said.

113

"I was just thinking I might go to the cinema," Peter stammered.

"Sounds like a good idea in this weather," Jeannie said, and she didn't appear to be curious about exactly what was playing, either!

Later that evening, Peter came by again and met Jeannie. When they left, their hands remained straight down by their sides, but when they turned the corner, Peter slid his hand into hers. She held his warmly. They gazed at the sky full of stars as they ambled down the hill to the bus stop on their way to the cinema in Brighton. And, there, in the cinema, sitting so close, he slid his arm around her. Who cared what was playing?

A week later, they went to the movies again, and after the film was over, they strolled along the streets of Brighton. Suddenly Peter turned to Jeannie and said, "I know we are too young, Jeannie, but I feel like one day we'll be married." He wasn't even feeling shy when he said it. It was more like–just the truth. Jeannie turned to him and giggled, but then she placed a big kiss on his cheek even if that woman standing near them at the bus stop was making noises about doing things in public.

From that day onwards, Peter was a man–and a happy man. He knew his future, his wife-to-be, and the mother of his children. He knew everything; he walked taller; he smiled more; he breathed deeply, and he loved just about everybody.

"When?" he said to Jeannie later.

"When?" she answered.

"When! You know what! When should we tell our parents?"

Jeannie giggled and said, "In six months."

Peter turned to face her and offered her his hand. They hugged briefly, then turned and walked towards their school bus stop. Jeannie smiled, and Peter grinned, hoping his smile was like a butterfly kissing her forehead.

THE CINEMA

Peter went round to Jeannie's, but nobody answered the door, so he went back to the pub. Her mum and dad were there. Jeannie had left an hour before, they mumbled. Where had she gone? Brighton? On her bike?

"'Course not!"

Peter parked his bike where he saw hers parked against the wall of the pub and hopped onto the bus to Brighton. He wouldn't find her, he was sure, but he had a better chance if he went to Brighton than if he just stayed home. The bus ride seemed interminable, but he jumped out as soon as he was within walking distance of the cinema. He charged up and down the hills, his bright young detective eye flashing left and right, looking for a red scarf. He went to the cinema and asked them if she had bought a ticket. No. He scanned the street up and down and across. People everywhere, laughing and smoking, walking, holding shopping bags for the new clothes they purchased. He was just about to buy one ticket when he saw her moving quickly in his direction.

"Jeannie!" he yelled.

"Peter! What on earth are you doing here?"

"Mum said I should go to the cinema. I tried to find you, but anyway, here you are!"

"Yes. I was just going to the cinema."

"May I pay for your ticket?" he asked.

"You needn't do that, Peter. We're friends, aren't we?"

Peter felt like they were more than friends as he looked at the nape of her neck.

"Just this once, then," he said shyly.

"Well, all right, Peter."

Peter bought popcorn again. They sat side-by-side. All Peter could think of again was her knee so close to his. The lights dimmed, and the film began.

Peter slid his arm around her cautiously, but he didn't dare touch her shoulder. He tried to seem casual, but his heart was racing madly. Peter hardly saw any of the film and couldn't possibly tell anybody what the title was. All he could think of was Jeannie's neck and her breasts, which he hadn't truly noticed that much until he saw just how the light from the film made them seem so round and soft when he stole a glance at her.

Peter wanted to kiss her on her lips as he had so often imagined, right here in this very cinema. He stole a glance at her lips, her laughter: her eyelashes. Did she lean into him ever so slightly? Did he lean towards her without even breathing? Did they finally touch lightly, like the wind blowing gently into their ears? Was that all? No passionate kisses? Just dreams?

"Good flick," he said casually as they were coming out of the cinema, hardly remembering a thing about it.

"Not bad. Next week's is better," she answered.

Peter smiled to himself. He could invite her and get another chance at that promising kiss.

"Shall we go together next week, then?" he asked.

"I wouldn't mind," she answered with a sweet smile that made him fade into the sky.

They made their way back to Rottingdean without stopping for a drink. Neither could afford it, and neither would put the other on the spot, so it wasn't even a topic to be discussed.

The next week, same day, they met this time right at Jeannie's house. Her mum was already at the pub, and Jeannie said she was getting fish and chips down the hill on their way. Peter had already had crumpets and tea, served by Angela, but he said he hadn't had time for a proper tea.

"I could have fish and chips with you, then."

They were early and sat together, pouring salt onto the fried fish and vinegar all over the chips. Peter dug into the fish like he was starving, but he was only starving for her lips as he watched her chew her chips.

"Mmmmm," she said.

"Mmmmm," he said back.

That was the sole content of their conversation, but it was just fine.

At the cinema this time, Peter put his arm around her right from the beginning, and since they had already eaten, he didn't buy popcorn. After all, he had said only this once. But he paid for her ticket this time, anyway.

Peter couldn't remember the name of the film, or the actors or the subject matter. Her neck was positively pulling his lips to it. He adjusted his posture so that he could look directly at her. She seemed to adjust hers so that she could see him better too. He leaned over, cocked his head, and felt his lips upon her lovely, warm neck, ever so lightly. He felt her shiver and turn her head and her shoulder in such a way as to indicate she was ticklish. But she let him do it again and again. Finally, he put his hand up to her cheek and directed her mouth straight on towards his. He kissed her so lightly that she kissed him back, but harder, turning the direction of their encounter towards something like the passion he had anticipated in his dreams.

Before he realized what he was doing, his tongue was again licking the outside of her lower lip, which protruded ever so slightly, as if asking politely for entrance. She gently opened her mouth, his tongue slipping inside, reaching for hers. Like two tiny children, they played with the tips of each other's tongues, two children meeting for the first time. It was like making eyes shyly, only with their tongues. It was an exploration, a greeting: a passion.

It was only when she put her arm on Peter's shoulder that it turned into that passion and urgency he felt in his dreams. He grasped both of her hands and pulled himself towards her so that he could feel her breasts on his chest so that he could imagine and wish their clothes were gone and only their skin was touching and rubbing and hot against each other.

When the lights came up, Jeannie wiped her mouth with her handkerchief and looked away from Peter. He took the opportunity to wipe his mouth with his handkerchief and cleared his throat, and they both got up, pretending that nothing at all had changed. There was not one moment of doubt which route they each would take the next time they were so close they could smell each other's breath.

The next week they told her mother they were going to the cinema again. It happened to be the same film, but that didn't bother them. Instead, they went up to the cliff where nobody was around at all. Jeannie lay down in the grass, and Peter looked into her eyes as if he was speaking volumes, and then he kissed her mouth gently. She flung her arms around him and pulled his whole body onto hers. He moved so that he was lying on her leg. They were both panting uncontrollably by now, and he was mounting her entire body so that he could rub somewhere better—and he did. He could feel that passion that he had dreamed about so many times screaming to a height that almost hurt him.

Peter gently slipped his hand under her skirt and pushed it up and down her inside leg. She didn't stop him. To his surprise, she was panting as if to encourage him in the direction that this whole moment was taking them.

Peter turned to see if anybody was nearby, but nobody was anywhere around. He needed to press into her, to let her know how much he loved her and how much he had loved her in his dreams for so very long. He found what he wanted, entered her, and then, after a long pause, he yelled and lost control completely. He saw only her mouth, open and loud, too. This was his dream, the one he had practiced for years, and he collapsed onto her soft breasts and breathed hot air into her neck and stayed there, so warm, against all warnings, and never wanted to move away from her, ever again.

PARIS–SUMMER 1968

Paris called to Peter when he was eighteen, like a mother or a father calling to its child. Jeannie wasn't hard to convince, and they both took off for the ferry with light, summer hearts and visions of museums and Impressionist paintings, to a place to practice their French, albeit haltingly, and to find out what all the fuss was about with the rioting students.

It would be a weekend of discovery. They packed their rucksacks with toothbrushes, hairbrushes, toothpaste, underwear, scarves, umbrellas, cardigans, shorts, flashlights, matches, and handkerchiefs. It was amazing how much could fit into one rucksack.

Angela wasn't happy about it, but she remembered how she had wanted to go abroad and help clean up after the Second World War in some way. She even wanted to help in London, but soon she was pregnant, and that was the end of her dream. So she had given Peter and Jeannie a hot cup of tea, wished them well, and said to stay away from trouble. Of course, they were aiming right for the trouble. But Angela knew she had to say that. Maybe she thought Peter would remember it as he got nearer and nearer the tear gas and hoses and saw what happened to brave young people who knew all the answers to all the questions.

Jeannie's mother said, "You be careful, now. And learn some of that French while you're there!" She was fairly civilized when she wasn't tipsy. She meant well. Even Jeannie's dad meant well, giving her a big teary hug as Jeannie heaved her rucksack onto her back and left the house with Peter. Her parents had closed the door and probably went back to fighting. Jeannie said it was almost like they liked it because nobody got killed!

Jeannie got horribly seasick on the rough seas across the Channel. Peter kept his eyes on the horizon to calm his stomach while he held Jeannie's brow. Strikes were threatened in London for the next morning on all the buses and trains. They were glad they could get to Paris before that happened!

They found the youth hostel on Rue des Barres, close to the center of Paris and signed in. Jeannie stayed in the girls' section, and Peter plopped his rucksack down on the bed in the boys' section.

Neither was particularly political, and yet, being young, they were drawn to the student protests near the Sorbonne. It seemed there were protests around the world that summer against the war in Vietnam. Too many people were dying, Americans, in particular, but everybody else too. There was no sense to it, and if the American and other governments were not going to realize it, the young, who were next in line to die, took it into their own hands and let the world know they were finished with it.

They met up at the local café, Chez Mademoiselle, and had a truly French cup of coffee in a bowl and listened to people talking nervously about the trouble. American tourists huddled and talked. But they looked rather dirty and wore turtle necked shirts. Perhaps they were also students? A sound like a shot was heard in the distance. Peter looked up and saw a crowd of people charging down the boulevard in their direction. They looked mostly like young people—like students. He jumped up and grabbed Jeannie's hand. He didn't know if he should be running towards them or running away from them. But Jeannie pulled him towards the crowd in her usual fearless way.

"Let's go. They're there. We have to join them—swell the ranks."

Peter had never heard Jeannie talk like that and was amused, if not a little shocked. She must have been reading the *Morning Star* or something like that. He followed her, remembering his mother's plea, but the adrenaline was pumping. He ran straight for the crowd, joining it with Jeannie, and began shouting in French. Then they sang *The International*–only in French. At last Jeannie and Peter could practice their French! They were swept along in the crowd of men and women wearing black and navy blue turtleneck shirts.

A massive blast of teargas hit the crowd, and they all scattered. Peter pulled Jeannie over to a side street, both of them coughing, covering their mouths and noses as best they could while they ran. As soon as the gas dissipated, they all ran back into formation and shouted even louder.

Now the hoses burst water into the crowd. Jeannie and Peter found themselves right in the front line and were sprayed so hard that they fell down, pushed aside as the police came towards them. Peter saw a policeman grab Jeannie's arm and before he knew it, Peter was rushed towards him and rammed into his back so that the policeman shot away and let go of Jeannie's arm. Peter and Jeannie took off running in the middle of the crowd, yelling and managing to disappear by the time the policeman jumped up to run after them.

They ran down a street with a small group of people to recover themselves, and Peter wanted to see if Jeannie was injured.

"No, a scratch, that's all," she said. Peter grabbed her arm in the exact same place.

"Ouch, Peter! That hurts!"

"Thought so," he said. "Let's have a look."

"Don't be silly, Peter. It's really nothing at all. Just please don't grab my arm on that side for now!"

"No heroics, now, Jeannie!"

"No heroics–and also no fussing!"

Peter smiled at his brave friend and grabbed her hand. They looked at each other's faces and nodded and ran back into the crowd, which had moved another block along the boulevard. The fighting and yelling was only getting louder. People were being thrown into paddy wagons and taken away. Peter didn't fancy a night in jail. He pulled Jeannie aside to avoid the center of the chaos.

"What's going on, Peter? Let's go over there."

"I think we're fine right here, Jeannie. I don't want to learn to speak French in prison. Do you?"

"Why not? It's exciting!"

"Not I, Jeannie. I think we can be just as effective as witnesses as we can by being thrown in jail."

The ruckus was getting fiercer. Water was everywhere. More policemen arrived and were dragging students into their vans. Peter grabbed Jeannie's arm where it hurt, and dragged her away as she screamed, "Peter, let me go! That hurts." He held on and ran, pulling her away from an approaching pair of angry police officers.

Peter and Jeannie turned a corner and stopped, both panting hard, and Peter put his arm around her shoulders, encouraging her to move further away from the turmoil. She didn't seem happy, but perhaps the sight of those two policemen made it all a reality, and the idea of sitting in a café became marginally more appealing than sitting in a jail swearing in French.

They hurried back to the youth hostel and changed into dry clothes. They met outside again within half-an-hour, and after a light supper of spaghetti and another coffee, walked back in the direction of the demonstrations. Along the way, Peter's eyes caught sight of a French afternoon newspaper and a photograph on the front. There was Jeannie, being pulled up from the ground, the hose blasting her along, and there was Peter, crashing into the shoulder of the policeman who was sent flying. And there was another photograph of the two of them making a dash for it, with two policemen in pursuit.

Peter was shocked. What if his mother saw these photos in the paper or on television? He looked at Jeannie, who was looking at them as well, and knew she understood.

"Tomorrow we'll go to the *Musée d'Or*. Then back on the ferry. I know your mum would have a right fit if she ever saw these photos."

"I've got to telephone her now, so she won't worry herself silly." They found a public phone, gathered all the sous they could find in their pockets, and made a quick call.

"Mum, it's me," said Peter. "Everything's fine. We are going to the museum tomorrow and then coming home on the ferry. Not to worry!" He hoped the train was still running to the ferry.

"Peter, it sounds horrible there. I hope you aren't anywhere near all that fighting. Take care, love. See you tomorrow then."

"She didn't see them, yet!" he said to Jeannie.

"All right. Are we going back in now?"

Peter was amazed at this new person he was seeing in Jeannie. "Jeannie, can we just hang around the edges? I think we've done enough for one day!"

"Oh, come on, Peter. Really! Nobody will know!"

"Not likely, Jeannie," Peter said, and took her arm firmly and pulled her away from the fighting, while she leaned back towards the action like a sail in the wind, letting him pull her away like a stubborn child.

"All right then." She jerked her arm away and added, "But let's go and watch it all from the Eiffel Tower!"

First, they bought ice cream and wandered around underneath the huge Eiffel Tower and over to the Seine, then they got on the lift to the top of the tower. Far below, the city spread out around them and became smaller and smaller. In one section near the Sorbonne, they could see sparks flying, but they couldn't hear the shouting anymore. They saw the hoses, the vans, and the crowd surging and running. Peter felt guilty, watching from afar. But he told Jeannie he also felt a small part of this history, just to see her smile.

The next day, after a brief visit to the museum, they ran for the train, tossing their rucksacks aboard and leaping on it as it pulled obediently out of la Gare du Nord train station towards the coast and then on to the ferry home.

As she leaned over the rail of the ferry, Jeannie kept singing Irish songs as the wind blew her hair like it was on fire.

"Oh, Mrs. McGrath, the sergeant said,
"Would you like to make a soldier
"Out of your son, Ted...,"

A GREAT FATHER

Paris had become a misty past. All Peter could think about was Jeannie, lively person that she was. Every day he felt his love growing deeper for her. Some weeks later, he met her at the cliffs, and they went for a bike ride, pushing against the strong wind. When they stopped and tossed their bikes into the tall, swaying grass beside the path, they plunged down the gentle slope together, rolling and giggling in an embrace.

"Peter, there's something we need to talk about."

Peter couldn't imagine what she looked so concerned about, but he felt sure it would have something to do with her father and his drinking problems that nobody mentioned.

"What is it, my love?"

"Here. Feel here," she said, taking his hand and putting it on her belly, which was not as flat as it used to be.

At first he had no idea what she was indicating, but then he took his eyes from their hands and looked at her face. She nodded.

"Oh, my God! Jeannie!" Peter said.

There was a long silence. "Oh, my God" might have sounded like, "how horrible!" It could have meant, "Fantastic!" But whatever it meant, Peter could see that he needed to say a little more. Peter noticed Jeannie studying his face as he tried to come up with some more words. He was, after all, not even nineteen. So she couldn't be pregnant. But she could. He remembered now, that very first time, that passion, his inability to hold back, as he knew he ought to have done.

"So," he began. He paused. Her eyes pierced his own. Thoughts raced through his head. Escape! Run! Abortion! This can't be true!

"So, Jeannie, my love: are we going to be parents at this young age? Is that what you are telling me?" He looked down at her hand covering his.

She nodded with a little smile.

"Oh, my God! Jeannie!" he said, with quite a bit more gusto. They hugged and kissed and hugged again, then laughed and flung themselves onto their backs spreadeagled to look at the clouds racing across the sky.

Peter sat up and then leaned down close to Jeannie's face. There was another long silence like he was trying to say one thing, and another came out.

"When is it due?"

"In about six months, I think. That isn't long to get things in order, like, you know…of course, there are ways…to…"

"Stop it, Jeannie, don't even think about it for a moment. We'll get married right away. I love you, and I know you love me, and that's all there is to it. We knew we would get married, just not quite this soon. Your mum will be relieved, and my mum knows how I feel about you. I'm not going to college, except maybe a few evening classes, so I can almost support us. We won't have much, but we will manage, won't we, my love?"

"Peter! What a father you'll make! What a great father!"

Peter had wondered how he could ever make a great father without having a proper father himself, but if Jeannie believed in him, so he would believe in himself. He puffed himself up and yelled at the sky, "You hear that? I am going to make a great father!" He leaned down and kissed Jeannie passionately.

THE ANNOUNCEMENT

They went straight to Peter's mother. She would be easier to tell first.

"Mum, Jeannie and I have something we need to say," Peter said that evening at tea. Jeannie sipped her tea and fumbled with her history book.

Angela looked over at the two children. "What is it, my love?" she said, walking towards them, obviously looking at Jeannie's stomach and how clearly the cardigan fell out and not in, right about at the waist.

"Well, you know I love Jeannie, Mum, don't you?"

"Peter, get on with it. Don't you think I might be able to guess what it is? I wasn't born yesterday, as you well know!"

"All right, Mum. Jeannie is going to have a baby, and we're going to get married very soon. There it is."

After a silence that lasted a long thirty seconds while Angela paced back and forth, and while Jeannie and Peter squeezed each other's sweaty palms, Angela finally said, "Congratulations, son, and my new daughter. This is difficult news because you are so very young, but a baby is always a wonderful gift to the world, and yours will be well-loved by us all–if you're quite sure you want to keep it."

"Of course we want to keep it!" protested Peter. Jeannie giggled.

Peter was relieved to hear his mother's words. They were wonderful words. In a way, maybe it was how she might have felt about him when he was in the womb and when he was born: loved, welcomed, and wanted by her.

They were not so sure about Jeannie's parents. They had to plan how they would tell them with a little more care. Her dad would have to have at least two drinks in him, but not more than three. Her mum would only need one drink, but not more than three, either. They would announce it at the pub, so they wouldn't get a verbal blast in their ears. The next night, that was the plan.

"Peter and I want to join you and Dad at the pub after dinner tonight, Mum—just the two of you."

Jeannie's mother's eyes were searching Jeannie's face. After all, they all knew that Jeannie spent most of her time trying to escape from the pub and her parents. Would her mum realize that this change of behavior might mean something serious? Her mum wasn't born yesterday, either, it would seem. But her father, well, he might not even comprehend it, even after the announcement!

Later on, into the pub they walked, finding Jeannie's parents sitting at a table far away from the usual drinkers who hung out there and sang sea shanties into the night. Peter felt like he had to be on his best behavior.

"Sit down, then, Peter. Have a pint. It won't hurt you at your age. Jeannie, you can sip from Peter's."

"No, Mum, I am going to have a pint all to myself, aren't I, Peter?"

"I'll get this round," Peter said, so there would be no discussion after that.

Peter and Jeannie waited until they could count the pints and hear the slurs beginning.

"So, then," said Jeannie's father. "What do we owe this cozy visit to then, Jeannie?"

"Well, Dad. You know Peter here."

"Is he the culprit, then?" said her father.

Jeannie's mum put her hand over her bucked teeth and choked and spluttered.

"Dad!" Jeannie exclaimed.

"Jeannie and I want to get married," Peter broke in.

"Cheers, then," said her father, and they all raised their pints and took long sips.

"So, when's it due?" asked her mum. At least these parents didn't wait politely and pretend they didn't know. It was a relief for Peter and even for Jeannie.

"In about six months," Peter said.

"Six months then," said Jeannie's mum. She seemed to be doing figures in her head.

"Right then," said her father, taking another swig.

"When's the wedding? Next Saturday?" asked her father.

"As a matter of fact, we were thinking it would be good to have it rather soon: in about a week, just at the Town Hall, no frills," Jeannie said. "We can't afford them. A few flowers and bring the pub all down to cheer and have a free drink."

"Oh, me Gawd!" said Jeannie's mother. "What are you going to wear, and in that short period of time? We've got to think. Maybe we could get Peter's mum to sew up something nice for you, love."

"She's already started on it," Peter said.

"Well, that's nice. Told her first, I see," said Jeannie's mother, her mouth pinching.

"Yes," Jeannie said, "We knew we would have to get the dress started immediately–that's why."

Her mother mumbled and took another swig. Peter saw that look on Jeannie's face that meant it was time to leave. Her father had had enough to start in with the yelling and blaming. It was a precious moment–this saying it all in public–but couldn't be helped. The best thing they could do, though, was to down the last of their drinks and get up and go.

"You're not leaving so soon, me loves?" Jeannie's mum spluttered.

"Homework still has to get done," Jeannie said.

"Fat lot of good it'll do you now," her father mumbled, and Jeannie and Peter dashed out of the pub into the brisk ocean air and gave each other a big hug and a bigger kiss. They ran all the way up High Street, and Peter swung Jeannie around and around, but carefully.

HOME

On his last night in his childhood home, Peter scanned the sitting room: the flowery settee, the rocking chair, the green curtains, the antique side tables with lions' toes for feet; the Chinese vase for the umbrellas; the grandfather clock; the pen and ink paintings of Hampstead Heath; the old lamps that hardly worked anymore.

He and Jeannie would have nothing glamorous in their own place: just a double bed, a cot, a tiny bathroom with a separate w.c., a small kitchen area with no fridge; no view of the sea, but a lovely tree outside the small sitting room window. It was an upstairs flat, so there would be light, but even though they could leave the pram at the bottom of the inside staircase with its smooth wooden handrail, it would still be a flight up with the baby and groceries.

They were young, Angela had insisted, and it would be manageable. Jeannie needed her own nest. It would do. Peter would have to save for a rocking chair and two more reading lamps. Angela gave them a few dishes and some cutlery, teacups, glasses, a small frying pan, and a toaster. It would be just fine. Their friends from school who had just settled down with a baby on the way had even less. Peter just hoped the gas heater would be adequate when the cold wind blew off the ocean and through the gaps in the ancient windows.

Peter walked down Angela's hallway and into the kitchen and looked at his childhood, all spent around the wooden table with endless cups of tea, toast, and marmalade. He pulled out *his* chair and sat down. He had an eerie feeling just then as he looked at the floor. Wasn't that a blood-stain by his shoe: dark and spilled, old, but permanent? The shape of its splash pierced his brain and disturbed him, but he had no reason he could see for this. He leaned over and pulled his fingers lightly across the stain. Perhaps he had seen it over the years and never really took any notice. But on this last day of his childhood, it seemed to take on a mean-ing that only unsettled him as he glanced around the kitchen one last time.

It wasn't that he wouldn't even be back later on for tea with Angela. But it was his private acknowledgement of leaving his childhood behind and joining another group called adults, or grown-ups. It didn't feel dif-ferent yet. The baby wasn't born. He and Jeannie still ran and laughed and hugged and swelled with pride over their new status. But the lump in Peter's throat only got worse as he contemplated this moving on. An-gela had so wanted them to stay. She would be lonely now. Tea—they would come for tea. Angela could look forward to that. And she had her pupils. And she would have a grandchild. It would be just fine. Peter leapt up from the chair and dashed into the w.c. His throat squeezed and opened, but nothing came out.

"I'm home," he heard Angela call out.

"Home," Peter mumbled to himself, as he coughed and cleared his throat. Where was his heart now, if home was where the heart was? He put his hand to his chest and felt its beat quicken as he imagined himself kissing his mother good-bye and kissing his new wife hello; and then kissing his hand and putting it, yet again, on her growing belly. It would be just fine. He rubbed his eyes and strode into the kitchen.

"Just taking one last look, Mum. I'll be round for tea tomorrow or the next day, once I carry Jeannie and the baby over the threshold."

"You aren't going to put your back out, Peter, are you? You are teas-ing your old mum. Aren't you?"

"I am, but I might give her a piggy-back ride for just a 'mo' over our threshold."

"Should I come, Peter?"

"Mum. I think later might do the trick."

"Of course, son. Teatime–tomorrow or the next day. Cheerio then, my love."

"'Bye, Mum."

Peter loaded the last box into the taxi, got in, and as they pulled away, he stretched his neck for a final glance at his childhood home, then turned his eyes to the front to begin his short journey to his new flat and adulthood.

JEANNIE
LOSING HER MIND

Perhaps it was then, the night Jeannie started bleeding, the night they'd lost the baby that had given birth to their marriage. Perhaps it was those sad, barren months afterwards when they pretended everything was normal, but it was certainly around that time that Peter's love changed. From then on, there was a certain reserve, an appreciation that a life plan could alter its trajectory in a moment when one thing dies and another takes its place.

Love, in Peter's case, became a place he'd been wholeheartedly. Love had now become a place of honoring the past. He drowned his sorrow in his detective cases, which seemed to include disappearances of people who were later found quite alive. In his case, their baby would never be alive. They didn't even want to know if it had been a boy or a girl. Chin up! Get on with it! Try again, and again. And again. Peter loved Jeannie enough to stay with her if they never had another pregnancy. In fact, having a child would have been inconvenient, he'd reassured himself. He remembered her face that night in bed.

"Never mind, my love; we'll try again." He kissed her forehead. He didn't feel like trying. The one they'd lost happened without trying. They were so young. It would happen.

"No," Jeannie said, shifting away from Peter. Peter didn't move.

"I'm not ready to have another baby–I never was. Now I'm stuck with you, and there's no baby! I never wanted to have a baby! Never!"

"You aren't stuck with me, Jeannie. I love you, but you know why we married as well as I do. We can start again. We can even separate for a while if that's what you want."

Peter hesitated–perhaps that was what he wanted.

"That's what you want, isn't it, Peter?"

"No! No, my love! I love you. We're married. We'll go slowly. When the time is right...."

"No babies. I'm leaving!" Jeannie flung the blankets away and jumped out of bed, slung on her dressing gown, and strode down the hallway, yelling, "I'm done! I'm fine! It's fine, just fine! I didn't want the little intruder in the first place! I'm bloody free!"

Peter heard pans and the kettle clanging around in the kitchen. Twenty minutes elapsed. He didn't know if he should go and comfort her or let her be.

"Where are you, Peter? Can't you see I'm losing my mind?" she yelled, approaching their bedroom door. She kicked it open and brought in a tray with a teapot and a plate of toast and marmalade.

"Cuppa tea?" she said calmly, as if life had not altered one bit.

"That would be lovely," he said, holding his voice back to make it sound calm and normal. He sat up and let her settle the tray on his lap. She hovered a moment and then placed a blanket around his shoulders. He felt like a fool. It was a game he was learning to play quite well.

MOVING

It wasn't more than a year later when Jeannie became pregnant again. And in those first two years after Henry was born, their tiny flat rapidly filled with wicker baskets full of soiled nappies; clean, folded nappies on the shelves and tables; tiny blue outfits; knitted booties from Angela, wooden soldiers, painted wooden red fire engines—even World War I toy airplane models. Peter was constantly inventing new storage methods: a big box under their bed for blankets, shelves above every possible window and table, tall baby clothes dressers, and shelves above the w.c. for towels and sheets, hooks for cups, and a large dish rack for the permanent storage of plates.

One evening, when little Henry was asleep, Peter and Jeannie had their usual cup of tea to seal the day.

"I'm bored, Peter," said Jeannie. "I'm not fit for the life of a devoted wife and mum. I want to travel. This rain is driving me batty."

Peter hardly knew what to say or do. He just nodded and looked at her face, which seemed to be developing a smile that curved downwards, and two frown marks between her eyebrows.

"We've got to move, Peter," Jeannie said. "It's no use. Soon enough there won't be any place to walk. Henry has to play in the dirty laundry basket. I can't leave the ironing board up, can I?"

Peter knew this moment was inevitable. Money was tight. It had to be done, but where?

"I heard our neighbor is thinking of moving to a smaller flat. Can't afford hers now her husband's died," Jeannie suggested.

"We can't afford it, either," Peter said, "Unless I get a raise. Actually, I am up for one."

Jeannie's eyes sparkled. "You'll get it, Peter. But come to think of it, can't we just ask her if she wants to swap flats?"

"Ingenious!" Peter said.

"Bloody marvelous!" Jeannie said.

Within the month, the awful business of moving both flats out and onto the landings, and then inching the sofa and chairs back into their new flats proceeded, back and forth, with hundreds of cups of tea and chocolate biscuits in between.

Peter hoped this would finally quell Jeannie's complaints about feeling cooped up all day. Perhaps he'd come home from now on and be greeted with a smile and a nice hot cup of tea. Perhaps.

It didn't happen. Nothing he tried or was willing to try ever quite seemed to satisfy Jeannie.

Jeannie fussed over the baby blanket Angela had knitted. Her face took on the look of a sad dog.

"I couldn't care less about traveling now. I know my place. I'm a good mum, aren't I, Peter?"

"Of course you are," he lied. He could have wished for a woman easier in her traditional role, as he was in his. To ease her burden, however, he'd changed many nappies and sung many sea shanties out of tune. He'd washed dishes and carried out the rubbish. He worked by the gas fire, searching through documents and files he had brought home. They would manage. Everybody managed–most everybody. He reminded himself of a couple who had, in fact, not managed in Brighton just that year. The husband had murdered both his wife and child and then himself. They said it was his depression and no work, and they said he gambled away the little money the government gave them. No, he and Jeannie would manage. But not everybody could–not everybody.

Two more babies later–in spite of Jeannie's changing birth control possibilities–Peter only wished he had a moment to read the paper. He felt he was a good man. He sneaked a read at work and was relieved to have a place to go every day. Crying babies were driving him crazy.

NAPPIES

Peter began to study the spider in the corner, its web building, its fly-catching and devouring. He watched Jeannie as she flitted from sink to stove. She hardly ever hummed her folk songs anymore. At first, Peter hadn't noticed, but now there was a hardened silence as she worked and a tightening around her jaw that seemed new. The spider intrigued Peter, who could hardly keep his mind on his case or read the paper. Jeannie had lost the art of conversation somewhere along the way once their second baby, Oliver, was born, and then came little Cassandra. Peter had tried–he helped all he could when he was home.

"Jeannie, my love, let me put the nappy on Oliver," he offered.

She looked at him as the safety pin hung between her lips, then jammed the point into the cloth nappy with a harshness that made Peter cringe.

It seemed that Jeannie resented Peter for not helping, yet pushed his efforts aside when he tried to participate. It wasn't in his nature to bring up the issue, so he learned by her silence to at least see to the dishes or make melted cheese on toast with tea before she mentioned it. Peter knew his mates were dealing with these new marital expectations. The jokes at the police station, where he had been working for a while, re-flected all the new "women's lib" expectations.

"Here, look at my thumb," Ernie had said one day. "Purple!"

"How's that, mate?" John said.

"Bloomin' nappy, safety pin jammed right under my nail!"

"Better than in your baby, mate!"

They all laughed and inspected his thumb from a polite distance.

Peter noticed the jokes about women had toned down several notches in the past five years. They were less harsh but more humorous, particularly about the new role for men. No more sitting about like a lion while the lioness went hunting. These new males were expected to push prams with a smile and not let the old ladies' comments get to them, even the nice ones. Trailblazers, they were: they'd better be. Most of their wives were out slogging through a day's work all day, same as them. And the women weren't at all quiet about it these days!

WHERE ARE THE HUGS?

When he came home, Peter yelled out, "Hello, dear!" but he knew there would no longer be an answer. The kitchen door down the hall remained closed. Pans clattered behind it. Jeannie never came to greet him or hug him or even kiss his cheek. He remembered the warmth of their cheeks against each other when they were first married. It seemed so long ago. Where were her spontaneous hugs that there used to be? But now, his body ached in his loneliness. It was like he'd marched across a desert and had dried up like a prune, his tongue parched, his hands stretching for the water just out of reach. He walked into the kitchen and closed the door behind him.

"Hello, my darlings," he tried again like nothing was wrong. The children had already finished their tea and were clearing their plates. Jeannie stood by the sink, her worn apron streaked with grease and begging to be discarded forever.

"Tea then?" she said in a flat voice. The words were exactly the same every evening when he arrived home. It was as if Jeannie always looked straight through Peter. He knew his role.

"That would be lovely," he said in his civilized demeanor. If the children noticed their wooden speech, they didn't show it. Peter supposed they must be pleased to see him. He kissed Cassandra and Oliver and put his hand on Henry's shoulder.

"Have a good day then?" she asked him, as she did every night.

"Nothing exciting: same old paperwork; a suspicious burglary that seems to have been done by the ex-husband looking for his wedding ring. That's the day. Oh, and Richard is retiring."

Peter knew Jeannie didn't give a fig about Richard. "Silly old man," she said. But what else could he tell her? He tried to keep the conversation going, if only for appearances to hide away the reality of their deteriorating relationship.

"Henry's got a cold," Jeannie said.

"No, I haven't. It's an allergy."

"Sorry, love. It's a cold," Jeannie said, perhaps a little lacking in sympathy.

"I've got a cold, Mum," sniffed Cassandra.

"No, you've got allergies."

"It feels just like a cold, Mum."

"That's true. Now all of you finish your homework or your reading before you watch the telly. Go on."

The children sat back at the table, pulling open their satchels and pulling out their stacks of sky-blue covered notebooks.

Peter ate quietly, wondering about family life. He guessed most people just accepted it all. He even felt guilty when he questioned his own existence within this framework. He was glad he was a detective and could have a rush of adrenaline on a regular basis. Maybe he would have chosen another life if Jeannie hadn't become pregnant that first time. He wondered, as he ate his sausage and toast with jam, what that other life would have looked like. He'd have gone further than Paris for one thing. As he looked at poor, bedraggled Jeannie, he realized her own travel yearnings had been buried long ago.

Perhaps later–when the children were grown–perhaps later.

PETER'S IMAGINATION

Peter looked at Jeannie as she slept. It could have been that Peter was just over-imaginative. After all, that was his job as a detective. It was a positive quality to suspect the most unlikely people of crimes one couldn't imagine such nice people committing. But dragging his over-imaginative leanings home might not be a blessing.

He began to suspect Jeannie of horrible deeds. He imagined her having a lover. He imagined her setting fire to their flat. He imagined her hanging herself or their children. Sometimes he imagined he'd walk in the front door and say, "Hello! I'm home!" and she would step out from behind the door and bash him on the head with a pan or worse.

Jeannie's daily activities were indeed cause for concern. She was irrational. She complained about trivial things that didn't bother him one wit. She raised her voice at the children unnecessarily. Peter lurked about like he was a detective in his own home. When she wasn't looking, he would go through her mail and the pockets in her clothes. He couldn't understand her anymore. Was she just harassed over the piles of laundry to be done, or was there something chemically wrong?

Peter had ignored the clues far longer than he would have for a criminal investigation. He wondered what it was about one's ability to ignore the obvious with the people one loves or is supposed to love? Peter shrugged his shoulders involuntarily. The word love didn't seem to apply to his feelings towards Jeannie anymore. He had compassion for her unhappiness, but now she didn't bring out the love he had buried. It was like that old feeling was in a locked up suitcase, and the key had long been tossed into the sea.

Jeannie turned over and opened her eyes briefly.

"What's going on, love?"

"Can't sleep. This case is a stumper."

She turned back away from him and mumbled.

"I need to sleep."

"Sorry, my love," Peter said as he crept out of bed into the cold, raw morning. He put on his dressing gown, walked through the bedroom door, and closed it lightly and firmly. He peeked into the children's bedroom: such angels with their dreams and occasional nightmares. He loved them until it hurt.

Peter went into the kitchen and put the kettle on, turning on the BBC news automatically and softly. The news was always the same—great discussions about the economy, taxes, elections, and murders. *Murders*: that was the part of the news he waited for. It helped him put his own investigations into perspective. There were hardly any murders in Rottingdean. It was probably because everybody knew everybody else and remembered them when they fought as children and were forced to say, "Sorry," and then got on with it. But up in London, *that* was a different matter. Nobody knew anybody, so they didn't care, and then they murdered somebody. Nobody was looking or would come and make them say, "Sorry," and life could continue.

Peter poured the coffee and sat down, wondering about this new word he heard everywhere, "dysfunctional."

GOING CRAZY

Peter stared at the green bottle. He shivered as he remembered throwing it into the garden a few nights before. It now reflected the sun back to him. He observed his nose–rather red. He reached for his hand-kerchief and blew his nose.

Jeannie was still sleeping. Strange how her old habit of early rising, dressing, watching the children, and getting them out the door had given way to her looking like a drugged doll. He lifted the bottle and threw it down onto the dirt, but it hit a large stone and shattered into a hundred pieces, all reflecting his nose back at him.

He knelt down and began with his right thumb and forefinger, labo-riously picking up each shard, swearing at his stupidity each time he put a new piece into his palm.

He bit his lip and emptied the shards back into a deep hole he'd dug in the sod, buried them, then stood up and gazed at the sea. He stood stock-still for so long that the sun couldn't penetrate his freezing fingers. The wind kicked up and blew his hair all over his face. It felt like his legs were made of heavy stone, and his arms were two heavy anchors. He squinted at nothing. He sneezed but couldn't reach for his handkerchief again. His nose began to run. He couldn't lift his arm even to drag it across his upper lip. His breathing was shallow. He felt himself splitting into two people, the one who says *use your handkerchief,* and the other who just can't move. As he stood there, he began to talk to himself.

"What is the matter, mate?"

"Nothing much, just enjoying the view."

"Not true. You tell a lie."

"Good view. You must admit it is."

"True. But what's the matter with you?"

"I told you. Good view. Just relaxing, enjoying myself."

"Liar!"

"Okay. You win. I'm tired of it all. Exhausted. I need to rest. So, I'm resting."

"Looking at the beautiful view."

"Exactly."

"What about that glass?"

"What glass?"

"At your feet, you lazy idiot."

"Not lazy."

"Are, too!"

"Am not."

"Pick it up, then."

"I'm busy."

"Looking at the view…"

Peter felt quite crazy.

A HOUSE IN VERMONT

As she languished in jail, Catherine remembered the day that she and David had decided to go to Italy for their trip–just three months before he died.

What excitement! What joy! And then, a few months after she had been convicted and was now sitting in prison, she remembered him saying something about some silver cups and Benvenuto Cellini. What had he said? She had been thinking about something else and wasn't really listening. But now that she had so much time to listen to her own thoughts, she looked at the stars out of her small, barred window, and she tried hard to remember what he had said, something about six cups and astrological signs. He was always talking about Cellini, and she often didn't really listen. It didn't mean much to her. But he had said something about beautiful engravings on the cups, she remembered, and something else about only having six. After a whole month, Catherine put it together. There were twelve astrological signs, but he only had six cups. She wondered where the other six were, or if they were in existence at all.

It was sometime later that some men came into the prison asking her about silver cups. She didn't care to help them out. She listened but said nothing. It didn't make sense. If they had told her more, she might have been helpful, but they kept it all to themselves, so why shouldn't she? It made her wonder for years.

She made up a song about the cups.

Six silver cups,
Dancing in the sky,
Each one missing,
Something like an eye;
All the stars above,
Winking like true love,
Six silver cups
And all the stars above.

Catherine felt quite clever, and it kept her mind working. Then she made up a tune to go with the words and sang it every time she watched the stars if it were not too cloudy. It made her feel she was somehow in touch with David. In some ways, she didn't really believe he was dead. He had died, and then she was taken away that very day. It all seemed more like a dream; she thought she might just get out of jail, go home and there he would be. So she sang to him. It was some kind of time warp in her mind.

Catherine's whole life had revolved around David for so long, and now she was living through this horrible time in jail. What else was there for her to look forward to and who would be her friend when they all thought she was a murderer? She wished there was another place she could go to as the time drew nearer for her release. She didn't know where she would live or what she would do after twelve long years in jail.

"Here, love," said a fellow prisoner named Jillie. "What you going to do once you get out of here? It's coming up soon. Can't just hang out on the streets, can you?"

"No. I'll find my way. I don't quite know, but I will think of something. I don't think I can go back to our house. I heard that his legal wife is living there now. After all that work I did on it. It doesn't seem fair. But then she had a baby, and the baby needed a home, so that's it. I will have to think of some other way."

It wasn't long afterwards that she got the letter from David's mother in Vermont. In earlier letters, she had hinted to Catherine that she might be giving Catherine something once she got out, but to be given her whole house in Brattleboro and a small income was astonishing! She knew Brattleboro slightly, and she felt she could make a new start there. It was too late to find a husband and have a family, although she had desperately wanted to. Thirty-four was the very outside limit to take a chance on having a baby, and that would be her age when they let her out. She spent her stargazing time planning another life, perhaps teaching astronomy.

"I got a letter from his mother," she later confided to Jillie. "She's leaving me her house in Vermont."

"Well, what a fine turn-up for the books! What a lucky lady you are then. You might've thought she would have shot you dead for what you done! Oh, sorry, 'course you didn't do it."

"I didn't," said Catherine softly. She listened to the music in her voice as she said it. She said it like someone who, indeed, was telling the truth.

"I wouldn't mind being you. Why not you stay 'ere in my place, and I'll take that lovely 'ouse in Vermont!"

It was silly, but it was after that comment that Catherine began to appreciate her luck. David's mother loved her for some reason, knowing full well that she was innocent. But why should she get all the money and the house? Didn't she know about David's so-called son? Of course, his son, Peter, would inherit their house in Rottingdean, and David's mother must know that. Catherine felt better once she thought about that.

Freedom: it almost frightened Catherine. She had read the papers and knew all the news that had gone by in the last twelve years, but she didn't know a lot more. She heard rumors when new women entered the jail. Some roads were one-way now; everybody had a television and a fridge. Times had changed in that way. But she wondered how they might have changed in other ways. Had they forgotten her? Probably: twelve years was a long time. Maybe they would just let her creep away and start a new life without headlines and announcements that might damage her chances.

SLEEP

Over the years, Peter had lived a quiet, planned existence. Being a local detective was exactly right, and later, working in Brighton suited his more ambitious years.

Life had rushed along: cricket matches were played; netball matches were won; concerts were played; new uniforms were bought and worn; tea was drunk with two spoonfuls of sugar in each; Jeannie learned to cook and sew and even quilt in Peter's mother's class. They became close as Angela admired Jeannie's fine work.

But Jeannie had stopped giggling long ago and just smiled now and again.

Yes, indeed, time moved everybody right along in its usual, familiar way. Books were read by the fire, the war receded into history, and everybody had a television. There was dancing in the streets, happiness, fun, loud colors, trips by others all the way to India, gurus seeking followers, Americans following in thousands, love in the air, love for everyone, no more war, no war, no war! No war! No bras, no authority, question authority, question your leaders.

Where were the women? They were coming out of the closets–all the closets. Laws were changed. Men became secretaries. And men became nurses, as well. Women rose in the ranks and yet could not seem to get beyond a certain step on the ladder–but up they climbed anyway–together. Support was everywhere; don't go through strikers–support them. It was all on television now. But you could sew at the same time, but prick your finger a lot more, but what's a little blood compared to that blood all over the television? And in Brighton, political party conferences arrived like clockwork–loud voices changing thoughts and women's voices pushing through.

The years had flown by, raising Henry, Oliver, and Cassandra: working, visiting Grandma Angela, tea parties, birthday parties, with no highs and no lows until the day Jeannie shoved him into the kitchen stove.

"Go to bloody hell!" she had shouted, her face fierce with anger.

"Ouch, you b....., I burned my hand!" Peter yelled back.

"Serves you right," she said, stepping away.

Several months before that, she'd frequently been angry or moody, more demanding, and more sullen. Peter was busy and thought it would pass as it always had done before. Peter felt that he was a patient man. His feet met gravity with a solidity his children felt as they stepped on his large feet and shoes as he walked them all over the living room, holding their hands high in the air.

Now Jeannie thrashed in her sleep; Peter never slept deeply and was on guard in case she turned over and accidentally smacked his nose again. When she turned, he turned away from her arm swinging over to his side. Constant nighttime vigilance was becoming a habit. He didn't realize it at first, but his sleep deprivation invaded his sharp memory, which flushed his face as his colleagues witnessed his inability to dredge up facts he really did know. He thought it might be an idea to sleep on the settee regularly at least once a week to recuperate. But he feared her anger at such a suggestion, so he put it off for a day when she might be happy.

Those days never appeared; Peter was just plain exhausted. He could hardly lift the kids anymore. He developed dark circles under his eyes. He drank more coffee during the day to stay alert. One day Jeannie was finally in a good frame of mind, even singing folksongs as she watered her daffodils.

"My love," he started. "Take a look at my face." *Why not do the direct, detective method?*

"God, look at that blue sky, at last!" she said.

"No, love, take a look at my face."

She looked, blinked, and looked away.

"Well?"

"What?"

"My eyes: bags!"

"So? Look at mine!"

"No," he answered, "Let's look at mine for the moment."

"Peter, love, would you move that pot over there, please?"

Peter moved the pot, then came back and stood by her again. He didn't speak or remind her, and strangely, she just kept sprinkling the daffodils until they were soggy.

"Oh, Peter, love, could you turn off the hose?"

Peter walked over to the outdoor hose tap, turned it off, and then walked back and stood by her.

"What's going on? Why are you just standing there?"

"You haven't looked at my eyes yet, really."

She opened her eyes very wide, put her face close to his, and looked at his eyes for a long moment.

"There you are!" she smirked.

"What did you notice?"

"Peter, love, what's going on? Don't treat me like I'm a suspect!"

"Can't you see how tired I look?"

"Of course, we're all tired. That's life, isn't it?"

"Well," he tried, "I was thinking I might sleep on the settee now and again to get a good night's sleep."

"And what's the matter with our bed?"

"To tell you the truth, you're tossing and turning a lot lately, and it keeps me awake."

"Suit yourself," she said, turning away like she was in a trance.

That night Peter started off sleeping in their bed, then crept into the sitting room and lay down on the settee. Now he was the one tossing and turning. By 3 a.m., he trudged back to their bed and slipped in.

"Peter?"

"Just turning over, love. Go back to sleep."

He lay awake for an hour and then somehow drifted off to sleep.

DISGUST

"Peter," Jeannie said the next morning, "I toss and turn because I can't sleep next to *you*. I'm sorry, but I just can't. Last night I knew you were in the sitting room, and I slept soundly. Perhaps we could try it again tonight?"

Peter felt a swelling in his throat. He wasn't sure if it would be relief or sorrow.

"Of course, Jeannie. Let's try it again tonight."

He turned the pages of his book and went on with the mystery. Somehow his life as a detective didn't seem as glamorous as the detectives in literature, but at least he wasn't caught up in a drug habit. His worst habit was worrying about how to make enough money to get through the second fortnight of the month. He never went shopping, tossing what they needed into his bag. He checked the prices first. He even walked by bread until it was a day-old sale. Food was cheap, so he never saved much, but it was the one place they could cut down, however small.

He couldn't help noticing the money that was spent on drinks at the pub. Jeannie's generosity would bankrupt them. After two pints, she bought rounds for everyone in her group on the slightest pretext. Peter avoided the pub now and made his excuse the need to save money on babysitters. It was becoming lonely at night after the children were asleep. An hour watching television dimmed his brain and his eyesight and made his muscles cramp. He preferred sitting under the lamp and reading his mysteries.

"Daddy," said Cassandra, peering around the doorways. "I can't sleep."

"Come here, my love," he said. She walked over in her bare feet, and he pulled six-year-old Cassandra onto his lap.

"Would you like a story again?"

"Yes, please," she said, laying her head against his shoulder.

"I'll make it up, then!"

"Oh, I love your stories."

But no sooner had he begun his story than he heard her soft breathing that indicated she was already asleep.

Peter carried her back to her bed, tucked her in, and kissed her forehead.

"Good night, my love," he said. It was this love that was so deep that he couldn't consider parting from Jeannie, no matter how difficult she had become.

Peter got up, checked Oliver, and left the door slightly ajar. It was cold in the bedroom. He sneezed and went back to the gas fire by his chair. He felt glad in his soul to be ushering these children into what he imagined would be a good life, but then, he felt a dragging on his heart when he realized he was fooling himself. Jeannie's growing brand of insanity was pervasive. It had to affect the children. But what could he do? He'd already very gently suggested therapy. Jeannie had actually laughed in his face and said, "*You* go!" How can you tell someone they need help? Must they always fall on their face to see the problem?

Peter opened his book and scanned a page.

"Hello, love!" came the call from the front door, and then it was slammed.

Peter leapt up and raced to the door. "Jeannie, love, please be quiet. Cassandra was just getting to sleep."

"I'm being quiet!" she said at the top of her voice. She slung her coat onto the hatstand, and as it fell to the floor, she tramped her wet shoes down the hall, burped, and headed for the bathroom.

Peter felt a wave of disgust for her. They were in and out of the same bed, but their love had completely evaporated. He couldn't stand her breath and kept turning away from her as she snored and choked the air in and out. He knew they would be eating a lot of potatoes for the next week, eggs and potatoes in many varieties. He hated his life; he hated his wife. But he adored Cassandra and Oliver, and he ached for his dear, eldest son, Henry, who was unfortunately quite aware of what was happening to their family.

JEANNIE SLEEPING

Most of the time, Peter came and went, kissed the children, and pecked Jeannie *hello* and *goodbye*. But lately, pecking Jeannie's mouth had turned into brushing her cheek and looking somewhere else. Some days he ran into the house and straight into the w.c. When he emerged, Jeannie pointed to his tea, and he was happily diverted to the table and the chatter of his growing children.

On this particular day, when Peter got home, the children were glued to the television eating crisps, and Jeannie was apparently upstairs fast asleep on their rumpled bed. The kettle was hardly warm, and there was nothing on the table to suggest supper was on the way.

Peter put down his briefcase, kissed the children, and took out some frozen peas, chips, and hamburgers and set to work.

"Henry, come and lay the table, love," Peter said quietly.

"Can't I finish this program? Two more minutes?"

"All right. Two minutes."

But Peter didn't notice when Henry came in. His mind was churning. He looked at the peaked and tidy rooftops down the street and checked the cloudy sky. Rain was imminent.

"Dad?" Henry said.

"Yes, son?"

"Mum isn't waking up. She's been like this since we left for school this morning. She just grunted, 'telle,' when we got home, turned over, and went back to sleep. What's wrong with her?" Henry put the forks, knives, and dessert spoons in place; then he took the glasses down and laid them perfectly at each place.

"I'll go and wake her, Henry."

"Don't bother. She won't wake up."

"I'll give it a try," Peter answered, turning the gas very low and walked to the stairs. When he looked back down the hallway, he saw Henry standing at the door, watching him with a face too serious for Peter's liking.

Peter climbed the stairs, dreading her temper. He stood over her for what seemed to be a very long moment. Jeannie's mouth was open, and her slightly buck teeth, now beginning to yellow, made her look like she was smiling in her sleep.

"Jeannie," Peter whispered. She turned over and buried her head.

"Jeannie, love. Time for dinner." Peter gingerly put his hand on her shoulder. At first, she didn't move. He gently jiggled it.

"Go away," she said gruffly.

"Jeannie. It's suppertime. Your tea will get cold."

"Fuck off!" she bellowed and put the pillow on top of her ear.

Peter only felt sad, way down deep in his being. His throat felt dry as he tried to piece together this new puzzle. It was true that she got home so late the night before that he had to go to sleep before she got in the house. He had now been sleeping on the settee for weeks. He opened one eye when she came in but didn't officially wake up. Jeannie clattered down the hall and into the kitchen, rustling pots and pans, seeming to forget that the house was full of her sleeping family.

Peter left her and slowly went back downstairs into the living room.

"Tea's ready," he said to the children.

"Oh, Dad! Can't we watch it while we eat? All our friends are watching this program."

"No, you cannot. It's getting cold. Do I have to turn it off or will you?"

Henry turned it off and patted the other two who slithered off the couch and onto the maroon Turkish rug. They crawled to the door where Henry grabbed one of each one's ears and pulled them up to standing, pointing them down the hallway to the kitchen table.

"Where's Mum?" Cassandra asked.

"Silly! You know she's asleep!" said Oliver.

"Dad, she needs to wake up!"

"I can't wake her right now," said Peter. "I think she had a sleepless night. We'll let her catch up."

"You can't fool us, Dad. Mum's depressed," Henry spluttered.

Peter had no word for Jeannie's sleeping needs until that moment. Of course, she was depressed. He felt a little relieved just to have a name for this strange behavior.

THE KITTEN

When Oliver brought the kitten home, he hadn't asked Peter or Jeannie if he could have it. As Peter looked at the little furry thing with those large green eyes, he imagined himself saying, "Take that kitten back, you know we can't have an animal right now." But instead, the kitten's eyes beamed into Peter, who found his arms receiving the small bundle from his hopeful son. Its black, fuzzy body with a white face fit right into Peter's palms. He drew it to his chest and sighed. The bond was instant. This wasn't Oliver's kitty; this was Peter's, next to his heart, next to his filling lungs, next to his soul.

The little eyes blinked back at Peter, and for a brief moment, Peter wondered if he had been a cat in a past life. He felt protective and loving, as he had when he held his own newborn babies. This kitty was an instant new member of the family, its innocent eyes softly allowing itself to be held and loved. His long silky fur just asked for a hand to smooth it down again and again, and its tiny purr was like a melody to Peter's ears. He could hardly let it go, but he held the little kitten out to Oliver, who scooped it to his own chest and began the petting that produced the purring.

"You love this kitten, don't you, Daddy?" Cassandra asked.

"No doubt about that. I hope Mum feels the same: she prefers dogs, you know."

"You'll convince her, won't you, Daddy?" said Oliver.

"I'll do my best. But we all have to agree. Just be sure to let her hold the kitten before you ask. She'll fall in love just like we did."

Peter reached out and tickled the black fur between the kitten's ears. The purring amplified like a tiny engine, and Peter felt he couldn't really stop.

"Mum's coming," Henry said, looking out the window.

"I'll go into the kitchen, children. It's all in your hands."

"I got you to agree: Mum's a pushover. Watch this," said Oliver with a smile.

The front door opened, and Jeannie struggled in with two bags of groceries. She put them on the small table stand and exhaled a huge sigh.

"Hello, love," she said to Cassandra. "Well, who's this?" she added as Oliver pushed the kitten into her empty palms. If only she would draw it to her breast, she'd fall in love.

Jeannie held the kitty at eye level and as far away as a book one might be reading. The purring had slowed from an engine back to normal, but the blinking eyes continued.

"He's lovely, Cassandra and Oliver, but you know we can't have a kitty right now. Sorry love, but you'll have to take him back again and tell the family we all need to think about exactly when we can have an animal." She handed the kitten to Cassandra and brushed off her hands like the kitten had left hairs on them.

"Mum!" squealed Cassandra.

"Don't whine," Mum said.

"Please, Mum," she tried.

"Sorry, love. We can't. You have to talk things like this over with Daddy and me first. Now, off you go." She sighed again as she tossed her coat onto the hook, heaved up the grocery bags, and started down the hall.

"Peter!" she raised her voice. "Come along and help me with the groceries. My back is killing me."

Peter tossed the paper down onto the kitchen table and went to help with the groceries. He took both bags out of her hands and kissed her cheek. Jeannie continued down the hallway to the kitchen, but Peter went over to Henry and Oliver. He reached out, petted the kitten, and the engine roared.

"Wait here," he said, and marched down the hallway with the determination of a mother cat protecting her young.

"This time we're going to keep the kitten," he said in a firm voice. "This time it's their turn."

"I told you I can't do one more thing. You know I will get landed with all the work!"

"What if I take over the work with the kitten? I'll feed it."

"Fine! You feed it then," Jeannie yelled, stomping back down the hall. The children huddled together as she fired by and out of the front door. "And empty the litter box!" she added.

"Here's your kitten, children," Peter said. "But you have to feed it and empty the litter box."

"We will!" they all sang together. The engine roared.

WHERE'S THE CAT?

Months later, a few hours after sunrise, while Peter was doing foot-work research, or snooping on a case as he liked to call it, he remembered that he had not fed the cat. He knew the children had forgotten to do it. He had been unusually rushed and dashed out, kissing his children and leaving them to Jeannie, who was still asleep.

Hopefully, someone might notice the cat circling their legs and purr-ing with intention. Peter went on about his snooping, following the so-ber drunken man, a suspect in a robbery three nights before. It was one of the tamer moments in Peter's job, but the man held his bundle and scurried along towards the antique shop that doubled as a pawnshop. The man entered, and Peter held his ground a few doors down and across the street. Not long afterwards, the man came out empty-handed. Peter knew exactly which pub the man was now headed towards, so he went into the shop and found the goods in question still on the counter. The case was now nearly closed.

Meanwhile, the cat hovered in the back of Peter's brain. How unusual for it not to circle his ankles. It was a missed touch, something Peter depended on to start his day, a signal to his brain that there was uncon-ditional love in his own life. It niggled at him the whole day. When he opened the front door that afternoon, he fully expected his usual kitty

169

greeting—a kind disinterested stance, a looking away, and then washing its face to let Peter know he had duties to perform. But there was an empty shadow in its usual place, a vacuum where the cat usually sat.

"Jeannie, love?" he called out.

"Tea's ready," she called back.

Peter hung his hat and coat and pushed down the hallway and into the bright, warm kitchen. Jeannie stood by the stove, hand upon her hip.

"Where's Kitty?" Peter asked as he kissed Cassandra and sat down.

"He's gone," Oliver said, holding out his cheek for a kiss. Peter kissed his cheek.

"He's probably dead," Cassandra pouted.

"No, he's not. He's in love, spending time with that cat down the street," Peter said.

"Finish your tea," said Jeannie.

Peter kissed the pads of his fingers and laid them on the cheeks of Henry, as usual.

"No cat then?" he turned to Jeannie.

She moved about the table and only said, "Hmmm. Oliver, drink your tea while it's hot. Stop fiddling with your food."

Peter put down his cup. The detective in him had been alerted and even slightly alarmed.

"Jeannie, what's going on?"

"Nothing, love."

"Jeannie, love, where's the cat?"

"No idea. Do I follow Kitty around all day? He's as free as I'd like to be, that's for sure!"

"You're free, Jeannie. If you need to be, go out and look for the cat. I'll get the tea and read the children a story."

Jeannie had been unusually grumpy lately, and Peter wanted to give her a sense of space and freedom that they both knew to be impossible. Only last week, she had stopped washing the dishes, and they all piled up until nothing clean remained on the shelves.

"I'll cook as long as you like," she had said to the gaping mouths, "but if there are no clean pans to cook in, I'll have to stop until there are, won't I?"

Oliver and Henry were just about old enough to help with the dishes and could even cook simple things. Their grumbling stomachs got them to the kitchen sink with hardly a complaint as the stew bubbled on the stove into its final day. Jeannie made stews now—potatoes, carrots, onions, peas, and beef or lamb—and they lasted four days. Then the bottom of the pan was burned, and someone had to clean it. It was the only one big enough for a four-day stew.

Peter tried again. "Did you feed the cat this morning, then?"

Jeannie shot Peter a look that alarmed him, but he didn't quite know why. The detective in him wanted to press on, but the husband kept his mouth closed and ate his sandwiches and washed them down with sweetened tea.

Then in walked the cat, stepping daintily into her bed, curling up, closing her eyes, purring, falling asleep, and not noticing the surprised looks on everybody's faces.

JEANNIE AND THE CAT

Two days later, Cassandra sat, looking horrified, in the overstuffed chair except for her large blue eyes that stared at the dying cat. Jeannie had pulled the knife out of the bleeding cat that writhed in its last moments and moaned its final meow. The puncture wounds from the dog's bite oozed dark blood. Jeannie wiped her face with the knife still in her hand, smearing her cheek with blood. Cassandra watched as her mother sped down the hallway into the kitchen and the knife clattered into the sink, the faucet on it full blast.

"Damn, damn, damn that dog!" she heard her mother yell. There was the sound of a scrub brush that went on and on. Cassandra slipped off the chair, tiptoeing towards the kitchen as the front door opened, and Peter came in, slinging his hat on the hat stand, dropping his briefcase, and heading towards the bathroom.

"What's wrong, my little darling?" he asked, bending down and kissing Cassandra briefly on the forehead.

"Mummy murdered the cat," she said, her glassy eyes looking up at Peter.

"Mummy didn't murder the cat," Peter said, standing up, his jaw hard.

"...a lot of blood," Cassandra added.

"Mum!" he yelled, striding straight down the hall and into the kitchen. Peter's face pinched into a shocked, muddled, opened mouth face of disbelief.

"Jeannie!"

"Peter! I had to do it!" Her face looked like she'd battled a lion, and the lion had won.

Peter stared at the dead cat, his child, and his wife. It reminded him of the occasional bloody moments on the job. Was this happening in *his* home?

"What's the matter with you, Jeannie?

"With me? With me? I saved the cat from its agony; that's what the matter is! With *me*!"

"What happened?" he asked, stepping towards the knife in the sink.

"Oh, Peter, the cat was mauled by that horrible dog next door. You should have heard her shrieking in agony. I didn't know what to do. Come here, child," she beckoned.

Cassandra stood motionless, looking at Peter, then Jeannie; then she turned and ran down the hall, climbed back onto her chair and crossed her arms. When she looked up, there was the dead cat again. Not one movement did it make. Its injured eyes were open, and they seemed to stare right at Cassandra. Jeannie raced down the hall, followed by Peter.

"My love!" Jeannie said, kneeling before her child. "Mummy had to put the kitty out of her misery. Mummy loved kitty, just like you." She hugged her stiff daughter. Peter gathered some newspapers from the stool, wrapped the kitten up, strode back down the hallway and outside, tossing it into the rubbish bin. For a very uncomfortable moment, he imagined Jeannie stabbing the kitten with a look of glee upon her face and triumph in her eyes. He began coughing and coughing until he felt sick. He went back into the house and washed his hands in the kitchen sink.

"I don't love you anymore," he heard his daughter saying. "You're not nice to Kitty. Where's Kitty? Where's Kitty?"

Peter walked back into the living room.

"Kitty went to heaven," he heard himself say. He hated himself for that. Kitty was in the rubbish bin. But how could he tell her that now?

"She doesn't understand," he said, looking at Jeannie's stony face. Jeannie got up and brushed past Peter.

Peter went to the child and picked up her small hand and held it between his large, protective hands, clean and cold.

"Kitty is dead now. Mummy had to put her out of her misery."

"Misery?"

"Kitty was hurting very badly. Mummy was trying to help kitty. If I am hurting, will Mummy do that to me?" Cassandra asked.

Peter gathered his arms around the child and hugged her tightly.

"Mummy would never do that to you or anybody else. We go to hospitals and doctors and get medicine to make you feel better and not hurt."

"Why didn't Mummy do that?"

"I think the kitty was dying anyway, and she had to help it die."

"I don't love Mummy now."

Peter hugged the child and thought, *neither do I.*

THE STORM

Once again, the rain took over the day, and their summer plans were aimed back indoors. The thunder shook the house, and the lightning threatened fire. The wind took up the show and tossed small branches along the street; flags were torn to threads. It was impossible to sip tea and feel protected by the brick house while the windows that rattled at the bumping noises just the other side of the door made it feel like a great giant had come knocking.

Peter huddled in his chair with Oliver under one arm and Cassandra under the other. His tea was cold, and the children were quiet.

Where was Jeannie? She should have arrived home with the fish and chips by now; should have been back half an hour ago. Perhaps she had gone to fill the car up with petrol and got to talking with her mum? Or maybe she went to pick up that chair from the boot sale they'd finally paid for.

"Daddy, I'm afraid," Oliver said.

"Come now, Oliver, it's a summer thunderstorm. Remember last summer? We sat in this very place and cuddled just like now."

"No, you went out to shop and didn't get home until we were all scared to death!" Oliver said

"Sorry, my little loves, yes, that's true. Mum is doing the very same thing right now–probably stopped at Granny's to see if she and Grandpa were managing all right."

"We could telephone them," Oliver suggested.

"Let's wait a few more minutes, and then if she hasn't come through that door, we'll give them a tinkle."

Besides the storm outside, the only thing they heard now was their breathing, as the three of them snuggled in the warmth of familial security and listened to the crashing and banging outdoors and for the sound of the front door handle.

A roar of simultaneous lightning and thunder shot all three out of the chair and over to the far side of the room away from the window. Peter went to pull the curtains across the window to further enclose and protect them.

"Can we phone Granny now?" Cassandra asked.

"Let's hope the lines aren't down." Peter bit his lip as he said it when he saw Oliver's glassy eyes staring up at him.

"Probably they're right as rain," he added and pulled Cassandra to his chest. Oliver took his hand as they proceeded down the hallway to the kitchen and headed for the phone.

Oliver reached it first, took the receiver off, and handed it to Peter who nodded for Oliver to dial.

The line was dead.

"Hello, Gramps, is Jeannie there?" Peter said into the silent phone, looking at the expectant eyes of his children. "She's on her way home then?" he asked. "Right then, all's well there? Good. Cheers!"

Peter cringed at his lie, but the fear on their faces pushed him to extend the truth for as long as he had to, even as he felt dread to his very depths and wondered where Jeannie really was.

Half an hour later, as the children finished their hot chocolate and Peter finished his tea, the latch of the front door wiggled like the giant had arrived.

The children ran down the hallway to hug Jeannie. Through the door came their Henry, drenched and shivering.

"Gawd, it's a bloody waterfall out there!" He looked around. "Where's Mum? I've got something to tell her. Hello, me darlings!" he said to Cassandra and Oliver, patting them on the top of their heads as he always did.

"Mum never came home," said Peter. "Must have gone back to Gramps for the duration."

"Didn't phone?"

"Not . . . herself," Peter stretched the truth again.

Peter put the children to bed, sat awhile with Henry while Henry finished his book report, and then suggested they retire. It wasn't until three in the morning that Peter heard her come in the front door. He pretended he was asleep.

DETECTIVE AT WORK

Peter strode across the street as if it were a stage and he the star. His chin was tipped upwards, his pace determined, his eyes like an owl's, piercing his black-clad suspect with hardly a blink. The street was narrow and he turned left to follow the figure at such a distance that it would not betray a sneeze. Yet when he reached the corner, it was gone. He turned left again like a dancer and pushed on into a stride, his breath burning his lower lip. The wind swept up the dirt from the garden along the road and swirled it into his wide eyes. He blinked rapidly to keep his eyes open for the sight of this figure in black.

A stone flew in front of his feet; he jumped aside and glanced left. A coat tail flapped as the figure climbed the wall nearby, and Peter heard a thump on the other side and a moan. It was a female voice. He turned to follow her, sprang up the crumbling stone wall and over, only to see her round the corner of the old, damaged house. He guessed she was in her thirties in some kind of disguise with her white fringe blowing under her black cape. Even with all his agility and his self-confidence, no matter how she leapt and lunged, he felt unable to catch up with her. He called out, "Stop! Police here!" but it only seemed to spur her onwards.

He rounded the corner, panting like a runner finishing a race, and could see that she had quite disappeared. There was a closed gate ahead.

There was a broken wall to the left. There was a garden shed to the right. Peter stopped and stood still, listening as if for a train whistle in the distance, trying to hear sounds beyond his own puffing. The wind shifted and blew his fair hair into his eyes from just under his hat.

Then he heard her panting. He crept over to the shed and stood outside the metal door that hung an inch ajar. He quietly put his hand on the door handle and breathed in, then jerked it open, ready to pounce. For a second, he saw her face, and then he felt the shovel crash onto his head; he fell to the ground and felt her shoe smash his palm as she threw herself over his downed body and dashed out of the nearby gate.

As he lay there, half-conscious, he felt that he might know that face. He stood up, placed his hand on his bleeding wound, and began to comprehend the serious nature of his obligations–those of a husband and father, as well as those of a detective and a trusted representative of the people of his village. He wiped his cheek with the back of his bleeding palm, then aimed his aching body towards the open gate.

THE FIGURE

A few days later, Peter was making his way towards home after work. The sky had darkened more than usual at this time; an overcast sky and night had both arrived. Across the street, the figure moved into the murky shadows. Peter froze. The figure melted like chocolate into the blue of the darkness between the branches. The person's height was the same. The movement was light and furtive, like a young person. Peter's misty breath clouded his vision.

The figure darted around the trees and along the brick wall into the narrow walkway and seemed to beckon him forwards, yet tiptoed away just as he neared his goal. This puzzle compelled him to follow the figure at its own pace. Why was he being teased like this? Who was it, really? Was he in danger? Would he be jumped and surprised? In spite of these thoughts, Peter moved closer.

As he turned the corner, all Peter could see was the heel of a boot disappearing by the street lamplight. When he reached that location, he turned and looked up and down the street. All was eerily quiet. The cat figure had escaped. Or was it ready to pounce? He stood still and listened with all his professional hearing he'd taught himself: the slight breeze, the piano notes in a house down the block, a dog barking far away.

Peter's heart was racing. His eyes narrowed as he cocked his head. After five minutes, he realized he'd been outwitted. Peter walked towards home, musing over the possibilities.

As he opened the front door and began to hang up his coat, he noticed a pair of boots by his feet. He couldn't help leaning down and feeling the soles. There was damp mud on both of them.

The house was dark and still. He closed the door and made his way upstairs to their bedroom. The lights were out except for the small night light in the bathroom. He pushed open their bedroom door and saw Jeannie sleeping. He walked to her side of the bed and laid his hand upon her back. Surely she must know that he knew who that figure was now? And yet, there she lay, breathing deeply like she did when she was asleep.

Peter lumped this event into the category of unusual happenings regarding Jeannie and decided to never mention it to her. He washed his face, brushed his teeth, and got into bed. But sleep would not come. This night he would sleep right beside her in their bed. How he longed to reach over and pull her to him, but also, he wondered who this strange person was who had shared his body and his bed for so long.

Later in the night, he felt her hand across his back, and he moved towards her as if this night were the same as other nights of long ago. He put his arms around her and tried to forget his misgivings. A powerful surge of fear and excitement overtook his logical thoughts, and he pulled her to his body and gave in to a primal heat that won over reason.

The Churchyard

A few nights later, Peter stepped out of the flat and went downstairs to be under the stars. The summer rain and the moody wind of yesterday seemed to have blown away across the Channel. What was left above was an invitation to the depths of the universe, an array of bright and faded stars, a sense of the vastness where the earth hung, small and fragile. Peter felt an unusually eerie feeling with absolutely no breeze at all to lean into. It was as if he were supposed to wait for the clocks to push further into the future, while at present, they waited, still as stone.

The children were asleep. He paced away from the flat as if he were a thief of space and time, as if he had cut the cord of responsibility that tethered him to his family. He didn't say to Jeannie, "I'm just popping down to the pub." No, he just left, not quite freely, for the guilt weighed heavier with each step upon the stone path. It was the pub he aimed towards–at least at first. But when he got to the corner, he turned left down the hill. The old church pulled him towards it while the pub's laughter diminished, the usual dart players getting drunker by the moment.

The church was closed and locked; only a small light flickered at the front doors. Peter followed his feet. He was working at a level of instinct now that he knew so well. It wasn't a sense of logic that moved his feet.

It was more of a pull of something like gravity that made his body go to this dark place where bones lay from the twelfth century. As he turned under the entrance arch and through the wooden doors that were only two hundred years old, he shivered as he thought of Pip at the graveyard in *Great Expectations.*

The bells were quiet–not even a wisp of wind shimmered by to give an echo of their existence. Peter could barely see his feet, but he kept walking up the long, stone pathway towards the lone light. He stopped and listened. Faint laughter filtered through the cool air from the Plough Inn down the street. The splash of a fish or frog from the pond near the pub brought Peter back to the moment of darkness around him. He didn't know what he was looking for, but he knew there was something to find. He had stood by the old front doors many a time in the past during the day, but now he stood very still and listened.

Beside him, there was a creaking. Peter stiffened, his head and body poised in extreme alert. He turned imperceptibly towards the sound. A footfall on the path around the side of the church made Peter want to flee. Yet whoever was there surely had a full view of him by the yellow light at the door. Peter stepped out of the light, backing into a shadow like a turtle pulling in its head. The moments of waiting were interminable, but these were the excruciating moments he lived for, not the drudgery of paperwork. If a person was hiding there, they had the same right to be there as Peter did. Yet, who would be wandering around the old churchyard instead of playing darts at the pub? Peter's heart quickened so much that it thumped in his ears: another footstep, another, fading back behind the church. In the darkness, Peter had to make up his mind what to do. Jeannie would guess he'd gone to the pub, in any case.

He heard the footsteps leaving on the stone path, and then it was all quiet and dark again. He started into the night, following the faded sound of retreat. He stopped and cocked his head: someone breathing over by the oldest raised stone coffin.

"Who's there?" he ventured.

A sudden gust of wind swept through the graveyard. The breathing grew quiet as the figure disappeared over the low, crumbling old stone wall and left Peter to wonder if he had been a witness to something mysterious that he would only know by the light of the morning.

INSOMNIA

When Peter awoke, it was dark. The dawn chorus had begun, but the house was eerily quiet. Jeannie was fast asleep, as were the children. Peter slid out of bed and headed towards the door.

"Peter. What's the matter, love?"

"Sorry. I didn't want to wake you. Just need to go to the loo." He rubbed the bump on his forehead.

"Oh," she mumbled and turned away as he stood motionless. He heard her breathing take up its deep, challenging sounds.

Peter turned back, shoved his cold feet into his slippers, and then proceeded out the bedroom door, which squeaked. One of these days he'd oil the hinges. He'd been saying that for years now. He sighed: he never would oil the hinges. He closed the door gently behind him and looked into the children's bedroom. Three lumpy beds exuded a deep mixture of sleep and gravity. He closed the door, which also squeaked.

The noises of a stranger creeping through the graveyard the night before had unsettled him. He had trained himself to think pleasant thoughts first thing before the reality of baser lives necessarily entered into his detective brain. But this surprising event left him cold and curious and slightly apprehensive. After all, it could have just been one of the homeless old men, and Peter had merely intruded into a quiet space where someone slept. How did those poor creatures manage through the rain and wind? Peter imagined a white-haired man, hunched up with a dirty sleeping bag under a plastic tarp, pressed under the ledge of a centuries-old stone grave, just a few inches from a skeleton inside, long dead to the cares of an old homeless man.

Peter walked to the kitchen, closed the door behind him, and was pleased that at least this door remained obediently quiet. He put the kettle on without even realizing he was doing it. He yawned and tried to think of something positive, but the darkness of the frightening night before stuck in his brain. He knew that even a nice hot cup of tea wouldn't remove it. Peter went over the strange evening in his head again and again. There was a deep dread that he couldn't shake. He'd have to get dressed and go out into the foggy morning and see who was sleeping in the graveyard. Meanwhile, he prepared the teapot and sat down to take the only quiet moment that day might afford.

It required a woolen jumper under his coat and his warmest scarf. He pondered about a hat. Well, it wasn't raining, and the fog might lift, with the sun coming up. He'd go hatless and wrap his brown scarf around his ears until the people started emerging from their houses to begin their working day.

Peter left the house without a sound. It was an easy ten-minute walk to the church. As he walked down the hill along the stone wall, he blew out the warmth from his lungs into his scarf and pushed out his lower lip to breathe warm air onto his freezing nose.

Peter worked his way down then up the hills until he reached the pond and the church. He turned into the churchyard and stopped to listen. The birds had finished their morning song, it seemed. The milkman was surely not too far down the road. Peter closed the old gates and surveyed the church, so old, so loved, yet so seemingly haunted with nobody there to tend it so early. It was as if the church and the graves had their own nightly existence, quiet and dreamy, far from the bustle of the traffic yet to come and the contemporary villagers whose lives did not include the dead and gone, except to brag of their centuries of residence like they were relatives.

Ahead of Peter was a man walking briskly towards the bus stop in his bowler hat carrying his umbrella. Sunny though it was, they all knew from childhood how the weather could change in an instant. Peter gripped the handle of his own umbrella. At worst, he could poke a foreign object with it.

Peter stood before the wooden gate, which he'd closed firmly after him last night. His eyes caught the fact that it was slightly ajar. Either someone had followed him out, or someone had gone in after he left, perhaps this morning at dawn. He pushed the gate open as it squealed like the moaning of a cat. He walked up the stone path towards the ancient church, scanning the leaning tombstones on either side. He hovered before the front doors and listened like he expected a ghost to appear. Was that a crackle he heard on the left? He listened again: no sound. He shrugged his shoulders and proceeded around to the side of the church where he had stood the night before.

A homeless bundle lay on top of the stone coffin and turned, mumbling to itself. Peter quietly mumbled, "Sorry," and back-tracked around the sleeping lump and up the slope towards the coffin he knew might hold the secret of last night. The leaves and grass made noise no matter how lightly he stepped. As he approached that coffin, he leaned over and put his outstretched fingers around a damp, dirty blue knit scarf. His eyes scanned it, his fingers feeling along the weave, along a familiar–a very familiar–knit pattern.

What was a scarf knit by his mother doing there? Was that Angela last night? He rolled it up and put it under his arm. He poked around the rest of the area with his umbrella, but everything rested like nature had left it. As he turned to go, he noticed a footprint. It was from a small shoe, a woman's shoe. He pulled out his flat detective kit, laid the foot-long plastic paper across the print, and pressed it evenly. As he did, he could tell that it was about the same size as his mother's shoe; he would try to match them up with women he suspected. He hardly suspected his mother, but together with the incriminating scarf, she would, indeed, have to be his first suspect.

Peter snickered to himself. What did this suspect actually do? There was no evidence of a crime: just a person out of place in the middle of the night. Very suspect, thought Peter–but still, a blind alley. What in the world would his mother be doing in the churchyard in the middle of the night?

THE CEMETERY

"Mum," **Peter** said that evening, his teacup perched on his knee.

"Yes, Peter, my love?"

He wished she wouldn't say, 'my love,' just when he was about to become a detective with her–his own mother.

"What were you doing outdoors last night?"

"Outdoors?" she said, eyes wide like a child caught sneaking forbidden sweets.

"Yes."

He waited.

"I wasn't outdoors. I was knitting by the telly. Look here! It's almost finished." She held up the green and white afghan, destined for the foot of his and Jeannie's bed.

"Mum! The churchyard, in the middle of the night! I went there today and found this blue scarf by a coffin," he said, holding up the bedraggled thing. "The coffin was too old even to read its inscription."

"Ah, yes. I'd forgotten exactly. Sometimes I go for a little walk at night to look at the stars if it's a clear night and not raining."

"Mum. The cemetery at night isn't a place you would want to be, would you?"

"Of course not. I just wandered in. Never did that before. I thought I might challenge my fears of the dark and the dead."

"Couldn't the dark streets do that well enough?"

"To tell the truth, love, I was visiting your father's grave. I don't like to do it during the day. He had a decent funeral, but I didn't cry just then. I couldn't cry. So now, son, I go there and, I am sorry to say, I still cry."

"Ah, Mum. Sorry to intrude."

"No, no. But you understand, don't you, Peter? It was such a scandal. I don't like to give the villagers any more ammunition than they already have against me. We moved in soon after he died, and there was a lot of whispering. Can't be helped, I suppose. But I can't let them see me crying. No more questions from those snoopy women!" She took out her handkerchief from her cardigan sleeve and blew her nose.

"Of course, Mum. No more said." But Peter then realized that his father's burial plot couldn't be where he'd heard her last night. Those graves were centuries old. His father's grave was way back as far as the property line behind the church.

"Mum," he ventured.

"Yes, my love?"

"Never mind. I'll have another cuppa, please." Peter had an uncomfortable feeling that his mother was lying. Why would she need to lie about his father's grave?

LOVE IS GONE

Peter couldn't immediately recall the exact moment he knew he didn't love Jeannie at all anymore. And anyway, what was love? It was passionate at first, and then it was the joy at sharing their young children. It was even the making up after a fight. But where was the line when it altered and the glint in his eye she used to see changed into a bored, hard stare? It happened over years, subtly, so that he didn't see it happening. He had become impatient with her outbursts, but, somehow, he had still loved her through that.

Perhaps it was when she blamed him for all the wrongs of men towards women? He was so fed up with that! Perhaps it was when he felt the need to pull Cassandra and Oliver, and especially Henry, away from her so that Henry could go on feeling fine about being a man: his son, so bright and kind, so observant, polite and jovial. He now knew it was when he felt a deep need to keep Henry out of earshot of her ranting. The love he had felt for her seemed to be absorbed away from her, sucked out of her heart, and into Henry's. Peter invented errands so he could get him away from those moments that were brewing behind her furrowed brow. Peter sent Henry on more frequent visits to Angela's house, up the hill on the corner of Nevill Road and Sheep Walk, always

193

to bring her sugar or to fetch her homemade biscuits and take them back for tea.

The love he felt had burned into fear and anger at what she was doing to their family, to him, to the contentment that should have sheltered them from the outside. Now negativity permeated the inside of the house, and his job's negative side needed balance. With this balance gone, Peter got irritated and found it a relief when Jeannie went to the Black Horse. The fact that she would be drunk upon her return was alarming, but he knew his love had died when he was willing to trade that evening peace with his children for her rude remarks when she crashed through the door at eleven twenty-five. Then her face was haggard, her eyes angry; her speech slurred. Her beauty had disappeared like a sponge had sucked it up and left her skin dry and wrinkled.

JEANNIE'S ANGER

Peter looked forward to his children's smiles when he got home from work, but he dreaded the next abusive words that would inevitably pour from Jeannie's mouth.

"Tea's cold," she'd said when he got home.

"Sorry, couldn't be helped," he answered as he put his briefcase on the chair.

"Always sorry! Try changing your schedule. Then you won't have to apologize for your existence."

"Jeannie!" he almost started in, and then he just stopped and changed the eternal subject.

"Hello, love," he kissed each child on the forehead as they buried their heads in their schoolbooks. Their silence was disturbing. What children would be so quiet when their beloved father got home, except if there had been anger and threats in advance of his opening the door? And yet, the children didn't complain. Once in a while, Peter caught young Henry's eyes looking up as if to say, yes, she's been shouting at us.

Peter felt helpless watching week after week as his children's faces appeared sadder and the days peeled on. He couldn't make it home any earlier. This job was very serious and involved high up political people.

It had to be done exactly right, or the hours were inevitably longer. A murder of a secretary and the new DNA he was learning about kept him busy in London as well as in Brighton.

Jeannie grumbled as she poured his tea. She grumbled as she clattered his plate in front of him, re-heated. She grumbled about the mud on the kids' shoes and the holes in their socks. She mumbled about the piles of laundry and the overdue bill at the corner grocers. Peter could hardly eat, listening to her endless moaning about life. He leaned into his food; all that could be heard was the clinking of his knife and fork on the plate.

Peter turned on the radio to pretend that sound was okay, and their life was normal. The kids looked up and smiled at him. The warmth of their existence pulled Peter up this torturous path. One day he would reach the top and be able to breathe again. But the hill was steep and long, the wind pushed his chest, and he stumbled backwards.

As usual, Peter asked himself where that love had gone. When had it evaporated? He had hardly seen it coming. It was just sitting there like a lump of clay, soggy, heavy, and solid. This realization was something he could not just brush off like a fly. It was something that welled inside his throat. He remembered loving Jeannie with such a great passion that he would have died for her. And now, it was more like she wasn't the same person that he had once loved so far inside his being. She was now an unhappy woman, complaining about everything, driving him and their children crazy. He had tried. He had indeed tried. And he wasn't a bloody "male chauvinist pig," as she had claimed several times.

That was just the new way that couples dealt with hard times: name-calling. He knew he wasn't one of them. He was conscious of everything going on around him, the women's movement, and all the things that men had taken for granted that were not fair to women. He was a good son; he knew of his mother's hardships. He washed the dishes as a boy while he imagined himself as Sherlock Holmes. He knew how to iron: he'd ironed many quilts; ironing was a part of life, not drudgery. He liked to fold the laundry and iron a crease in his trousers and along the arms of his clean white shirts.

Peter loved beauty in antiques as he did in people like he had loved Jeannie's beauty when she was young. She'd had a way of laughing at life that made him love his own life more. She had enough energy to take on the world and catapult it into space, sticking her tongue out at it all. That was the beauty that he loved.

And now? Now she was different. The beauty was hard to see, even when he tried to look and catch a glimpse of its old place in her face, her stance, her walk: her eyes, those eyes: dark eyes, brown and mysterious to him, full of laughter and light. But not now. That laughter had been gone for years, it seemed. He couldn't will the love back. He'd tried. He used to need her. He used to like her to be near him, to hold his hand, to nuzzle up to his neck, and kiss him. But now, when she approached him, he found himself backing off for fear of a touch that wouldn't feel right; a touch that meant something that, in truth, was gone like the famed green flash of the setting sun over the ocean's horizon.

Instead of depth, when he looked into her eyes, he saw a blank wall of resentment and even hate. He couldn't do anything to change her vision of him. He wished she would stop going to her new women's group. He wondered what they talked about there. Hadn't they gone through that already, years before?

She was quite ruffled each time she came home from that meeting. He had put the kids to bed, read stories to them, checked their homework, tossed the ball back and forth, joked, helped them with the dishes. He had done it all while she apparently griped about him in her group.

Peter hated to admit it, but he started to truly dislike that group. Why couldn't she go to a music group instead? Why couldn't she take up ballroom dancing or something? Why couldn't she stay home? She was just like her parents, sitting in that horrid pub he now hated. This group seemed to be an enormous eight-headed monster tearing their marriage apart like the currents rolling underneath the top of the ocean and pulling Peter and Jeannie in opposing directions.

Now he didn't even like Jeannie. He hated himself for admitting that. He would rather have kept it out of his conscious mind. He had enough hatred to deal with in his job—people hurting each other, killing animals in a rage, stealing from their neighbors, tripping up old ladies. He didn't need hatred in his home with his wife and children. But there it was.

One night Jeannie came home from the pub, and he knew she had been drinking too much. He tried to ignore it.

"Hello, love," she said, as always. "All the children asleep, then?"

He nodded. "Want a cup of tea?"

She smirked at him. Her body gave her away, loose and unguarded. He looked at her in disgust, and the thought of divorce flickered through his mind. That's what the Americans did, not the British! Then the thought of their children shot through his mind. Children needed a mother, even if she was a bit crazy. Indeed, she might just be a bit crazy.

"What do you think, Peter, love? I've had enough to drink this evening?"

"That's evident."

"You don't have to be like that. I have a right to have a drink if I like."

"How many drinks have you had, then?"

"Not that many. First, we had to drink a toast to Sylvia and Geoffrey for their twentieth anniversary. And then, of course, we had to toast the boys for winning at cricket. And then after that, Cynthia and Stephen are getting engaged."

"That makes at least four pints."

"No actually, Peter, I think I had about six. I have to pee...."

Peter watched her wobble past him towards the toilet. He felt a surge of disgust. The thought of making love to her was abhorrent right now. The idea of touching her depressed him–scared him.

When she came out of the toilet, she turned back towards him. He backed up.

"What's the matter, love?" said Jeannie. "Let's go have a good time!"

Peter backed further away, saying, "I have to use the toilet."

How long could he stay in there trying to figure out this whole nightmare? Maybe she would fall asleep on the settee while waiting for him. He heard Cassandra crying.

"I'm going," he said, emerging from the toilet, and went into the children's bedroom to calm Cassandra. He put his hand on her face and rested it there to calm the nightmare away.

Jeannie crashed into the room. "Go away. This is my job, remember?"

Peter was shocked. He'd never said it was her job. What was she thinking? He backed off and squeezed out the door. Cassandra started screaming again. Peter listened and felt hurt for his daughter, who had finally just calmed down so nicely.

JEANNIE

Peter opened the front door and didn't say his usual, "Hello! I'm home!" Instead, he listened to Jeannie, like the detective he couldn't help being, singing that loud Irish folk song his mother used to sing.

"Oh, Mrs. McGrath, the sergeant said,
Would you like to make a soldier
Out of your son, Ted,
With a scarlet coat and a big cocked hat,
Now, Mrs. McGrath, wouldn't you like that?
With your too-ri-a, fol-di-diddle da, too-ri, oor-ri, oor-ri-a"

There was something forced and harsh in her voice. Her song wasn't about Ted losing his leg in battle, but more about an angry woman who didn't like what she was doing, most likely the laundry, but who was singing fiercely to make the work tolerable.

Peter felt like he was spying on his own wife. But lately, she had been so strange in her highs and lows that he couldn't ignore the symptoms of something that wasn't fun and creative but rather morose and deep. Upon occasion, Peter had felt his moments of desperation and boredom and hopelessness. Still, mostly he could put these forces behind him with the centuries of security inherent in a cup of hot tea. It was as if the tea, the ceremony of accepting the hot mug into his hands, begged one to cancel out the bitter moment and produce a smile of gratitude instead. It was a communal offering, and Peter was reassured that there was another human being offering him, at the least, a temporary solution to the extraneous world that insisted on crushing his desired calm state.

The problem was that Jeannie frequently forgot to offer him a cuppa these days. He'd taken to hurrying into the kitchen and making her the offering instead. It was as if he knew that she needed it more than he did, no matter how many criminals he had detected that day.

Peter slowly closed the front door, took off his hat and scarf, and hung them on their hooks. Jeannie was now bellowing, *too-ri-a,* in a vicious way that had nothing to do with the song. He froze. He had a very uncomfortable fleeting notion that he was hearing a strain of insanity in her voice. He held his breath and stood very still. It felt like he couldn't even get into the kitchen in time to soothe her mood with tea.

> *"Well, if I had you back again*
> *I'd never let you go to fight the King of Spain*
> *For I'd rather have me Ted as he used to be*
> *Than the King of France and his whole navy.*
> *With your bloody too-ri-a, fol-di-diddle da,*
> *Too-ri, oor-ri, oor-ri-a!"*

Now it sounded like she was tossing the laundry somewhere up against the back door or over onto the kitchen table.

"Mum!" Henry yelled from inside the kitchen.

Peter rushed into the kitchen to find a delicate blouse of hers flung on top of the stove, bursting into flames. He grabbed it at the same time as Henry, tearing it in half, and landed on the floor where he and Henry stamped on it until the fire was out. Jeannie grabbed her ironing water and tossed it all over the smoldering shirt.

"Jeannie?" Peter said.

"What's the matter with you lot?" Jeannie smirked. "Never seen a nervous breakdown? So! Good! Have a bleeding look!"

She grabbed the hot iron from the ironing board and slammed it on the floor, the plug sparking out of its socket. Then she flung open the back door and ran out yelling, "*Too-ri-a, fol-di-diddle da, bleeding too-ri, oor-ri, oor-ri-a!*"

And then she fell face forward onto the cold, wet grass.

"Get on with your homework please, children. Mum's a bit over-wrought. Henry, put the kettle on; there's a good lad. I'll see to Mum."

Peter was somewhat afraid of what she might do to him. Actually, he'd rather leave her there. But he had to sort it out while the children pretended to be working in their notebooks.

"Jeannie, love—come back in now. Have a cuppa. Henry's put the kettle on. It's warm inside. Come along, there's a good girl."

Jeannie flashed her bulging eyes at him, and her wide mouth underneath her bleeding nose spewed out, "I am not a bloody *girl!*"

"I didn't really mean girl, did I? It's…oh, never mind. Come along now—the children are watching."

PETER

Peter took the razor and looked at its deadly edge. He couldn't fathom why he was so careful not to nick his fingers–habit and years of Angela protecting him from the outside world. He'd heard that single mums were over-protective.

The outside world got to him in its own, usual pounding way. He saw the hypocrisy of kindness over anger. He saw the smiles with the hardened eyes. He practiced his manners obediently, shook hands, even bowed slight, humbly, as a child should. He had said *thank you*, and *please*, *sir*, and *sorry* with due diligence after many years of Angela's reminders. But the world seeped in, and it was never what it was supposed to be.

Peter remembered the nursery rhymes that Angela had read to him. They seemed quite jolly as she almost sang them. He heard her singing *Bobby Shafto's Gone to Sea*. He'd become Bobby Shafto. He'd be a sailor and conquer the world. It was only much later that he realized what that would entail, seeing the local sailors who'd returned to marry their girl-friends. But they were already promised to others, and the pub was the place they went to drown their sorrows.

Reality had pushed into Peter's mind, right through the school rules, the quiet evenings as Angela had sewed, and he did his homework. His desire to be a detective was partly a need to satisfy the contradiction he kept seeing between the necessity of manners and the reality of poverty, crime, and hardship. Peter had stood back from the world and tried to put the pieces together. Up until now, he'd managed to fool himself–he solved riddles, caught criminals, upheld justice, shook the proper hands, spoke harshly to the criminals when necessary, and went home to tea and said his robotic words to Jeannie.

Now he was deep in depression, like he was in an endless hole with high, slick walls, and he was at the bottom. No matter what, he could not climb out. How he'd tried! How he'd smiled at Jeannie and the children to hide his own growing devastation.

Not today–not today. Maybe never–maybe never. The psychic hole sunk a foot as he raised the razor to his cheek. It struck him as funny, or hysterical, that he was at this demeaning fork in the road. He stared at the razor and admired its power, and held it to his throat to see how it would feel, and then he dropped the razor into the water, wiped off the foam, blacked out, and collapsed onto the bathroom tiles.

"Daddy, I have to use the loo," he heard from a long distance away. "Daddy, unlock the door. I'm bursting!"

The door! The lock! The razor! Cassandra! He reached up to the lock from the place where he was lying on the floor. He collapsed back onto the tiles as he flicked the lock open. His body blocked the door.

"Daddy!" yelled Cassandra as she pushed against the heavy door. It wouldn't budge.

"Get Mum," he mumbled and passed out cold.

"Daddy!"

"Daddy!" she screamed. "Mummy! Mummy!" Cassandra yelled as she ran downstairs and into the kitchen. Clattering footsteps thumped up the staircase.

After Jeannie and the children managed to push the door open enough for all of them to squeeze in, they all stood around him: Jeannie, cold and stern, as usual. Cassandra sat down on the potty.

"What's happening to Daddy?" Cassandra asked Jeannie while Jeannie bent down, kneeling against Peter's back.

"Get up, and come and help me with the children."

Peter opened his eyes partially, swallowed, and looked up at Jeannie.

She seemed to have blurry horns growing right out of the top of her head. Her arms splayed out like wings about to take off after her clawed toes whisked him away and dropped him into the sea. He closed his eyes and waited for some kind of brutality on her part. When he opened them, she had gone and only Cassandra knelt nearby watching him.

"I almost peed in my pants, Daddy!"

"Sorry, my love," he murmured.

"Can you get up, Daddy? Have you hurt your arm?"

A little kindness was all he wanted–a little witness–some concern. After all, he was not a block of wood, just providing an income so they could eat.

"Thank you, Cassandra, my sweet darling. Give your papa a hand, then," he said, offering his hand and not letting on that his shoulder stabbed with pain.

Peter groaned as he slowly pushed himself up with the help of Cassandra's immense pulling, puffing, and leaning. He bent down in spite of his pain and kissed her on the top of her head.

"You are so precious to me, little Cassandra. Thank you for helping me up."

"Why did Mum walk away? She could have helped you better than I did. She's big."

"I don't know, really. I just don't know."

BREAKDOWN

Two days later, Jeannie broke down at teatime at Angela's house right in front of the children. Peter was shocked. He only wished she could have hidden in the bathroom or gone off on a quick walk to the shops or stayed in a corner somewhere. But Jeannie had fallen apart yet again right in front of her innocent children!

She screamed at them. She yelled at Peter. He reached out and grabbed her by the arm and said, "We're going for a walk! Now!" and he yanked Jeannie down the hall and out of the front door, adding, "Sorry, Mum!"

Peter dragged Jeannie to the car and sat her down. He got into the driver's seat and drove the car away from the eyes of curious villagers, up to the cliffs where the sea was loud, and nobody could hear a woman going crazy.

Peter parked the car and went around and opened Jeannie's door. He took her hand and pulled her up and out. They walked, as they had begun to do lately, to exorcise their anger away.

As they went along their path, watching the sun disappear over the hills, a chilly wind swept the tall grass into motion. Peter remembered how they had fallen in the grass right about there and made love so long ago. He remembered how his bicycle had plunged off the cliff, and he was able to buy a new one somehow.

"What a way to spoil our day with Grandma, Jeannie!"

"Who cares what I spoil? I'm tired, Peter. I'm beat. I need a break. What's happening to me? What is going on? I feel like screaming!"

"Then scream," Peter said as the wind blew his hair in all directions. "Scream all you want here–nobody will hear you." Peter was horrified at Jeannie's recent violent outbursts, which seemed to come out of the blue–no real reason–they just burst out.

So Jeannie screamed at the wind and the sea. She screamed at the grass and the sunset. Then she turned to Peter, who, though concerned, was trying to avoid the whole scene–just to let her get it out of her system and calm down. He pulled her along and led the way on the part that was narrow. Jeannie screamed until she'd almost lost her voice.

They were silent now as they walked the familiar path. He was afraid he would say something to spark off her temper again, and she didn't talk either. For a split second, he thought about the razor again. The ocean crashed below. After a while, they stopped, and Jeannie started in.

"So, is this a talking to?"

"Of course not! I'm not your parent. But you have been drinking rather...."

"So, it is a talking to!"

"Well, all right, maybe it is."

"And why would I be drinking, may I ask?"

"Jeannie, I have no idea why you have started drinking when you know darned well your parents...."

"You leave my parents out of this. It is nothing to do with them. Take a look in the mirror. That's who it has to do with." She swayed along with the grass.

"Jeannie, you are becoming very unreasonable. I'm doing everything in my power to keep this family going. I make the money. I help with the children. I do bloody everything!"

"You see! That's the point. You 'help' with the children! Why can't *I* say that? What if I said I was perfect and keeping this family together because I *help you* with the children? And I work, too, Peter. If I were paid like a man for the same work...."

"Jeannie, please, let's not talk about that again. I can't fix all the wrongs of the world!"

"Right, then. You don't have to mention how you earn the money for the children. I put in my hours, but the only difference is, you're a man, let's face it."

Peter kept his mouth shut and stared at the distant horizon.

The silence was overwhelming, so Peter began to walk again, up the narrow path with the crashing waves below to his right. Jeannie followed along, and then she began to cry.

Peter pulled her towards him and put his arm around her, but she shrugged it off and dropped back behind him. She was screaming. He could just reach out and hug her. He could try to be helpful. It seemed that a hand was what she really wanted–human warmth and understanding.

He put his hand behind him in a subtle way so that she could choose to take it or not. When he looked around and saw her hand coming towards him–he saw that she was too close to the edge. He reached farther to grab her hand. But her face changed to alarm. Her mouth opened to let out a deathly yell! And then she was falling and screaming, her arms flailing into the sky and then downwards, the sound of her scream diminishing rapidly. He yelled again. "Jeannie! Jeannie! Oh, my God! Jeannie!"

Jeannie's last look stabbed into his soul, her mouth wide, her eyes bulging in shock and surprise, and her voice echoed, as she fell, slowly, rapidly, endlessly! In a moment, she was just gone. Gone!

"No! Jeannie! My love! No! No! Help!" he yelled. "Help!" Peter screamed into the wind. His mouth opened wide. He fell onto his knees and yelled again, "No!" and buried his face in his hands. He uncovered his face and looked down through his tears, then dropped face down onto the grass as a black cloud enveloped his mind and canceled everything out.

And then there was a strange calm. There was the sound of the ocean breaking on the rocks below–the crash, the ebb, the hush, and again, the rhythmic crash.

People in the distance were running towards him. Now he was crying as he struggled up and crawled over and hung his head over the cliff, staring down. Her body lay still and broken across the sharp boulder jutting out from the cliff.

A helicopter came then, or was it later? He didn't know; he couldn't remember; he didn't care. She didn't catch his hand. She fell. Why had they walked so close to the cliff? Cliffs had never bothered Peter or Jeannie–they always liked them. He had never felt dizzy or scared–he had even felt thrilled by the height. And now? And now? Her body lay limp and still far below him.

The green grass at the edge of the cliff caressed his cheek. He couldn't quite remember where he was, but then he heard the voices and looked at the crowd of people charging up the hill. Some rushed up beside him, but the rest ran up to the cliff's edge and leaned over it–they were murmuring to each other and looking back at him.

"Did he push her?" he heard one of them whisper. Peter groaned, and they all turned to stare. Someone was helping him stand up. He got up slowly while a woman in a tartan scarf steadied him on his left and a stocky man held his arm on his right. The wind was churning up into a fierce cloud chaser. Peter's hair slapped against his face.

"You all right, then, Gov?" said the round man who Peter recognized as their butcher. The woman seemed familiar–her smelly breath indicating she had run up the hill from the pub.

"I'm fine," he said, but staggered as they held firmly to his arms.

A flash of Jeannie's face going over the cliff knocked him into a swoon. He turned and stumbled back towards the cliff.

"No, Gov, that's not a wise idea," said the butcher, still in his bloody apron. The butcher and the woman both struggled to lead Peter away.

"No!" he yelled and shook them loose. "Sorry," he said, as he turned and headed quickly back to the cliff and the muttering crowd gathered there.

They looked at him, and two young men held up their palms as if to stop him. Peter stumbled forwards, but they caught him and swung him away from the cliff. The crowd turned to observe them, then turned back to watch the rescue efforts down on the rocks–the stretcher being carried by the ambulance driver, the crowd forming on the pebbles below.

The indifferent waves crashed towards the shore without hesitation, onwards, nearing the rocks, then diminished and died while the next ones surged to their destiny.

"I'm all right now," he said, and the people guiding him gently let him go. His gait had steadied, but they were walking him away–away from Jeannie.

"I have to see her," he spluttered, looking back over his shoulder.

"She's being transported in the ambulance now," said the woman.

"Is she…I mean, is she…?" Peter said.

"We don't know," said the butcher.

Peter broke away from them and started running down the hill. He reached the ambulance just as they slid the stretcher inside.

"I'm her husband!" Peter yelled.

A man reached out for Peter's hand and helped him climb inside. Then they sped four long miles into Brighton to the hospital. Peter just stared at Jeannie's bloody face. She looked dead.

They took her out of the ambulance so quickly that he hardly noticed a nurse taking his hand and leading him to a desk. He choked back his tears; his chest was heaving; his breath caught; he couldn't see the words of the papers he had to sign.

The police arrived for a statement. Of course, they knew him well. He understood their need to question him. Out dribbled the answers. He suddenly knew how it felt to be on the other side. The questions were a blur. They were confirmations of the truth that had just broken him in half.

They drove him back to Angela's. He dreaded that moment when the children were going to ask, "Where's Mum?" At least the police had said she was still alive.

COMA

The next morning as Peter drove to the hospital, gritting his teeth, afraid of what he might see, he went over those last moments, the sense of her behind him, the energy coming his way from her, how he turned to reach out his hand and how her own energy catapulted her forwards, then how she twisted and stumbled and flew off the cliff–that scream, diminishing like the end of a song–his shock–his disbelief–his own desire to reverse what he saw–to have caught her hand and drawn her towards him in a warm embrace far from the present and back into their remarkable past, full of laughter and love.

The children were at Angela's. She was the best grandmother anyone could wish for–always there, loving the children; countless projects to teach and pass down; her stories that she used to tell Peter; the songs he'd almost forgotten pouring from her memory into their ears. The children were safe for now.

In what state would he find Jeannie? He dreaded this moment as he pulled into the parking area and got out. He found out her room number and made his way there. The hospital halls were grim with so many people waiting to be seen, in wheelchairs or rolling beds or along the long line of uncomfortable chairs, young and old, all waiting endlessly.

When he arrived at her door, he hovered and took a deep breath. He reached for the door then decided to knock first. It was a tentative knock, more a warning than a polite notice of permission to enter. He heard no reply, so he gently pushed the door ajar and saw Jeannie lying still on the far bed, one leg propped up in the air. He moved cat-like as he made his way past the other patient and stood at the foot of Jeannie's bed. Her eyes were closed. Tubes were attached everywhere. Her face was severely bruised, her hair swept back, exposing her forehead covered with bandages. Her left arm was in a cast. It seemed that life and death hovered around her like they were in a gentle battle or dance.

Peter had been told of her comatose state, but somehow it only really penetrated when he saw her in this deathlike posture. The doctors said she could easily die or could easily awake. They had no idea, he realized, what was happening to her. He pulled up a chair and sat by her side. Reaching over, he gently slid his hand into hers as it lay limply by her side. It was cool, almost cold to the touch. He studied her fingers, scraped and bruised and inert.

Peter looked at Jeannie's puffy, purple cheek and her left eye, swollen shut. He looked at her head, wrapped up like she wore a turban. It seemed as if her drooping mouth was held down at the corners–permanently stitched downwards. He looked in horror at her broken leg, surrounded by plaster and held up by a sling, her arms wrapped in solid casts down to her fingertips. He felt queasy and could hardly push a word out of his mouth. Although she was comatose, part of Peter was relieved that he need not talk.

Peter pulled up a chair and nudged the dripping water bag aside. It seemed to hang heavily against his hand. Tubes were everywhere; a bag of yellow and red urine hung by the bedside. Peter retched and looked away.

"Jeannie, my love," he said, turning back.

She made no sign that she had heard him. He reached for her three exposed fingers on her left hand. They felt cold and dead. He squeezed them gently then put his hands back in his lap. A middle-aged nurse came in with a cup of tea.

"Thank you very much," he said.

"These patients hardly ever remember their visitors, love. It's mostly a total blackout for them. You might as well talk to her anyway. Sometimes, I've heard that the sound of a voice pierces through that blackness. It's worth a try, isn't it?"

"Thank you," Peter said again, his cup clinking in the saucer.

The nurse left, and Peter calmed his nerves with a hot sip, that comforting warmth trickling down his throat.

"You're alive, Jeannie. You've made it through."

She didn't move her eyes, her mouth, or her nose. She looked quite dead—white and dead.

"Tea's hot," he said, looking back over at the other patient.

He sat for a few quiet minutes wondering how the children would feel to see their mother in this state. He'd put them off a bit longer, but soon enough their clamoring would get to him. They would be sad and shocked. But they would have to see her eventually. No one knew how long she would be like this or if she would ever become normal again.

Peter's chin dropped to his chest. A lone tear escaped his right eye, and he quickly wiped it away and furtively looked to see if anybody had seen his momentary lapse of composure. Then he felt a fool. Men cried more openly these days—one wasn't a sissy anymore. One was a whole person with feelings. But the memories of his childhood tears and the teasing about being a wimp dug deep and still bound him to silence.

"The weather's improved," Peter said. "It's not so windy; still cold, but not much rain. One of these days, I'll wheel you out into the sun."

Would she ever get out of that hospital bed, open her eyes, smile? Talk? Would she ever hear his words again and laugh at his occasional wry humor? Would she ever ask about the children?

"Oh, Jeannie, what have we done?" he whispered and choked and kissed the tips of her fingers, one-by-one. "What have we done?"

Without warning, tears now flowed down his cheeks. It didn't look at all hopeful. Peter felt lost deep down to his very soul. He took out Blake's poetry book and read a few words aloud. Even if she couldn't hear him, the sound of his own voice reading poetry kept him going, one foot in front of the other; back out of the hospital, back to work, back to the children and teatime and supper and homework and lights out, and television to numb it all away—until the next day.

ANXIETY

Peter's anxiety was churning up his stomach. He felt hungry, and his body ached. They said she was out of her coma, and he could finally talk to her instead of a body whose soul was locked away from his words.

Peter winced as he noticed a fleeting thought that flashed through his mind before he could censor it–why couldn't she just have died?

"Oh, God!" he mumbled to himself, imagining a slap across his face. Did other people have these horrible thoughts? Of course, he didn't wish that she had died! Death was permanent–the end of everything. In fact, now their conversation could continue. Peter realized, in horror, that he didn't want their conversation to continue.

Peter walked in the doors of the old hospital. Nurses or nuns or both sped down the halls, each carrying a heavy load. He asked at the information desk if Jeannie had been moved–not yet.

Perhaps she was sleeping again. He walked towards the same room and was gently told to wait, so he went and sat in the hallway so long that his head fell forwards in a doze.

"You may come in now," said a young nurse.

Peter grabbed his briefcase and shook himself awake, wishing for a hot coffee. His stomach clenched, and his mouth was sticky and dry. He pushed the door ajar as the nurse disappeared down the hallway, and he walked up to Jeannie's bed, glancing at her raised leg in its cast.

Peter was miserable watching her lying there, looking so dead. But a secret part of him was relieved not to have to talk about what had happened. Who would bring it up? They would have to bring it up soon enough. Should he just stick to the weather for now–and ask her how she feels? He brought the book of Blake's poems again. Perhaps, this time he might get a response–she'd always liked Blake. He brought a few postcards of oil paintings–of Bacon's swirling figures. He brought her favorite photo of a Modigliani nude sculpture: a tall, thin being that Jeannie had somehow identified with. He'd rejected Degas' pastel, *The Laundress*, as he didn't want her to dwell on the misery of the endless mounds of laundry inevitably piling up at home no matter how hard Peter tried to get through it. Again, he pulled out of his pocket the notes from the children–he'd read them to her before, but perhaps now she might actually hear them. He brought things that might remind her of the beauty of life–he brought her inspirations to go on living.

"Hello, love," he said, and kissed her clammy forehead.

Her eyes moved slowly in his direction, but her face still looked like stone. Her hair was bedraggled and damp. Did she even recognize him? He pulled up a chair and sat close by. The other patient still lay comatose in her bed hidden partially behind a curtain, surrounded by gurgling blood infusion equipment.

Peter felt awkward. Jeannie's eyes accused him of something, but her mouth remained inert. He wished for a hot cup of tea now. He'd settle for tea–something else to draw his attention naturally away from her stern-looking face. He shivered and wondered if that look would stay fixed in his brain forever. Was it his fault? Had she been suicidal? Was she just plain crazy?

"Glad to see you back in the land of the living, Jeannie, my love." He felt completely idiotic. What did she know about how she had looked dead before today? Her eyes began to close, and he felt so alone again. He reached for her limp hand but pulled back just before he actually touched it. It seemed she was half alive and half dead.

"I brought you poems by Blake. Shall I read them to you?"

Her eyes opened halfway. She seemed to nod. Her eyes closed again, leaving him sitting there wishing he was somewhere else where he could have a conversation. But where was that? Not in a pub. The silence in that room pulled the corners of his mouth down as he fumbled with the pages, looked at her pale face, and began to read–she seemed to have fallen back into a coma again.

HENRY

"I want to see Mum today, Dad," Henry said, his new voice cracking on "today," his knife scraping his plate.

"Let's wait a day or two, Henry. You know she's in a coma. She can't really hear you."

"Sorry, Dad, but I need to see her alive; I don't care if she looks dead. I have to see her. Please, Dad!"

Peter began clearing the dishes away. Henry stood up and carried the soup bowls over to the sink. Henry was practically a young man now. He certainly had a right to see the reality of Jeannie's plight. Peter had planned a quick trip to London today to check on some DNA research. It was an urgent matter of timing–the culprit could escape before they had the evidence to arrest him. But what was a trip to London compared to that crease between his son's eyebrows?

Peter admitted to himself a sense of shame that somehow he was involved in Henry's mother's tragic fall. He couldn't see those questioning looks Henry might have shot him over his homework, but here was a pure request from Henry's heart.

Perhaps Peter could just send him to the hospital alone. But Henry would melt at the sight of his mother's fragile state and would need Peter's comforting words to get through it: words of hope; of the temporary nature of this coma; of a future with Jeannie, lively and talking about silly things again like bugging Henry to take out the rubbish or make his bed or help his siblings.

"All right, Henry. You can skip school, and we'll go to see her right away. Perhaps I can still get to London as well. Would you like to go up to the lab with me?"

"I'd like that very much, Dad. I've always wondered where you worked in London." Henry shot Peter a cheerful smile. Peter realized he's just set up a father-son moment. He never planned things like that— too American. Peter put his hand on Henry's back as Henry placed the bowls in the sink. He patted Henry's shoulders and smiled at his son with his new fuzzy mustache, and he felt his own upper lip stubble and remembered how once it had grown in so soft and delicate.

Jeannie had been comatose for three weeks now. Sometimes she woke up. It was unpredictable. Peter was losing hope. How long would this go on?

"Mum!" Henry said, as they entered her hospital room. She had fewer bandages around her head. At least she looked slightly better.

Henry walked over to Jeannie and stood by her bedside, his arms at his sides. He looked sad and shocked. Peter went around to the other side and bent over and kissed Jeannie's bare, but purple and yellow cheek. Henry shuffled a little and then bent over and kissed her other cheek.

"She can't hear us, can she?" Henry asked.

"Probably not," Peter said.

"She looks terrible!" Henry spluttered.

"She looks better if you can believe it."

"Let's go. I can't stand it a moment longer."

"Calm down, Henry. Stand here and be with it." Peter winced at what he felt was American psychobabble.

"What's there to be with? She looks dead. Maybe she is dead?" Henry put his ear to her face.

"No, she's breathing. She still looks dead." Henry turned his back to Jeannie and Peter, holding his stomach as he rushed out the door and down the hall. Peter jumped up and hustled after Henry, catching up with him at the lift.

"I can't do this. Why did you let me come?"

Peter kept his mouth shut, got into the lift and stood back while Henry pressed the button for the ground floor.

"I don't want to go up to London today. Sorry, Dad. I think I'll just go to school now."

With that, Henry took off, hurrying out the hospital door and down the busy pavement. Peter limply raised his hand to wave. Henry never looked back.

"Damn," Peter said, turning towards the train station and the DNA lab. This balancing act was getting him down. What would Henry tell the children? They might never be able to get to sleep. Peter felt split apart down to his very soul. How many lives was he responsible for now? Peter held himself in check and felt rather British and stodgy.

Rights

One day bled into another as Jeannie's health deteriorated. As Peter looked over at Angela sipping her tea, he knew that the doctors weren't ready to tell the truth that Peter knew just by being with Jeannie. This new coma couldn't last much longer. And yet, did he hope it would, just so he wouldn't have to tell the children the truth? At the deepest, darkest, most private part of his soul, he violently wished that she would just die. Even the children might be relieved. They would all cry and cry. They loved Jeannie. Of course, Peter loved Jeannie, a woman with spirit and life and, yes, a large dose of anger. Death seemed a word hardly used around the truly dying. Peter somehow felt he was not allowed to talk about it, though it was always on his mind. He felt he needed to make practical decisions, like where to have her buried in the churchyard and where the funeral would take place. Yet that would be toying with Nature's plan, which had mostly seemed to have been taken over by plastic, rubber tubes, and medications. As the days passed, however, nature appeared to Peter to be asserting her power over the conceit of the medical establishment.

Peter made calls to the minister who was sworn to secrecy, inferred by Peter's whispering voice. These details were not unknown to Peter, but he'd never had to make the actual arrangements for one of his own family. It was about all this that he wanted to talk to Angela, but Angela mostly kept her mouth shut and her thoughts to herself, for which Peter was grateful.

"What if…?" she said, while the children played outside in the tall grass.

Peter only looked up briefly, but, by then, she had looked away. It had to remain unspoken for some reason. But now Peter knew he wasn't the only one thinking about it.

The telephone rang.

Angela motioned for Peter to pick it up.

"Yes. I'll be right there," he said into the phone. "She's not breathing well," he said to Angela as he pushed his chair back under the table. He stood and drank the remaining tea in one gulp as if to energize his next moves.

"I think I should take the children."

"Oh, Peter. Let them stay here. Why should they see her…now?"

"To say goodbye, Mum. They have that right."

"We didn't used to let children see the saddest parts of life."

"Perhaps that was a mistake, Mum."

Angela looked up. There was a very long pause–was she thinking about what had she hidden from him? He longed for his full rights as a child, even now. He longed not to have anguished throughout his childhood to know the truth. He wouldn't add mystery to his own children's right to know.

He turned and opened the back door.

"Children! Meet me round the front. We have to get to the hospital immediately."

Henry stood outside the door, quite tall and almost grown, his eyes unflinchingly asking the question.

"She's dying," Peter said, and he saw Henry sigh, as if relieved to hear from his father the truth he already knew.

GOODBYE

Peter, Henry, Cassandra, and Oliver stood by Jeannie's bedside in the hospital.

"Mum," Cassandra said. "Wake up, Mum!"

"Don't be silly," Oliver said. "She's dead."

"No, she isn't," cried Cassandra, grinding her eye with a fist.

"No, she isn't," confirmed Peter, dabbing his eyes with his handkerchief.

"But she will be soon," said Oliver.

"You can touch her," Peter said.

No one moved. Then Cassandra lifted her hand slowly and moved it to Jeannie's cheek and lowered it to make a slight touch.

"She's warm," cried Cassandra, sniffling and searching for her handkerchief up her jumper sleeve with the other hand.

"That means she's alive," Oliver said. "She'll be cold when she's..."

Peter said, "...when she's dead. So touch her now, and remember the warmth of your mother."

"Dad, what warmth?" Henry said, as if this question might hide his grief.

"Did she read you stories when you were little? Did she put her arm around you? Did you rest your cheek against hers–her lovely warm cheek?" Peter yanked out his own handkerchief again and blew his nose, looking away, his eyes glassy. "Sorry," he added.

"I remember," Oliver said. "Her cheeks were soft and warm." He moved towards her, reached her cheek from between the tubes and the oxygen mask, and rested the back of his quivering hand there for a whole ten seconds. Nobody spoke. It was as if the last of her energy were electrically being pulled into Oliver's hand so he could go home and treasure it forever.

Jeannie's breathing began to falter.

"Dad!" Henry said, the truth of the moment defying his reserve.

"I'm afraid she is taking her final breaths," said Peter. "Stay or leave; it's up to each of you, individually."

The three children stood watching while Jeannie struggled to breathe. Peter had the urge to run out of the room, but for the children, he stood and witnessed Jeannie's last breaths. He put his arms around Cassandra and Oliver and gave Henry a long, steady look. Henry took Cassandra's hand.

Jeannie's throat began to rattle. Peter reached to her forehead and rested his palm heavily across it. Did her eyes strain to see through her last moments alive, to see whose hand rested so firmly on her forehead? Peter thought so. He forgot the children. He leaned in and kissed her lips and said, "We're all here, Jeannie. We love you." The rattling became louder. Her eyes didn't seem open even a little now. They dropped deep into their dark sockets and stopped moving.

There was one last, lingering noisy rattle and expiration, and then she didn't breathe in again.

Peter kept his hand on her forehead. Cassandra and Oliver turned to look at him. He needed to lift his hand and comfort his children. Her forehead already seemed to be cooling. He wanted the rest of the heat left to smother his palm, but the children were buried in his coat now, weeping uncontrollably. He put both arms back in place around Cassandra and Oliver and looked at Henry, who stood stock still, watching his mother's face become stony. Peter was horrified to notice a huge sense of relief coming from behind his own tears.

"Say goodbye to your mum," he said, wiping their tears away.

"Goodbye, Mum," said Cassandra, her bottom lip quivering.

"Goodbye, Mum," Oliver said, quietly observing his mother's face, perhaps realizing that it would be the last time.

Henry stood still, his jaw firm, looked away and didn't say a word.

It felt like an hour before they finally all backed away. There didn't seem to be anything to do or anywhere to go. The silence of her death was interrupted by the nurse coming in again to check Jeannie's vital signs.

"Would you like to wait in the hall?" she asked.

"Sorry, but I think we ought to leave now," Peter said. "I'll return later, but these children need to be with their grandmother now."

As they left Jeannie, all of them took one last look from the doorway, and Peter pretended for a fleeting moment that she was just sleeping.

NONSENSE

It wasn't until one afternoon several weeks after the funeral, as the children worked in the kitchen on their homework, that Peter could even imagine himself in that scene with Jeannie. He sat in the sitting room, his book slumped on his knee. He pinched his eyes as they began to shut, and the scene of Jeannie and himself, high upon the cliff, came to him like he was a distant spectator.

He couldn't hear the voices or the words–only the gestures spoke volumes. He remembered that his back was turned–she was falling–he moved to reach out his hand–she fell. He couldn't remember her scream, but he imagined her body as she plunged down to the rock and the ground below. He saw himself throwing his frenzied hands out–too late– to catch her, and then he imagined himself gripping his head with his mouth wide, yelling something while his body slithered down into the grass.

Peter backed up the scene in his mind, again and again. This time he was right there, as close as her breath. She was following him; then she slipped. He thought he had turned, but not in time–he reached out to grab her hand–her hands. They were both stretched out before her, her face contorted while her eyes flashed like a frightened animal–at first with a horrible look of surprise following some other, perhaps angry expression.

But that look dissolved before Peter could catch it in his brain and put it neatly somewhere to recall later. It just disappeared into the startled face, full of fright as she slipped away from his helping hand. Did their fingers touch and slide away from each other? Had he stepped aside from her just as she reached out and lost her footing? Was the energy of her body moving towards him or falling away? Peter watched the figures in his mind with their dance so silent. Was this their last interaction–their last true conversation? Was this their last honest moment?

And where was love at that very moment? Was it his arm stretching out to save her? He rewound the scene yet again. He saw himself, turning aside, lunging towards her, failing, failing–failing her. After that, he saw himself again from a distance, falling onto the grass, fainting, unable to further comprehend the devastation that lay below, the crowd rushing towards him above while another group dashed towards her battered body at the bottom of the cliff.

Peter picked up the book from his knee and tried to focus–he had no idea what he was reading. He blew his nose and blinked his eyes awake. Something was missing, but in the light of day, in the place where everything fits nicely, he could not grasp it. It was like his hold on the book, so firm and yet, so easy to let go. He put his handkerchief away and gripped the book grimly with both hands, as if, somehow, it would make everything right. How could he ever make everything all right again?

But Peter had work to do. What was he thinking–that he had time to read a mystery? He put the book down, still on the same page as yesterday, and stood up. The children would expect their dinner soon. His work as a detective demanded urgent solutions. There was no time for this nonsense. He went through the kitchen and into the back room and began to sort out the laundry. Then he walked back into the kitchen, turned on yesterday's leftover stew, and began to stir, hardly seeing his children as they did their homework.

FIGURING IT OUT

Peter cried himself to sleep every night, so long after the inquiry—
that inquiry. He was numb all through it. He couldn't feel his arms as
they hung stiffly down his sides. He couldn't hear anything at all, and he
walked out of the inquiry in the same trance that he was in when he went
into it. He couldn't even think about his children. He wanted to die, too.

Peter was quite surprised that he was required to have a psychiatrist
for six months before the case would be closed, and he was also required
to join a men's group. What a waste of his time! Couldn't they see that
he had children to raise?

He had moved the family within easy walking distance of Angela's
house so that she could help out with the children. They were learning
how to quilt and sew beautifully while they listened to stories Angela told
them about the war. The children were glad they didn't have wars anymore. That is what Grandma said. "No more war!" she always said. That
is what they said on the television about the Vietnam War and World
War II, or was it what they shouted? It was like a part of the food they
digested every day. No more war! Angela embroidered it into her quilts.
People bought them. They hung them in their sitting rooms. Enough!

Peter spent endless hours trying to figure out what had happened that horrible day. He had thought of himself as the ideal father and husband– he was, damn it all!

The men's group that he had to attend had formed right there in Rottingdean. Some American man called Frank had started it, imported it right from California, where there were apparently hundreds of men's groups flowering. There they were again: *bonding*.

Peter would have preferred a wife to talk to, but at least he could tell these men he was innocent. At first, of course, they joked that he was some kind of hero, throwing Jeannie off the cliff. But when they saw Peter's face, so sad and serious, Peter could see that they realized it wasn't a joking matter. They even apologized because that was the rule of Frank, their group leader–men had to apologize to other men. Men had feelings, for goodness sake! Maybe wars wouldn't start if men got into their feelings, Frank proclaimed.

Peter had to deal one-on-one with yet another American, a therapist named Helen, assigned by the court–a woman even. He wondered at all these Americans leaving their own shores to tell the rest of the world how to act. He wondered at their own huge country where it seemed to Peter that everybody walking down the street was probably a big mess.

WHERE

One night Peter woke up with a pounding in his temple that almost pushed his vision sideways. He stumbled out of bed and lurched to the w.c., where he vomited into the toilet. He had not had a drink the previous night, but he remembered sitting in a slump for hours at home, hardly able to look at the bright light from the television, and unable to read either.

Visions of Jeannie, her hand held out towards him, her face contorted, almost surprised, as she fell past his jutting hand that perhaps had even touched her and slipped away. He questioned his reflexes. Surely he could have caught her hand? He could have saved her.

Images of her angry face all through the years alerted him to a secret desire that she would disappear somehow—not die, really—but just not be in his life anymore. And here it was. She was gone forever. And he hadn't caught her. He imagined now that he had loved her as he had from those very first days they were together when love remained forever. Where had that charming girl gone? Where had his daring darling gone, cycling dangerously down hills, challenging every blockade, rushing into the Paris crowds and *gendarmes*? That wonderful, lively energy had gone over a cliff, and a bright flame was extinguished.

Peter put his hand gently on his temple and held it there to transfer the pain somehow from his head out through his touch. It was early. There were rustlings in the children's bedrooms. It was time to be a parent, put the kettle on, mix the oatmeal, and set out the bowls, toast, butter, and jam.

A door opened, and Peter looked towards the dark kitchen beckoning him forth. He willed himself up out of his easy chair and cleared his throat. He practiced his smile. His cheeks cracked like they were solid ice. He cleared his throat again, ready for a performance of jollity, ready to send the children off to a good day—ready to put his pain away for a while and not transfer it to them and ruin their whole day.

"Dad, I feel terrible," Henry said, so tall now, hanging onto the door handle. "I don't think I can go to school today."

Perhaps Henry had the flu. Maybe Peter also had the flu. At least it would rule out a tumor in his aching brain. He hated that thought scampering through his mind—he never used to be a hypochondriac. He felt Henry's forehead again—a slight temperature.

"Go back to bed. I'll bring you a cuppa, love," he said, forcing a smile.

The door closed again; Peter sat back down and stared at the kitchen sink. The day was hinting at sunshine, which at least would keep his spirits higher than yesterday.

Peter also had a fever; it was clear. He had the flu—he would live to care for his children, see them off into the world and then, perhaps, have time to go over and over that moment one more time, slowly, and try to remember something else. There was something else to remember. He could feel it. But there was a fog around it, and the time was so short between his job and the children that he just couldn't grasp that something. It flitted through his fingers before he could clutch at it and bring it down and look at it—at that *something*.

Henry's Story

Young Henry was a lot like Peter: stoic, calm, and private. After Jeannie died, he took on the roles of mother and father, helping Cassandra and Oliver with bathing, correcting their homework, and setting out their tea.

Peter still had to work but managed to come home by half-past-five or earlier to greet the children who were often at Angela's eating supper, then take them home to finish their homework and get them to bed. Peter liked to see Henry's soft, caring concern for these younger, motherless children. Henry dared to kiss their foreheads goodnight. Peter knew Henry was copying him, parenting like he did. It was a relief for Peter, who sometimes felt that he just could not cope for another minute with the tragedy and emptiness that had become their lives.

The children were too old now to tell bedtime stories. And yet, Peter would build a fire, they would gather together on an evening, and he would tell them about when they were young, how he'd been to Paris with Jeannie, and what a spark of life she had been. Perhaps they were looking into the distance of their minds where a younger, daring woman resided and forgot the one who screamed at them and made them cower in the corner for fear of her threats of violence. Peter invented better times than there ever were in their family. He made up silly stories about the kitty, carefully avoiding its bloody end. He made the children smile, and he saw the hidden tears. But his men's group had encouraged him to let the children know they could talk to Peter about Jeannie, no matter how she had strangely fallen over the cliff.

"Henry," Peter said one night. "Tell us the story of when you were a young boy, and Mum had to get you down from the tree."

"Yes, tell us again!" begged Cassandra.

"I was four or five," he began. "I was a monkey." The other two laughed, and Oliver said, "You still are!"

"Oliver!" Peter said.

"Well, I spent every day for hours on that limb before it broke, and I came crashing down amongst the leaves."

The kids giggled.

"That was the day I was up there trying to get the kitty–she was stuck."

The children nodded, quiet and wide-eyed.

"I called her and called her, but she still climbed higher. I remember the very moment I stepped up to that flimsy branch. Mum…," he looked at Peter, who nodded, "Mum was just saying, 'Henry, don't climb any higher!' But I didn't listen. I wanted to save Kitty."

"Save the kitty!" chimed in the younger children as they always did in this part of the story. "I put all my weight on that branch, and there was a horrible crack. Before I could grab a stronger branch, I bounced off other limbs and fell to the ground. The kitty had leapt up and onto my branch and came down with me, all the way to the ground."

Peter had a momentary, horrible vision of Jeannie crashing down the white cliff and breaking a branch, which might have saved her fall.

"I remember that," Cassandra said.

"No, you were too young to remember that," Oliver said.

"But I remember the story."

"So, now I remember that you only cared about the kitty, not me," continued Henry. "I broke my arm. Kitty just landed on all four feet and started to clean her paws."

Cassandra and Oliver smiled.

"It hurt a lot–my arm," Henry said.

Peter said, "Remember, we got you to the hospital in Brighton right away and mended your arm."

"Yes," Henry said. "But nobody cared or noticed me very much. All they cared about was Kitty, and she was fine."

Peter reached across the settee and stole his arm around the back of Henry's shoulders and gave him a slight fatherly pat. Henry wasn't too old for that, anyway.

The Men's Group

Peter felt that the introduction of compulsory therapy was an extreme intrusion into his private life. It increased his use of "those Americans," with his mates often telling him to shut up. His men's group, on the other hand, held him together in ways he couldn't begin to understand.

"Evening all," he said one particularly stormy night.

"Cheers!" they responded somewhat gloomily from their circle of eight.

"It's been a rotten week!" he started. The men all looked down, scratched, coughed–looked anywhere else but at Peter–except Frank, who seemed to have his eyes rudely glued to Peter's nose. But Peter continued.

"I thought I'd start right in tonight. I feel a bit of a fool," he said.

"No," said Frank, "We are all fools here, so no need to bring it up. A fool is open to being a child again and is able to laugh at himself. Go on, Peter."

"Plenty to laugh at then," he smiled from one side and glanced very briefly at Frank, while the others shifted in their seats, looked at the ceiling or the painting on the wall of the fox and hounds and men on horses in red and black with whips and black, shiny boots.

"To tell you the truth," he said. They all looked at him from lowered heads, eyebrows still covering half of their eyes. He wanted to tell them the truth. He couldn't even tell Jeannie the truth most times. But the truth seemed to have a mind of its own in this room. The silence was long. It seemed as if the preciousness of what was to come in this circle from the new man left hardly a moment to breathe.

"Oh, forget it. Yes, I forgot what I was going to say."

"Peter, let's try that again," said Frank. "Just say, to tell you the truth once again and see what happens. Nobody's perfect here."

A grumble of approval went around the circle.

"Right. Thanks, mate. That's what we're here for, isn't it?"

Another murmur of approval. It wasn't the House of Commons fracas, but a distant relative of it. It was deeply English, but this powwow circle sat in its own uncomfortable revolution like it had never before happened in the history of England.

"So, once again," Peter said looking at Frank, who nodded, "....to tell you the truth, I'm not sure I killed her. Sometimes I think I did. But something deep inside me," how he hated saying that, "knows I didn't kill her. And yet, in some way, perhaps I did. That's the truth. She fell over the cliff, but she was so sure-footed. It doesn't make sense. I look at my work as a detective. There's always a cause somewhere. I find it all the time in other people's lives, but I feel blind and can't see my own life here."

"That's what we're here for, as you said, mate," said the burly man, John, whose wife was in prison after a brawl at the pub.

"Cheers," mumbled the group.

"Keep working on it, Peter," Frank said. "I feel something deep is emerging here."

THE GRAVE

Peter stood by the grave. The darkness of the familiar ancient leaning tombstones surrounding it comforted him. The sounds of the leaves rustling with the hint of winter calmed him. He looked at the clouds covering the black sky and the twinkling stars that had greeted him on his visit last week. He checked his watch for no reason. He shifted his stance, noticing that the flowers around the grave were withering in the twilight.

Was it ever time to forget Jeannie? There she was in her youthful beauty—with that smile that had lured him in so long ago, that energy for life and that freedom that she personified. And now, there she lay in the cold earth, silent forever—not an Irish song ever to hum again while she folded the laundry. As he stood there, visions swept over Peter of their cat bleeding to death, of Jeannie's descent into that horrible depression, and of her verbal abuse. He tried to switch off this gloomy picture in his mind by imagining her good moments, like when she was laughing with the children on the Brighton pier, spitting into the ocean, her head thrown back in a moment that stole its way into an otherwise very ordinary existence.

Yet the years of negativity won, and Peter felt forlorn that he was relieved she was dead and gone. The guilt over this fleeting thought almost made him sick. He had visited her grave so many nights, trying to

243

get over this latest disturbing thought process. He talked to her, then laughed cynically.

"You're listening to me, finally!" he mumbled to the mound of dirt that would be sinking imperceptibly over the years.

He turned and left, careful to close the gate, glancing at the pub over the way–a place of solace, a moment of escape. The bright lights in the windows invited him to go over. He pushed the door slowly and perused the scene–same old geezers; same darts players; same anti-social reader in a corner. Was this his choice of escape? He let the door close again and backed away.

A walk to the sea might do the trick. He glanced back up the street. The world was quiet as if it were waiting for something. His shoes on the cobblestones were the only sounds, besides some notes from a piano player that filtered into his ears. He threw his long scarf over his shoulders and realized there would be nobody waiting for him at home on this cold evening. The children would be fast asleep at Angela's.

Upon his tenth step on the cobblestones, he caught his breath and felt a severe lack of Jeannie in his life. Even with all the horrible scenes of the past years, at least there had been something to bat against. Now there was just the lonely air with no resistance and no one who cared that he was a male chauvinist pig, although he was not one of those, no matter what she called him. He went into his circular defense in his head and felt her company in those condemnations.

He picked up speed as he reached the shore. The nearby pub was noisy. Jeannie's parents might be there right now. Everything else was closed. The echo of the waves offered the comfort of constancy that was no longer in his life.

He walked along the stones and allowed the water to touch his shoes. He resisted a mad desire to tear off his clothes and dive into the cold salty sea and swim away until he was pulled down and his lungs filled with the thrashing, uncaring ocean.

PETER REMEMBERS

Peter coughed violently. His flu was over weeks before. He took out his handkerchief and covered his mouth, closed his eyes, and turned his head away.

Dr. Helen Carpenter sat immobile. After a while, Peter put his handkerchief away and settled himself back into his usual position. He still didn't speak. He stared at the oil painting on the wall behind her head of a local scene before the piers had disappeared with the crumbling of the cliffs, the car from the twenties, and the horse and cart.

Helen Carpenter said, "Do you want to tell me what happened just now, Peter?"

Peter finally altered his gaze to meet her eyes, those penetrating eyes, and her full-on willingness to hear his words without criticism.

He took a breath.

"Right," he said, gathering up his courage. "At first," he began, "my mind went quite blank. I saw, in my imagination, of course, my hand reaching out to save Jeannie. I saw my mouth open wide. I saw the sea and the rocks below the cliff, and I saw her falling. And then my mind went blank. And when I replayed the scene, it had all changed," he said, his voice now hoarse. He stopped talking and looked down at his hands. He moved them like he was reaching out again to save her, but his splayed fingers became a grasp and his arms pushed together as if he were tossing something aside. When he talked now, his voice had altered and became low, almost like a growl.

"You see—what happened just now," he started, then grabbed his handkerchief again and began to cry. The therapist leaned forward, her gaze never blinking, never altering.

"You see," he began again, sobbing, "I didn't save her, in fact. Sorry! Sorry!"

He stood up sharply and ran past the watercolor paintings, the Victorian desk, and the bright-colored bookcase—out of the room, through the hallway, and out of the front door towards the sea, the cliffs, and the dark stormy sky.

Peter didn't see the shoppers' faces, nor the traffic lights—nor did he hear the honking. He ran like a swarm of bees was chasing him, like it was a matter of death or life, his life, her death, his death, her life. Peter ran down the cement drive and over to the edge where he could look back at the white cliffs that eroded slowly in the rain, with a history as old as the world itself.

Then he looked up at the cliffs and imagined her body cascading down, perhaps bumping along the way against that branch that might have saved her if only she had grasped it. Couldn't she have grasped it? It wouldn't have broken. Surely it would have saved her? But it was as if she were boldly taking her punishment. He knew her well. She had some kind of conscience. It had just been lost somewhere along the way—lost in a cloud of greed or sadness, or recovered memories. Peter wiped his eyes and backed the scene up again in his mind. Yes, she had fallen over the cliffs. Horrible! Horrible! But this time, she was coming at him from behind, ready to push him over the cliff! He didn't reach out just then. He jumped aside, and after she kept going forward, he reached out in disbelief, reaching for his lost love, his shattered trust, his willingness to believe her life was worth saving while he now understood that his life— to her—was not.

Peter turned and slowly walked back up the wide road from the bottom of the hill. There was a small crowd gathered at the top. The pub was open. He wanted to go in and drown his memories. But there was no more drowning out to be done. He had remembered the truth, the act that had happened so quickly. It had blocked itself out and down into the realms of impossibility, the places where the darkest secrets reside, locked away from memory.

He walked quickly instead along Main Street and back up to Helen Carpenter's office. There she sat, waiting. How did she know he would return?

"Come in, Peter," she said, as if a bolting patient was as normal as knocking back a pint of beer.

Peter sat down and gazed up at the picture of the cliffs.

"Sorry! So sorry!" he started. "I know what happened now."

Helen sat there as usual and listened. He felt heard, not judged. She seemed to hear him so well, nodding just slightly. He didn't cry this time. Like the detective he prided himself as being, he told his story, boldly looking at Ms. Carpenter, telling her the awful truth.

"Jeannie had actually meant to kill *me*–my beloved Jeannie, lying so still at the bottom of the cliff, almost out of her misery." There was a long pause while Peter blew his nose, sighed, and sat with the silence. Then he continued.

"I don't know what to do now. I didn't have a real father, so I have no role model, as you say. Even our new house seems so empty. The children need me: I know that. But I'm not sure I am taking her place. You know what I mean? I will try, that's all I can do, isn't it? She meant to kill me! She meant to kill the father of her children! Oh, God save me!"

ANGELA'S SECRETS

After that session, Peter withdrew into his quiet place. It was a place of peace where nobody bothered him, nobody needed him, nobody wanted him. If they did, his countenance held them back. He was safe there, his eyes either down or fixed into the distance. Something churned in his head, but no resolution presented itself–too many pieces of information and no road to link them. In order to drown out the persistent memories of the cliff and Jeannie's death, Peter pushed himself to think about his right to know more about his father.

His long life had produced no solid clue as to who his father was, where he lived, or if he really died. Peter pondered the branches of the elm tree high above his head. His search felt like all the buds were at the ends of the smallest branches, and each one was going backwards towards the trunk, the solid joining of all the pieces into one whole–one answer.

Every day of the week, Peter took the children to school. He made them breakfasts and dinners, and laundered their clothes. Without their mother to share this work, Peter did all of it and somehow managed to solve a few crimes at work along the way. He was grateful for his work. It blended so well now with single parenthood. He could work at odd times of the day and night when he wasn't feeding the children or driving them somewhere. Angela was a blessing. The children went to her house after school almost like they lived there. It was just up Nevill Road, not five minute's walk. From her home, they discovered all the corners Peter had haunted as a boy. Grandma gave them tea and toast with jam and taught them how to knit and quilt more complicated things.

Peter felt his life and work were like a continuation of watching his Mum knit and quilt. He would take a piece of the puzzle, lay it out before him and fit it into the growing quilt that held the other pieces until all the colors balanced and the clues strengthened into a solid answer as he fit the very last piece into the pattern. His feeling of satisfaction each time he finally solved the puzzle was strangely akin to finding out more about his father.

But that puzzle was a mysterious giant, clawing to get solved, to get done with, rather like that Cellini saga. He couldn't piece things together for that one in such an easy way. They were all in his head, tucked away now over many years, panting for the next bit of information. His puzzle was far from complete. Every time Peter was on the verge of solving it, a new doubt emerged, and he felt it was possibly mostly his imagination and a deep-seated need to find his father that pushed him too far away from pure facts.

"Mum," he tried asking Angela again.

"Yes, love," she answered, straightening her glasses and looking up at him.

"While they're out playing, can you tell me more about who my father was?" It was daring. It was a straight question, not a hint.

"Peter, my love, I'd rather not, if you don't mind."

Peter's face fell from the inside. How could she be so cruel not to hear his plea? Surely it was his right to know about his own father!

"Mum, please tell me about my father. I have to know. It's my right, isn't it?"

Angela removed her glasses and rubbed her eyes, glancing at the door. Children's voices laughed just outside.

"All right, Peter. It's true. I always think about it for my own self, don't I? But it's true, love. You have a right to know something more about him before I die."

There was a long silence while Peter stood holding his breath, glancing at the door, which might burst open at any moment with hungry children.

"David was…," she faltered. It was like she had forgotten. It was like she was reconsidering Peter's request. More silence. Peter hovered still like a hummingbird at the nectar.

"What, Mum?"

"His name was…," Angela dropped her chin onto her chest. "Sorry, love, can we talk about this later?"

"Mum, you're getting old. Sorry to say that, but it's true. How much later must I wait? What if you die? I need to know more. You said his name was David. What are you hiding?"

"It won't be much later, but not right now, love. I just need to think about it a little more. You're a good boy…."

"Mum, please. I'm a man. How many times must I tell you that?"

"Of course, you are. But to me, you will always be my boy. I can't help it, love. I just can't help it."

Peter thought of his own children. Perhaps he would feel the same one day. No, he never would do that. He wouldn't call one of his grown sons *a good boy*! Never!

Peter felt a growing surge of anger at his mother. Not only was he not a bloody boy, but also, he had a right to know more. His rage was so close to the surface now that he realized he felt like punching her in the face. But he smiled instead and said, "Would you like a cup of tea, Mum?" Angela looked up from her inward space and said, "Yes, son. That would be lovely." And the subject was dropped, yet again.

MICHAEL'S PLANS

Michael visited Holloway Prison several times a year, even for years after Catherine had left. It had become a place to go all those years, where he had met people working there before she left and where he continued to have friends there after she left. After twelve years, it was almost a second home to him. They all knew him—they knew not to breathe a word to Catherine about who he was. By the time Catherine left, they had expected him to turn up anyway and have a cup of tea, and tell them about his ailing wife and son, or whatever else was going on.

In his agony to make a change after Janet had died, some years before this day, Michael needed to do something different, so one day he booked a flight to New York, hired a car for a week, and drove up to Vermont and into Brattleboro, where he made discreet inquiries.

He found out where Catherine lived and followed her for days—shopping, to the library, to the Unitarian Church, and even to the movies. Yet, Catherine never seemed to have any idea that someone was following her.

Now, back in England, so many years after Catherine had left prison, Michael picked up the ringing telephone early one morning.

"She's on her way back to England," said Vicky, a voice he knew so well from the prison staff. Michael took several shallow breaths. This was the call he had waited for and stayed alive for. He felt his body shaking all over.

"Thank you very much. I owe you for this."

"'Course, mate; you already done me plenty of favors." Michael could not remember any favors he had done for this kind woman. He had just talked to her for so many years they had both become quite white-haired. Wasn't she a redhead when he first started to visit there? It wasn't often, maybe once or twice a year, but they developed a bond anyway, and if he did her favors along the way, it was just a part of his life. He couldn't remember at all. She was just a fine woman: friendly, easy to talk to.

He dressed in his usual pressed fashion and made his way to the airport. He had to see Catherine immediately, but he would remain anonymous.

Catherine had finally come back to England from the States. Michael found out that Catherine was staying at the Churchill Hotel near Oxford Street. He would take the Tube down to Marble Arch Station and wander about, checking to see if he could see her walking out of the hotel. He wore his brogues again, thinking of his old grandpa, and remembered the years he had spent just watching Catherine. But he couldn't quite tell her he was there. If he did, it would all come back to the same problem: she would find out she had gone to prison because of his cowardice.

Michael checked his horoscope every day to be sure he was doing the right thing. It said, *"Do not push your luck. Hold back and wait for the right moment. Be patient."* Michael was being very patient. He still ran for forty minutes every day on Hampstead Heath first thing, rain or shine, to keep fit mentally and physically. He sold enough antiques these days to earn a reasonable living, especially as he was alone, now that his wife, Janet, and his son, Geoffrey, had both died. Once in a while, he would make a great deal of money, and the pressure was off for weeks. Sometimes he had to borrow for weeks, sure to find another deal. His mates knew he was good for a loan, and that is just how it went, year after year.

Michael had observed Catherine from the day she arrived in London from Brattleboro. He took to holding up the *Times* in front of his face so she wouldn't recognize him, even after all these years. He watched her go into cafés and get on buses, and he knew she had become friends with a man called Christopher from the Churchill Hotel and the pub nearby.

It was all a great distraction from his loneliness. It had been years now since Janet and Geoffrey had died. Michael had taken up visiting with a long freed fellow prisoner of Catherine's named Gracie, who had become his mistress. But he suspected Gracie might finally invite him to be her tenant when she found out about the valuable silver cups.

Michael wanted to confide in Catherine about why he didn't tell the truth and keep her free from prison. He felt quite guilty, but, also, he had felt, watching those two beings he loved die little-by-little, that he had done the right thing where the right thing had hardly been decipherable to him. But he felt he owed Catherine a great deal. He just didn't know what that would turn out to be. Meanwhile, perhaps she was back in England to find the six silver cups that were bound to be in her sights. Otherwise, why would she come back?

That first day Catherine was in London, he followed her on the bus. He was shocked to find out that Christopher's mother, Maureen, who lived in the East End, was friends with Gracie.

He knew he was a fool, phoning Catherine, and then hardly saying a word. But he also sensed that she was getting close to those cups. That would solve all his problems. Although he was managing well enough now, he still had so many debts left to pay after the difficult end-of-life expenses for first Geoffrey and then Janet.

Alone at home now, Michael pulled out his six cups and polished them until they gleamed, longing to see the other six, and longing even more to sell the whole lot and make his fortune.

MICHAEL MEETS CATHERINE

Michael hardly ever went to see Angela in Rottingdean now. It seemed to be a longer journey to Brighton, and then on to Rottingdean than it had in his younger days. Despite his age, he kept up the running, especially on Hampstead Heath near the ponds, if only to fool himself that he wasn't getting older like his acquaintances. And he didn't drink a drop now, nor did he smoke anymore. In his own eyes, he was a perfect angel, really. He just had a conscience, and he had a mission. He knew he had to find those cups and that Catherine, to whom he owed a lot, was the only person who might lead him to them.

Michael felt a bit silly, following her around London, making those ridiculous silent phone calls. But he felt very alarmed when one day he noticed that he wasn't the only one following her. Now he was sure he couldn't contact her. They looked like MI5 agents, and he always shunned the law. So now he watched them, as well as Catherine. And he watched his horoscopes in the *Daily Mail*. One day it was clear he should make his move. The horoscopes had said quite plainly that it was time for him to meet this person in his life that he had so patiently avoided meeting.

Michael spruced himself up even more than usual and went to the London pub next door to the Churchill Hotel. Upon entering, he was startled and pleased to see her sitting at a table, her back to him. His heart was beating so quickly he thought he might just drop down dead. All this time, when he visited her in prison, Michael had made Catherine think that he was called Mr. Smith. Finally, he would tell Catherine who this Mr. Smith really was, that silent man who had visited her all those years.

Michael came up behind her, and with his most polished accent, asked if he could sit down. She was polite and strangely didn't seem very surprised at his sudden appearance.

Catherine showed him a seat with her gesture. She must have known. But how did she know who he was? Yet, almost before they could say two sentences or take a bite of chicken or taste the delicate wine, several Scotland Yard men came up, grabbed Michael, removing his shoes and escorting him out of the pub to the paddy wagon waiting outside, driving him off to jail where they locked him up.

It was not fair to Catherine! How did they know he was going to meet her there? She had looked stunned. He was sorry, but what could he do?

Shortly afterwards, Catherine found out where they had taken Michael and took a taxi to the jail.

Michael knew that it was this very moment to tell her the truth. He had nowhere to hide and nothing to hide.

"I am not Mr. Smith, Catherine. My real name is Michael–Michael Evans."

"Evans?" she asked. "That's my surname!"

"And I did not kill David!"

A GOOD FATHER

It was easy to see why Jeannie had been angry. As Peter worked through his therapy, he was forced to see Jeannie again, slogging through the day with the laundry, the shopping, the cooking, and cleaning. He had to see his Jeannie, once so lively and daring, bent over the sink so many more times than was required of him. He had to notice, beyond the discipline and endless endurance of getting to work every morning that, in fact, he read two newspapers a day with cups of tea and had chummy chats at the office while Jeannie listened to *The Archers* while she worked. But how could it have been different? He needed to earn their living. He was good at his job, which paid well enough now. Jeannie was bright but had little education. She had seemed so happy with their first child.

"She was happy," Peter said to Helen, but his voice lowered, and there was silence while he thought about his claim.

"Well, at least, at first. Our baby was a joy, especially after Jeannie had miscarried. Actually, we were very poor. I did what I could, but perhaps it was harder on Jeannie than she let on."

Peter remembered how she used to sing Irish folk songs while she folded the laundry. But now he remembered how she might complain of the endless ironing of his shirts and how her back hurt, or was that later—

years later? She seemed to smile when he arrived home, and she prided herself on that cup of tea already waiting for him, complete with milk and sugar and some biscuits alongside.

"She loved our children; I know she did."

"Always?" Helen asked.

"Of course!" Peter defended. Again, Helen sat there in that eternal silence while Peter backed up and rethought his answer.

"Well, not always. There was the cat problem, and I think she took it out on the children. She couldn't face what she had done."

"Did she take that out on the children?"

"Of course she did!" Peter heard the echo of his certainty, his willingness to blame Jeannie without a trial—guilty before proven innocent.

"Well," he added, "It seemed pretty certain at the time."

"Fine. Let's talk about your feelings again. We know Jeannie must have been having a hard time, making it easy to see her as the problem. What else can you imagine was going on with you?"

"Me?" Peter pulled back. And then he remembered how Helen had cautioned him that he needed to see who he was in this dynamic relationship.

"I wasn't perfect, of course. I expect I was happy with our arrangement. She was a good wife and…"

"You, Peter."

"Right." Peter lowered his chin and tried to imagine his existence apart from Jeannie's. It was impossible. Everything he did was with or about Jeannie and the children. Well, not everything—not everything.

"I used to go for a quick drink with my mates after hours—just a quick drink—part of my job, really. But, in truth, other men skipped it and went straight home to their families."

"That's all quite understandable, Peter. What happened when you got home?"

"Well, as I've said, tea was ready. But after a while, she didn't kiss me hello. I remember that first time. She was too hurried. Maybe something was burning on the stove. I overlooked it. But it happened regularly after that. It was a sign. I see now that I chose to ignore it. It was about that time she claimed she was too tired for intimate relations, and when we finally did get together, there was a lack of response that, I see now, I also chose to ignore. She was obviously accommodating my needs, but, I'm afraid, hers were most likely not met."

"Go on," Helen said quietly.

"Now I think about it, I don't remember ever thinking about her needs. How pathetic it feels. It all started out so passionately. And in the end, it was probably a one-way street. She hardly ever complained, but I see now, she just withdrew from me over time. We almost never had relations in that last year. That's probably why I stayed for those drinks–it numbed my heart and body. I froze up and continued being a good father–I think I was a good father."

Here Peter looked at Helen, whose face gave nothing away. He was left alone in his thoughts. *Was he a good father, in fact? What was a good father? Where was the father Peter needed answers from now?* Helen didn't have to voice those questions, but Peter knew these answers needed to be forthcoming.

"At least, I thought I was a good father–the way our children hung on me, beseeched me for kisses on their foreheads–jumped on my back for piggyback rides. They loved my stories at bedtime. I was a good father. It did not matter how tired I was."

"Where was Jeannie then?"

"Oh, at the pub. That was her habit, you know."

"Where you might have gone before coming home?"

"Very likely," Peter confessed.

DAVID'S EYES

One day while Peter was putting the dishes away at Angela's birthday party, and the children were asking their grandma politely if they could go outside, Peter heard a knock at the front door. Angela went to answer it and Peter leaned against the kitchen wall, listening intently, curious to hear the story about some silver cups that were apparently buried under Angela's back deck.

In his usual quiet way, Peter greeted Mrs. Catherine Evans and Christopher, the man she had brought to dig up the cups. Peter strained to hear the words that they exchanged after the children had gone outside—something about his own father, David, who had buried the cups, about a map in a box that Catherine had found back in Vermont, and something about DNA. They had requested a shovel, and they were actually cheeky enough to ask to dig under the deck there and then and to do it all on the same day!

Peter dutifully provided the shovel and offered to help. They politely refused, so he went back around the house, but he crept back to the corner to watch and listen, eager to learn anything he could about his father.

"Peter," his mother called from the kitchen window.

Reluctantly, Peter walked back into the house.

"Mum, she's his other wife, isn't she?"

"The very one," answered Angela.

Peter's heart beat faster. He wanted to ask Catherine more, to discover if he looked like David–to ask things that Angela was so reluctant to tell him. Peter knew he had to hold his questions quietly in his aching heart, at least from Angela. She had made that quite clear. But here was his chance. He just couldn't figure out how to approach Catherine out of Angela's hearing.

And then Catherine twisted her ankle, and any hopes of privacy were dashed as Angela comforted Catherine with the required cups of healing tea. But Peter kept listening from the kitchen. He caught his mother's words–David was Peter's father–couldn't she see how like David Peter's own eyes were–his green eyes, his stance–his height? Peter felt warm in his heart to hear these words that Angela casually mentioned to Catherine and had never once told him. He tried to tell himself that these were meaningless facts about a man that he would never, ever meet. And yet, he couldn't stop the heat on his neck, the pinch in his throat, and the relief he felt from his toes to his nose, that he looked like someone–like his father.

Of course, his children knew about Catherine and David. Peter had told them all he knew, and Angela told them a lot, but not those urgent details. It was a story about David and Angela and Catherine, after all, and not about Peter. Or so it had always seemed until now. Peter knew his son, Henry, had eyes like him. But he never knew that his son also had David's eyes.

Peter brushed these thoughts aside, trying to deny their importance to him. And yet, the excitement filled his body with energy and joy that the puzzle was yet again moving towards completion. The matching pieces were finding each other and joining like a mending of his heart and a quickening of his breath. If only Peter could have shown David his wonderful grandchildren and let David know what a competent breadwinner he, his own son, had been.

Peter shook himself out of his daydreams and carried in some more biscuits and milk on a tray. For now, he would have to be satisfied with these new pieces of information. But the detective in him was not satisfied. His quest was not over–it was not dead. He would never stop his search, for he had an uneasy feeling that there was more to learn–much more.

THE HAIRBRUSH

Mention was made of DNA on television and on the radio. When Catherine arrived to dig for the cups, she had told Angela that DNA was why she initially leapt from her chair and flew back to England to find David's murderer. But Peter needed more. He had several cases that could be closed if he could use DNA samples. Perhaps he also could release a prisoner convicted without adequate proof that DNA could provide of his innocence. More and more people were being let out of prison in the USA when their DNA didn't match the items found at the crime scenes.

Peter turned on his new desktop computer. On a winter day, the bright light of his screen, its bright sky-blue color, cheered him as he, once again, searched the history of DNA and delved deeper to find out where others had sent samples.

He thought he might try it out using his personal items and match them up with anything he could find in his own life.

"Do we have anything here of my . . . of David's?" he asked Angela one Sunday at teatime. The grandchildren were outside running up and down the street in the drizzle. They never seemed to mind a wet face and a cold, red nose.

"I can't think right now, Peter." It seemed that Angela had become slightly fragile now, getting the first cold of the season. Perhaps her memory was a bit of a problem, but she could come up with some answers eventually. He said, "No matter. If you do think of something or find anything at all, I'd like to try it out on this new DNA."

Angela looked up and paused for a frozen moment. She cocked her head, and then she sat up quite tall.

"I think I have something." She got up from her chair, walked into the bedroom, picked up an antique hairbrush, and brought it in to Peter.

"Will this do?"

"I think so, Mum. That should be perfect, really."

Peter pulled a plastic bag from its box in the kitchen and put the old silver-backed hairbrush in it as if he were touching something that might bite him.

Armed with the hairs on the brush, he went home and pulled a few more from his own brush and comb and put them into a separate plastic bag. Then he packaged the items well, labeling them and putting them in an envelope, writing a letter on his detective stationary. He dashed down to the post office, where he sent his treasure off to the DNA lab. And then his wait began.

All the time Peter worked, he thought of the hairs that perhaps might reveal more about David. He felt that something was different. This new knowledge had changed so many people's lives in ways hardly imagined until recently.

ACTING STRANGE

Peter really preferred the old-fashioned ways, the fingerprints, the found suspicious objects, lots of spying like he did as a child: a deer-stalker hat–a pipe to chew on while he puzzled the pieces into a whole. Now he was required to better understand this new science of DNA. It was fascinating, yet it didn't fulfill his habitual detective needs: his handy magnifying glass, his feeling of satisfaction when all the pieces fell into place, and doubt morphed into a certainty.

It was the state of doubt that intrigued him. He enjoyed his moments of suspicion, although when he suspected his friends and neighbors, he worried that he might just give them the benefit of the doubt. After all, he had a reputation as a friendly person, one who might even look the other way at a teenager's descent into grabbing an item off a shop shelf and sneaking out without paying. He'd done it himself once when he was fifteen. He later went back and bought a toothbrush just to assuage his guilt about stealing from the kindly store owner who was so friendly to him.

This DNA course was exciting, too, but he knew most of his Sherlock ways would soon be taking a historical place in the annals of detective novels and his own career. He was proud that DNA was discovered by the British. However, it was much like going to school, getting good

267

marks, and going home without a great detective drama to relay at the dinner table.

Moving along through this new, inevitable history made him want to go back to Conan Doyle and ask him how he would write his stories with this new method. Perhaps Sherlock would test his own DNA and find out something unimaginable about his addictions or his deteriorating health. Perhaps he would commit suicide? No, that would never solve the crimes that awaited him. He would die a natural death, his fist in the air, holding the new DNA evidence that would justify all his intuitive discoveries.

Yes, Peter would go on being a great detective and then just cap it all off for the crowd with DNA proof! He would also hold his fist in the air to justify all the labor he had put into finding out the truth. He smiled to himself and thought that in his dotage, he would write mysteries about a contemporary detective who used DNA but really discovered the *truth* using all his wits and wisdom first. They were all going to want this new proof. The inevitable merged with the possible and made his success probable! He smiled at his homework and made a match. He would pass this course if it killed him. He would pass it with a wide smile, and he would be promoted.

Peter looked at his watch. Hearing a knock, he got up to answer the door. Who would come at this late hour? Strange.

He walked down the hall and opened it. Angela stood there, her face ashen, her raincoat dripping, her face wet with rain, or were they tears?

"Mum! Come in! Come in! What in the world are you doing here at this hour? Have a cup of tea, for heaven's sake. Come and sit in the kitchen."

"Oh, it's nothing, really, not to worry. It's just that it's hard to say. But that visit by Catherine has shattered my nerves. Nice enough old lady, really. Look who's talking! But digging under my deck was a bit of, well, a shock. It brought everything right back up in my mind. Sometimes…wouldn't it be nice to just leave the past where it belongs?"

"What did it bring up, Mum?"

Angela shot a look at Peter like he'd never seen in her before: anxious–afraid? He shifted his chair and stirred his remaining tea with the spoon.

"Oh, nothing, really," she mumbled.

"Mum, you're here when you ought to be in bed. It's dark and cold out. Obviously, something has come up that's unsettling."

"You're right, son: too many ghosts from the past–too many ghosts."

"Have another cuppa, Mum–soothes the nerves."

Angela chuckled. "You sound more like me every day."

"So, what did it bring up, Mum?"

"Nothing, really–it's all so silly. Like I said, it's in the past, isn't it?"

"Mum, why did you come over this late at night?"

"I'm bothered by it all–gives me nightmares, Peter, all that we lived through when you were small. I shouldn't bother you with it. But who else can I grumble to? Can't keep it stuffed inside forever, can I?"

Peter stirred his dregs with the spoon and didn't reply. The question hung in the air. The question that Peter didn't even know hung in the air. The air seemed thick with lies and deceit and guilt. His detective side felt it in his very joints. He cracked his neck. Here was where he knew from all his years questioning suspects that he had to sit tight. The question and the answer hovered above them like a specter, like a mighty bell about to be rung.

Angela wiped her eyes and warmed her hands by the gas fire. It was like she wanted to talk to Peter about something in the past. This was not normal, this strange behavior. What could she be thinking about?

But as long as they sat into the night, Angela just prattled on about the usual gossip. Nothing came out of her mouth that he hadn't heard twenty times already. Perhaps she just needed company, and that was all–perhaps.

"I was just thinking about your father, how he would have loved to have seen you all grown up, being a detective, being a father, even being the hero that you are, Peter."

"Mum, I'm no hero. What do you mean?"

"You know, Jeannie and all that–you know what I mean. The way you took on the children, kept your job going, stiff upper lip."

"No choice, was there? Not the stuff of heroes–just the stuff of necessity, wasn't it, Mum?"

"Well, we all know about that. We're all heroes in that sense. Remember the war, what we all went through?"

"I wasn't there, Mum!"

"'Course you weren't. But you know what I mean: millions of quiet heroes every day who didn't know it. They were just doing what any decent person would have done, weren't they?"

"Same as me, Mum. What choice did I have? You brought me up well, and I've soldiered on. I love my children. I loved Jeannie. There's no choice about it. What's a hero, anyway?"

"One who takes the bullet!" Angela said with determination.

"A hero doesn't let his wife fall over a cliff, Mum!"

"You said you reached out. You did your level best, didn't you?" Angela's face was almost angry.

"But, in the end, Mum, I'm no hero–gives me nightmares every night."

"Can't be helped–can't be changed, love. You got on with it and raised the children well–that's a hero."

"Well, Mum, anybody would have done the same. How about letting me drive you back home? Pick up your car in the morning."

On the short drive back to Angela's house, Peter realized he never heard exactly why she was so upset. It was the details that moved a case along, something to grasp at, not a generality. Angela had gone into her house now. But Peter just couldn't help it. He turned the car around to drive back up to her house to ask her why she had come.

He parked outside her house and turned off the engine. As he sat waiting for the courage to go in, he saw that she had just turned off all the lights. He got out of the car and went up to the door, paused, and then turned back and drove home wondering. What could she have meant to say?

ANGELA VISITS MICHAEL

As Michael waited in jail for his trial for supposedly killing his brother, David, he thought of his six cups hidden away nicely behind his coats and suits, and the other six missing cups that David had hidden somewhere. He wondered why the police had taken his precious brogues when they had arrested him in front of Catherine, her face looking on in horror and disbelief. Maybe DNA?

Angela kindly came to visit him, explaining that she had read about his arrest in the paper.

"They've finally got you!" she said cheerily. It was clear she believed in his innocence.

"Angela, you know full well I could never have killed David. I might have been jealous of him, but that wouldn't give me a reason to kill my own brother."

"I know, Michael, but why did you run away and let poor Catherine sit in jail for all those years?"

"You know I had my dear wife, Janet, shriveling up with her muscular dystrophy and needing constant help, and then, of course, my son, Geoffrey, sick since he was born and dying little by little every day. Someone had to care for them. I ask you, would you have taken them in? Who

271

would have done it if I had been falsely accused and gone to prison? Besides, Angela, you must know that I didn't kill him."

"Of course, I know it, but neither did Catherine, Michael. You let her go to jail. I can't ever forgive you for that."

"But I just couldn't risk it, Angela. The jury would have jumped to conclusions. Besides, I had no idea at that time that she would be blamed. I am so very sorry, but I felt I had no choice. I had no bloody choice!"

"Well, I do hope you can persuade the jury of your innocence!"

"I am not so sure. But thank you, Angela."

"Sorry! Time's up!" said a stern but polite, male voice.

"Cheerio, Michael," said Angela. "Keep your chin up, then. I will be praying for you quietly, in my way. I know you didn't do it."

"I appreciate that, Angela. We'll just have to see. Goodbye."

And as an afterthought, Michael said, "Oh! And how is Peter doing?"

"He's fine."

"You didn't hear anything about those silver cups, did you, by the way?"

"What silver cups? Oh, those. No, sorry. Best of British, then, Michael. Ta-ta!"

"You will tell me if you do, won't you?" he said. "Cheerio, then, Angela."

Later on, Michael thought it strange that Angela had not really answered his question about the cups. But it was good to have an old friend who he didn't have to lie to while he awaited his trial. Angela was a true friend.

Angela went home. She hadn't told Michael about Catherine's visit to her house, and she didn't tell him about the treasure Christopher had, in fact, dug up. It was Catherine–that was why. And Catherine didn't need any more trouble from Michael. This trial was more than enough.

PETER VISITS
UNCLE MICHAEL

Peter took the train to London to visit Michael in jail before his trial.

"Sorry, but are you related to Michael Evans?" a woman at the desk asked, her hair standing inches from her scalp, buffed and dyed red.

"Yes, he's my uncle," Peter said.

"Sign here, please, then," she said. Peter signed and went to sit down. He knew how long these waits were, so he'd brought *The Daily Mail*. As a detective, he knew he might get preferential treatment, but waiting without a newspaper was irritating to Peter, who was eager to get on with his cases.

"You may go in, sir," said a policeman, equally bored.

Peter folded his newspaper and stood up. The guard was pointing out the door with his eyes. Then he opened it and gestured for Peter to walk through. They entered a dreary yellow hallway that must have been painted at least twenty years before. Another door was opened to a bland, undecorated room where Michael was seated at a small, rectangular table. Peter shook Michael's hand.

"Hello, Uncle Michael."

"Hello, Peter. Nice of you to drop by. Have a pint, then?"

They both chuckled at this imaginary possibility.

"I've been following your case, Uncle Michael. It looks pretty grim in the papers. I swear *I've* never pulled a man from his restaurant and taken his shoes away."

Michael was quiet compared to his usual chatty self, and he looked at Peter as if to say, *go on.*

"I'm sure you're pretty nervous about the trial. I'm not sure what help I can be, but at least I'll be there cheering for you."

"That's not necessary, Peter. It's all pretty embarrassing. I didn't kill your father, but circumstances seem to point to me. It bores me to protest even one more time. Nobody believes me, in any case."

"I believe you, Uncle Michael. It's true, it looks from the facts like you did it, but I believe it was an accident."

"Do you?"

"I feel quite unable to help you. I'm supposed to be a good detective: Sherlock Holmes and all that."

They both smiled.

"You did give me that novel about Sherlock Holmes when I was a boy, didn't you?"

"You found me out, Peter. That I did. That I did. It doesn't help me now. Did you ever read it?"

"I swear I devoured it several times—once from the school library and a few times from the copy you gave me. I treasured it." Peter looked down and remembered how he'd felt bereft of gifts from his dead father and how this gift from one male relative to another bolstered his confidence and urged him on to become a great detective.

"Glad to hear it, Peter," Michael said, relaxing his eyebrows for a moment.

Peter looked at Michael without speaking. Michael seemed to be lost in a dream, perhaps of that very day David had died right before his eyes in Angela's own kitchen. Peter thought for the first time that, of course, he and his mother only moved in later, and that their kitchen had once belonged to David and Catherine.

"Angela came by yesterday," Michael finally said.

"She told me. She's a longstanding friend of yours, not just a sister-in-law, isn't she?"

"Very good friend," Michael said.

"Did you ever…," Peter started.

"She and David were married. It was out of the question, Peter. Of course, I was married, as well."

"Right."

Peter knew from all his detective years that people harbored secrets all their lives. Once a person stood before a judge and jury, things spilled from their lying lips that no other method could push from their closed-up hearts—but not until all pathways were blocked, and they had to explain their bizarre behavior. People needed to be understood, as if their crimes were a justification for their hardships. It was universal—people who were sane, anyway, hoped to be understood. Peter knew too much about the fallibilities of his fellow human beings. Certainly, Catherine was innocent. But Michael—there were reasons he could have killed David. They were fighting, in fact. It was a toss-up. He either did it accidentally, or he didn't, and David had actually fallen on the knife he'd held menacingly towards Michael.

"Well, I'll be going now, Uncle Michael." He couldn't help adding, "But I'll be right there silently cheering for you, never fear!"

"All right, Peter. Nice of you to come round. Let's go for a nice long drink when this is over, then. Cheers, mate!" Of course, it was an accident, Peter said to himself.

Peter got up and nodded slightly at Michael and left with a heavy heart. What if Michael had to go to prison? He'd surely die there. He was too old to suffer the indignities of prison. But when Peter thought about it longer, he remembered that, by his own silence, Michael had sent Catherine to twelve years in prison by remaining silent about the accident. Surely that deserved punishment! Peter hated himself for thinking that. But, really, it was preposterous! Part of Peter hated Michael for that. Part of him understood his crisis with his Down syndrome son and his wife with her debilitating multiple sclerosis.

Back in Rottingdean, Peter went to Angela's for tea.

"Let's go to the court together, Mum."

"I'd like that, Peter."

Peter understood that Angela was getting a little older now, less steady in her strong sort of way. Perhaps she'd appreciate an arm to rest on as they walked into the court to hear Michael's fate.

Peter and Angela leaned over their balcony seats and held their breaths. They were very surprised to see Catherine. Was she a witness?

The trial was very short. Just after the judge sat down and started to mumble his required speech, Catherine jumped up and shouted, "I killed David!"

The courtroom was in an uproar! Journalists were dashing for the phone boxes. By lying through her teeth, Catherine had effectively set Michael free, and why not? She knew she had already paid the required twelve years of that debt to society.

PORCELAIN TEACUPS

It was hard not to see what was obvious to the rest of the world, except when Michael's eyelids were pried open by a bright sun and a strong coffee. There stood Angela, the woman he had always secretly loved, with her hand upon her hip and her face as stern as an unsmiling lion, ready to slam the door in his face.

Michael's love for Angela had become mixed up like a swirl of autumn leaves with his duty towards Janet and Geoffrey, David's memory, and even Angela's will to hold him at arm's distance like she didn't even care about him.

This time, as Angela stood there, her stance perhaps firmer now than twenty years previously, he knew she still cared. There was a glint in her eye. He could tell she'd forgotten exactly why she always sent him away–especially that last time in the churchyard in the middle of the night. Was it the way she looked at him this day as if studying his aging face for the first time since they were young? Was it the way she looked down at his brogues and smiled to herself? Perhaps it was how she let him in with her usual reluctance but brushed against his arm as she closed the door?

Michael knew she remembered. He was sure of it now. How he longed to kiss her soft lips once more, to feel her melt into his arms, to feel her smooth cheek against his jaw. How he longed to speak with her with the fences knocked down and the barriers evaporated.

Michael took off his coat and hung it and his hat and scarf on the old rack she had kept in the hallway all these years. He glanced around to see the familiar antiques and small, framed etchings he and David had discovered so long ago.

"Come into the kitchen, love," she said, with no more formality, just to sit together with china teacups.

When they had settled into their places, Angela began to talk in a way that reminded Michael of another Angela, the one he had held in his dreams.

"Do you remember these porcelain cups?" she asked. "We drank from them years ago. I wonder if I've ever taken them down from that top shelf once in all these years."

The edge had disappeared from her voice, and he felt invited in–at last.

"David and I found those cups. I have six, and he had six. I still have my six."

"Not silver, though!"

"Not silver!"

"Wouldn't it be lovely to bring this set together, as they were meant to be," she said, her eyebrows elevating very slightly.

Michael could hardly answer. What was she saying? What did she mean? Would she buy his six porcelain cups from him? Did she want to sell her six to him?

"Yes," he said evenly. "That would be almost a kind of healing thing to do–for the cups, I mean."

"They would all look lovely along the top of that shelf there," she said, indicating a shelf along the top of the wall, well out of the way of her grandchildren's reach.

So perhaps she wanted to buy them. But he loved them and wasn't willing to part with his. The loss of the silver cups was too much already. Perhaps he could persuade her to sell her six.

"I couldn't part with them, I'm afraid," he said.

"Of course not," she answered.

Now he was stumped. How could his cups be here in this house while he lived back in his Hampstead flat? That would not happen unless he lived there at Angela's house as well. A little smile crept over his face. He looked at Angela squarely in the eyes.

"You naughty woman!" he said.

"Am I?" she nodded slightly and raised her eyebrows a little more.

He reached over and gently laid his hand upon hers. She didn't move hers away–just looked at his hand. The silence allowed the distant sounds of the sea filter into their minds as the warmth of their hands made Michael never want to remove his again.

Angela nodded but didn't speak. He obviously had to guess but hardly knew what to say–he dared not hope for what he thought she meant. His throat pinched, and his eyes watered slightly.

"Angela, is it too late?"

"Michael, my love! It's never too late!" She pulled out the tiny, colorful quilt from her basket.

He looked at her and the quilt he had given her so very long ago. She had kept it close to her along with their secrets all these years.

"Do you mean. . . ? Do you want me to . . .?" He was terrified of being presumptuous. Perhaps if he leaned towards her and kissed her cheek, things would become more clear. He began to lean towards her, but he didn't have to go far before her lips were upon his own, lightly, gently, lovingly–not passionately, no–but invitingly. Then she said softly, "I remember, Michael."

" Oh, Angela! I've never forgotten! I love you as I ever did. Not a day has gone by that I haven't dreamed of kissing you, not furtively like in a churchyard at night, but in the daylight, and more than once more!"

"It's the same for me, Michael!"

They leaned in once again, and their lips touched gently, like two people who had rekindled an old love that had never really died.

It wasn't long before Michael had rented out his London flat and had taken up renting a room down the hallway at Angela's house.

THE LETTER

It took six weeks. When the envelope arrived with the results, Peter ran out of his house and sat in his car to open the envelope in a quiet moment.

The letter read:

Dear Detective Evans,

It appears that your hair's DNA matches one of the hairs from the brush you say belonged to your father, David Evans.

However, there were other hairs on that brush, as well. Both types match your own hair; one is definitely your father, and the other could be as close as a son or an uncle. If you would like further information, do not hesitate to write. Yours sincerely, ..."

Peter sat, stunned. Who could the other hair belong to? Perhaps his son, Oliver, had used the brush when he stayed over at Angela's one night. It could have even been Michael, although his room was down the hall, and what would he be doing using a brush in Angela's room? He and Angela were just friends, after all, and he was hardly more than a boarder. In any case, Michael had not moved in by the time Peter got the brush.

Peter's brain was shorting its wiring as he attempted to go down his usual list. Something was not right. Something was amiss. The DNA before him had not altered, but now he saw it differently. His eyes blurred and turned glassy as a new possibility seeped past rules and known facts.

Here was David's DNA, next to Peter's. And there was Henry's DNA, next to David's. And there was someone else's DNA. He kept glancing back to this person's DNA and David's, comparing the finest details that were so very fine that he could hardly see the difference. It couldn't be Michael. He and David had two different fathers. Peter's courses on DNA were solid, but his ability to interpret these men whose hair gave their histories away was challenging beyond the worst final exam. After all, the courses were long ago. So much more had been discovered. Peter had read every article and went to refresher courses. DNA had changed the whole job of being a detective.

Peter had to be an expert–but he was no scientist. The similarities of all four of them were to be expected–they were closely related. But the puzzle remained as something Peter could not see, could not put together with all the vital information he had gathered over a lifetime. He shook his head. Doctors were not supposed to treat their own families. Perhaps detectives should leave the DNA to others who could look with less bias.

Peter bit his lower lip, grabbed his umbrella, and left the house. He squeezed his eyebrows together with his fingers, then slung his green scarf around his neck and donned his old knit cap that Angela had made for him years before. He needed to walk and think and perhaps have a pint of beer. The cold air would wake him up and help him to decipher the problem. There was a problem–a big problem.

Outside, the wind swept his hair across his forehead, and he headed down the hill in the direction of High Street. It was Saturday, and shoppers bustled along and wouldn't pay attention to him now. He wanted anonymous company–not easy in a small town. So he went to the Arkwright's Arms, the workingman's pub. He'd hardly ever been inside.

The warm air hit him as the fireplace flickered its orange welcome. Men in caps huddled in small groups talking sports, horse races, and betting. Peter walked to a corner and sat down. He ordered a pint. As he looked around and let the chatter of people grace his ears, he could feel the facts swirling around at some level just below his consciousness.

There was a solution rising to the top, ever so slowly. He looked like Angela, for sure. At least that was clear to him. But now he imagined his son, Henry, and David, grandson and grandfather. David would have been white-haired by now. Peter had only David's young photos to go by. Then he remembered Michael's young photos and placed Henry next to him. There was something more like Michael in Henry than like David—dark hair, same nose, crooked smile, same height. Peter's son, Henry, looked like Peter—always had. But Peter didn't look that much like David, more like Michael. Well, no, Michael was his uncle, so he could well look like Michael. But the DNA had shown Peter something that raised questions he thought he knew the answers to: David's DNA wasn't as close to Peter's as was Michael's. Peter didn't know enough, he realized, to know if that really meant anything.

Peter knocked back his beer and felt a loosening of his tidy mind. He sat back and relaxed, and a vision came into his head—Michael and Henry could be grandfather and grandson. He paused and felt slight nausea. And that would mean that Michael might actually be Peter's father.

Peter leapt from his seat, ran out of the pub, and began to run up Nevill Road. Angela would be home. Peter needed answers—not just DNA. He needed the truth!

DETERMINATION

There was a determination in Peter's run, head bent, up the hill that had become steeper and steeper until no matter how hard Peter pressed on, he slowed until he reached the top, his lungs pumping fiercely. He stopped, opened the wooden gate, and walked towards the familiar door. Even now, Angela never locked her doors, even after Peter had warned her of an uptick in crime in Rottingdean. Peter pushed the door open and yelled, "Mother!"

Peter never said, "Mother." She was Mum or Grandma and even Angela on occasion. He barreled down the hallway towards the kitchen.

Angela looked up from the large quilt laid out on the long, oak kitchen table.

"Stop what you're doing, now!" Peter commanded like a policeman.

Angela's mouth fell open. A door to the far bedroom creaked.

"Listen to me, Mum. I need to know the truth. No more lies!"

Peter could see that Angela was frightened. She froze, needle in hand. He shuffled a moment, then pulled out a chair and sat down, still panting. "No more lies, Mum."

"What are you talking about, my love?"

"My father! Who is my father?"

"I told you ages ago. You know David was your father."

"That's what you say. It's not true."

Angela's face dropped, and she looked down.

"Of course, it's true! Why would I lie about a thing like that?"

"Mum. You forget your son is a detective!"

"I can't forget that, Peter."

"And your son has access to DNA." Angela stared at Peter. "DNA can tell exactly who my father is."

"So, who is your father, Peter, if it isn't David?"

"You should be the one to tell me that! You were with someone else besides David!"

"Peter. Don't talk to your mum like that!"

"Then stop acting like you weren't there!"

"David's your father!" Angela said in a defiant tone.

"Mum, please! I know who my real father is!"

"Of course you know—it's David!" Angela stuck her needle into the cloth.

"Mum, don't pick up your needle again. Look at me right in my eyes and tell me there was no other possibility!"

Angela took off her glasses. "Peter, why go on like this? I was in love with David. We made an error of judgment, and I got pregnant. That's all there is to it."

"I'd say, Mum, you made two errors of judgment!"

"What do you mean? We only did that one time—that was all. But that is all it takes, I learned," she said, frowning, and then staring out of the window.

"Think harder, Mum. Weren't you seeing another person at the same time? That can be the only explanation."

Angela's eyes flashed at Peter's face and then away. She bit her upper lip. Peter squinted at her as his cheeks burned red. He turned to the window and socked his palm with his fist.

"All right, Peter. Sit back down and have a cup of tea, and I'll tell you the story."

ANGELA'S STORY

Angela remembered how, young and pretty, she had fallen in love—but not with just one young man. Angela fell in love with two young men. She loved each one differently. She flirted, of course—quite outrageously—she blew kisses, laughed at their jokes, and took separate walks with each one.

It wasn't fair. She was confused. Shouldn't she just love one man, and that was that? If her friends realized that neither one was *the* one, might they just stop seeing her or going shopping with her or giggling over boys? It was a crest of a wave for Angela. She was in love with two men or boys or whatever they were, and she wasn't a woman or was she, or was she a lady or was she a girl? After the war, men were hard to find. Too many women laughed together, eyeing the young men who managed to avoid war in the battlefields, no matter how glorious Winston Churchill painted their courage. Angela was pretty, and she wanted a wonderful, alive boyfriend. It wasn't her fault that two turned up!

There was David, charming David. And, then, there was Michael, his brother. How could she love one and not the other? They were like twins, hanging around with each other, going off to find antiques together, arguing over who found the best item at Portobello Road this time.

Sometimes Angela found herself skipping in between the two men while her girlfriends snubbed her for her forward ways. *What a flirt! What a selfish person, taking two men when there wasn't even one per girl to go round.* All those red-lipped women whose men never returned home lusted after the younger men just leaving sixth form, hardly a hair on their upper lips. It must have been a fine time for those men. The women were not happy. It took more red lipstick and shorter skirts and higher heels and even nylon stockings with a seam at the back to get their attention, and then *along comes Angela with her pretty face.*

Angela sewed the most beautiful dresses for herself out of found material. She was a clever girl. Might make someone a wonderful wife, she might.

It seemed she saw David on a Tuesday and Michael on a Friday, and even after a while, each brother still didn't realize she was seeing the other brother. Those brothers must have talked about antiques the whole time, and of course, money! But if they talked about Angela, it was most likely only in passing, a joke, not a competitive conversation.

Meanwhile, young Angela started teaching sewing classes to children in a local Hampstead primary school. The mothers would come and watch and tell Angela their sad stories about how their husbands died in the war. It was depressing to her. She didn't want to think about the war and the dying. But it was right there in front of her every time she held a class. Some of those women even asked Angela home for tea once in a while. But it never went further than that. She never found real friends.

One day David came by. "Would you like to go for a walk on Hampstead Heath?" he ventured. "Or perhaps we could fast-walk," he added.

"Girls can fast-walk, too! In fact, let's do it right now!"

And off she went, speeding along, hips swaying, arms swinging, across the zebra crossing and past the primary school and over the bridge, up past the Magdala Pub and down towards Parliament Hill Fields. Not to be outdone, David sped up his brisk walk and passed her with a grin. Anyone might have said it was a blossoming friendship, which could lead to something more serious!

Out of breath, they landed on the grass at Parliament Hill Fields and rolled down the hill. It was damp but not really wet—misty, but not soaking. It smelled green and good and fresh. After they had rolled down quite a way, David bumped into Angela at the bottom of the hill but didn't move away from her body. They were laughing so hard they didn't notice Michael in the distance walking across the bottom of Parliament Hill in their direction.

MICHAEL

Michael didn't see Angela and David on the grass. He was just going to meet a friend at the Magdala pub. He hoped to see Angela later on. He'd drop round.

He looked up at the airplane flying overhead, and then his gaze fell upon a couple in the distance. They looked like they were embracing, maybe kissing. They looked like they were in love. They looked quite taken with each other, like they were looking intensely into each other's eyes.

Michael looked away. Then his face turned serious, and he looked back as he got closer. His face fell, and he swore under his breath–that was bloody David! That brother of his was going too far–they had not even drawn straws. It just wasn't fair. She was their friend. It wasn't fair. And bloody hell, he should be the one kissing her! He loved her first–he loved her intensely. He was going to kill David. He was going to knock him in the jaw so he would never be able to kiss Angela again. He would then hit him on the head; so that all he could think about was how it hurt, and then that thieving brother of his wouldn't have the energy to hang around his lovely Angela.

Just then, David and Angela jumped up and started running up the hill, David chasing Angela. Michael pulled the miniature quilt that he'd found at Portobello Road from his pocket and studied his treasure. He stuffed it back in and carried on, not even looking at where they had gone or try to see what they did. But his mind couldn't help wondering if just over that hill, they hadn't fallen in the grass once again and kissed passionately. It wasn't fair! She was his love.

ANGELA

It was true–Angela loved David. But as David kissed her, she couldn't help imagining how it would feel to kiss Michael. They had the same lips almost, but Michael's were just a little more inviting. It was just a feeling. She wouldn't act on it. But she loved Michael just the same as David, so why shouldn't she kiss him, too? Thank goodness David wasn't putting his tongue into her mouth! She had heard about that kind of kissing, but she really preferred just lips, luscious lips caressing her own, tingling her very being, and right up and down her body to her very toes.

When she got home with her hair in a mess, her mother told her that Michael had dropped by and left an envelope with something thick and soft inside of it.

Angela rushed to her room and opened the envelope and saw a tiny and very intricately sewn quilt. The colors were not drab like all the dresses in the fifties. They were bright and light and lively. It seemed to her that her life had changed at that very moment. She held the quilt in her hands and smoothed it across her knees, the reds and blues delicately combined with whites and yellows, and studied the little stitches holding the squares together that seemed to tell a story. The hands that had made this quilt were clearly concentrated in each stitch, in each moment, in a realm of giving that would probably outlast a lifetime. She put it by her pillow that night; it was the last thing she saw before she turned out the light. And she then thought of Michael.

The next day Michael turned up at her door.

"Angela, love! It's Michael here for tea!" Angela's mother called.

Angela's mother seemed to like Michael. Later she mentioned his handsome face, contours perfect, carved like a Greek statue, his eyebrow slightly raised, almost like Laurence Olivier. She invited him in and made tea with her best teapot. David wasn't with him this time.

" Sorry, I didn't realize..." Angela said as she walked towards him, noticing Michael's eyes almost devouring her. She smiled at him and thought of the beautiful quilt.

"How nice of you to come over. I wanted to thank you so very much for that lovely miniature quilt. It made me want to gather all my old dresses together and cut them up and make little squares and put them together like a puzzle. What an idea! Perhaps I will do it!"

"Thank you. What an inspiration, Angela."

Michael stood at attention in his best clothes and shined shoes. How handsome he felt–like a gentleman, though only a very young man.

"Please have a seat," Angela's mum said and went out to prepare the tea. Michael leaned to his left, exactly where Angela was sitting and took her hand as if he had never done so before. He had, but only in play. Now there was something else going on. He could hardly explain it to himself, except that his heart was beating fiercely. *David and Angela lying in the grass, kissing.* He pulled her towards him and kissed her passionately on the lips.

"Michael!" Angela exclaimed, dabbing her mouth as her mother came in with the tea tray. Michael smiled at Angela. She would have to sit there now and realize that she really loved him better. She had felt his passion, his soft lips, his desire.

"I'll just go and get the supper ready, Angela. You have a nice chat with Michael. Lovely quilt, then, Michael. Just lovely," said her mother as she exited the door.

Michael grabbed Angela's hand again and drew her body to his, this time with his chest pressing into hers, his hand gently gathering her head towards him and her lips to his. There was no hesitation from Angela– she kissed him back. Was she thinking of David, of his lips, his caresses, his protestations of love? Maybe she loved them both. She threw her arms around Michael's broad back and pressed herself equally towards his body. Classical music came through the kitchen from the wireless.

"Come up to my room," Angela said. Michael got up and followed her upstairs and into her attic room. She shut the door and the two friends started by sitting across the room from each other.

"Come here," Angela said, patting her bed. Michael could hardly remember David at that moment. Angela's lips were warm and inviting. He knew he shouldn't sit that close to her on her bed. She smiled, her eyes penetrating his. Her mother was busy with supper. He couldn't help himself, got up, hesitated, and then threw himself at her, pushing her down with love and lust on the bed and kissing her with a pent up passion that had finally become like a furnace in his chest and loins.

DAVID

The next day David turned up at Angela's door holding a bouquet of daisies. It was teatime, and her mother was as gracious as she had been the day before with Michael.

"Come in, love. Angela will be right down." David stepped inside, holding the daisies close. He followed Angela's mother into the kitchen, and she put the kettle on.

"Lovely day, isn't it?" she said. "And lovely daisies, as well." David nodded and smiled back but felt tongue-tied to be witnessed now as more than the friend he had always been to Angela.

Angela bustled in with her big smile and wide eyes. "David," she said, accepting the daisies. "How lovely!" She took the daisies from his outstretched hands and pulled them to her nose.

"Mmmmm!"

Her mother poured the tea and invited them into the sitting room, carrying the tray in with perfect calm. "I must get on with the supper, so you two just enjoy your tea." She left them sitting side-by-side and closed the door softly.

David pretended to like the tea, but being his own man, he never really liked tea. It was a game though, and it required at least one cup. It was an excuse to sit together and gaze into each other's eyes over the edge of the cup. The saucer could be in his other hand, or he could leave it on the coffee table. He didn't smoke, so he couldn't connect with Angela that way, as he had seen other people do in cafés.

Angela laid her hand on his arm. He sat frozen and felt a tingle of excitement.

Angela giggled and pushed her thick hair back from her eyes. David smelled of Old Spice. Angela noticed it. She loved that smell. She leaned in and took a gentle sniff.

"Old Spice," she said.

"True. Do you like it?"

"I love it!"

David felt a small triumph, almost as if she had said she loved him. Again, this moment of their new way of being together was awkward. They used to laugh out loud together like children, roll on the ground, tussle, tumble, and play cricket in the park. Now they sat and could hardly figure out what to say, and worse, they could only just glance at each other.

Angela was in love with David–there was no doubt about it. But she wouldn't tell him. She might kiss him again. But she had to wait a bit. This problem with Michael had to be worked out. So they smiled and drank their tea. And then David leaned towards her and kissed her ever so lightly on the cheek. She blushed. She might have kissed him back right on the lips, but the touch of Michael's lips was too fresh. She felt confused–she loved them both!

Her mother came in and said, "Shouldn't you be doing your home-work, Angela?" She turned to face David. "It was lovely seeing you again, David, and I am sure you have homework to do yourself? Come again soon. Goodbye for now."

David shuffled towards the door. He'd got the hint. He paused, turned towards Angela, and looked into her eyes long and hard. Next time he would kiss her on the lips like he did before–soon–very soon.

THE LETTER

Angela expected to see Michael quite soon afterwards, but he never came.

The very next week, Angela heard that Michael had received a letter from a girl called Janet that he had been seeing quietly for several months. She apparently had written that she was pregnant and asked what Michael wanted to do about it.

David came by Angela's house with the news that Michael had married this girl because she was pregnant.

Angela fell onto the sofa, shocked and bewildered. She really did love Michael. But there sat David–so kind, so loving, so ardent–and she loved him as well. She was miffed that Michael had been seeing somebody else as well, but she could hardly complain. She pulled David by the hand and led him up the stairs to her attic bedroom. When she closed the door behind her, he pulled her towards him and kissed her on the lips, harder than he had imagined possible. And he put his hands up under her cardigan–she let him. He touched both of her soft, full breasts. He raised the cardigan, looked at her beautiful breasts, leaned down, and gently kissed each nipple.

And then he recovered himself and pulled her cardigan back down. But she leaned towards him and placed her soft, sensuous lips on his lips again. His resolve, and all the things he had been taught about respecting a girl who had to save herself for her husband, disappeared in a passion that filled his body to a place he had never felt in his life. He took her in his arms and held her so tightly that she had to cough. They giggled and then kissed again, this time with their mouths open a little, and then a little more and then wide with tongues lightly exploring. He pushed her down gently, softly. He kissed her neck and her ear and then moved his hand under her skirt. He didn't even mean to. It was like his hand had a mind of its own. There it was, caressing her outer leg–up, then down, in a rhythm that matched his racing heart. Yet now, he found himself yearning for the knowledge of the softness between her legs. He had to try to stop his hand, but his hand won, and over it went, across the mountain of her leg and down into the crevice that he suddenly longed for as he pushed himself against her outer leg to ease the urgency that swelled against his stomach.

Angela's breath became hot and quickened. It was loud in his ear, like it was inviting him to come closer and closer. She didn't push his hand away. In fact, she laid her palm on top of his hand as he pressed his fingers onto that dark, wonderful mound and inched it towards the softest place in the world.

THE MIRROR

Three months later, Angela looked in the mirror. It was a small mirror, so she glanced at her teeth, then held it away from her body, then altered its angle to check her waistline. Nothing seemed to fit these days. Buttons popped. It was something annoying in the back of her mind to be ignored if possible. But lately, no matter if she skipped breakfast and even lunch, she was gaining weight. She tried to see herself from the side view. She held her stomach in, but it came back out. She feared she could be pregnant. Her period was two months late, or was it three? She kept lying at school, saying she couldn't play hockey because she had a heavy period. She hated lying. Mostly, she was confused. Michael had married Janet, and David had disappeared, no longer coming by for tea.

"Angela, dear," asked her mother one day. "Where's David? We haven't seen him for weeks now, or is it months?"

"I don't know, Mum. I think he went to Italy. He's taking a year off before going into the life of a journalist. He's writing up a storm about antiques, I think. I heard it at school. My friend, Mary, collects antiques, too, and she got a card from David."

"He could have written to you, then, couldn't he have?" she answered with a tone of irritation in defense of her daughter's lonely existence.

"Mum, I'm still in school. He's now an official adult. I must look pretty young and silly to such a worldly man. That's all. He'll come round eventually. I wish I could go to Italy." She smoothed her hand across her rounded belly.

"Angela, what are you doing?"

Angela started.

"Nothing, Mum," she lied.

"What went on with David that he ran away like that?"

"Oh, Mum. I don't know. I thought we were getting serious." She had thought that about Michael, too.

"It looked like he was quite keen," said her mother.

"He seemed really keen, Mum. I don't understand him." Angela lowered her head. Her mother came over and sat next to her on the settee.

"What's wrong, Angela? Why are you crying? Why are you rubbing your belly? Why are you gaining weight when you never eat?"

"Mum, I haven't had my periods for two or three months," Angela said in a lowered voice.

The two women let the silence fill in the rest. No use confessing to her one-night stand with David, not to mention Michael. This statement brought it out between them without much else to ground it.

"What are you going to do if it, if you're…."

"Pregnant!" bellowed Angela, the tears pouring from her eyes.

"Pregnant," said her mother in a very quiet voice, whose eyes were watering. She breathed deeply and held Angela to her. She cleared her voice. "It's not the end of the world. David will marry you. He's an honest chap. You'll have to write him and get him to return for a quick ceremony at the Belsize Park Town Hall."

"Oh, Mum, I'm too young for all this!"

"Yes, Angela, but you are at the age when this sometimes happens to young people. They get married, and that's the end of it. Of course, all the gossips are counting the months backwards once the baby's birth date is known. Not to worry. You are not alone, love. It'll all work out for the best."

Angela blew her nose and looked with large eyes at her mother, the best mum in the world. Dad was long dead in the war. At least she wouldn't have the wrath of her father over this.

Angela flung her arms around her mother and bawled.

"Never mind, love. You'll see. David's a good lad, unless you want to...."

"Mum! Never!"

An Urgent Matter

Dear David,

I hope you are faring well.

I detest having to write this letter to you now. You must be having a wonderful life there in Italy.

I have to let you know that this is an urgent matter. I'm afraid our wonderful time together has resulted in a pregnancy. I really tried not to notice it at first, but now I am starting to buy new and larger clothes. Mum says you'll come and marry me and that you are a good, kind and understanding man, David.

I won't hold you to anything. It's clear you don't love me anymore. But I really need help now. Please come home. We won't live together, but I need to give this baby a name. Maybe you could help me? Peter sounds lovely for a boy. I can't think of a girl's name. I am hoping you'll come up with that one. You can figure out the month it will be born, of course.

Sorry to bring this news. I promise I won't hold you to a real marriage. But I know we're good friends and that you won't let me down.

Please hurry back, and let's get this over with so I can show my face!

Your friend,
Angela

"Oh, my God! This can't be true!" David yelled, shaking the letter in his hand. He looked around to see if someone had heard him—only the housekeeper, but she only understood Italian. David crunched up the letter and threw it into the wastepaper basket. He began to pace. It was a habit he'd just begun, as too much was weighing him down—too many decisions. Should he be a journalist, or should he go into antiques? And now this!

"Damn!" he yelled. The housekeeper jolted her head up and backed away.

"Scusi," he said to her, bending down, grabbing the letter out of the waste paper basket and stuffing it into his pocket.

"Damn her," he mumbled now and climbed the stairs up to his room. The job was there, they had written, waiting for him at *The Daily Mail*. They'd been impressed with his two articles on antiques and cricket. He had an offer, but now his year abroad was going to be cut short. He couldn't believe it. He didn't love her. He was very clear about that.

And yet, she was in a very bad spot. He had to stubbornly admit that he was an equal partner in their passion. But she had put his hand there! She started it! She should take the consequences! He could have waited. Or could he? He remembered his own passion, his drive to touch her there, to lie with his chest next to her breasts—those lovely breasts. He stopped himself. It was after his passion had simmered to a memory, right then when he was pulling up his trousers and looking at her smiling at him, that he knew without a doubt that this was not love—it was pure lust. Thank goodness he could go back to Italy soon, and it would be a natural ending to this beginning that had no hope of the love he'd imagined.

And yet, Angela and he had been friends forever. He couldn't let her down. In a way, their friendship was stronger than any love.

BUSINESS
BETWEEN FRIENDS

The bus was more uncomfortable than usual for Angela. David wrote that, of course, he was returning imminently and she wanted to look really beautiful. So she went into the West End and bought a tailored dress that hid her bulging stomach rather nicely. She felt a little sick as the bus bumped back home while she clutched her parcel. She liked the bus anyway. The underground was faster, but you could see everything along the way on the bus. She didn't climb up the curving steps of the bus these days. She wondered how much weight she had gained. Later in the week, she would go to the doctor's and find out. But first, she would do whatever David was willing to do and get that over with. She didn't buy anything like a wedding dress. But this white, frilly dress would do nicely in the Belsize Park Town Hall.

David arrived home on the train after crossing the channel on a very crowded ferry. He went straight away to her house and knocked at her door.

"Hello, David! Mum, it's David. He's here! Come in, love. You've really come home!" Angela said, shyly covering her stomach.

"Of course I did, Angela."

Angela looked at David's face. The old smile was strained. He stood at a polite distance.

"But I don't want you to get this wrong, Angela," he added. "We have agreed: this is business between friends, right?"

"It's just fine, David. Come in and sit down. I told you in my letters that we just needed to make the child legitimate. I would have been so sad if you had not come back. After all, it isn't just my child, is it?"

David looked up quickly at Angela's face as he sat down on a kitchen chair. She didn't mean to blame him. She was just telling the whole truth. Neither of them was old enough for all this, but it would have to get taken care of, and that was all there was to it.

"It's the day after tomorrow, then, as I wrote. We can just go down there by 10 a.m., and they'll do the honors. Just sign this and sign that, and it will all be over."

"Right, then. Seems pretty straightforward," David said, straightening his tie and smoothing down his blazer.

"Have some tea and stay awhile and tell us all about your adventures in Italy," Angela's mother said.

"Thank you. I've had a wonderful time. I learned so much in such a short while. I have been writing a story about it–about a famous goldsmith in the sixteenth century there in Italy called Benvenuto Cellini– quite exciting, really."

They had tea, biscuits, and sympathy, then bid a fond farewell until the day after tomorrow.

"Meet you here at nine-thirty then, and we can walk round to the Town Hall. Let's hope it's not raining!" David said, trying to sound enthusiastic. Her stomach was definitely sticking out. It would be obvious to anybody why they were standing there saying, "I do."

David met Michael in The Magdala pub in Hampstead that night. They both got roaring drunk and laughed their heads off about marriage and wives. Neither mentioned the silver cups. This was a time for celebration. The cups would come soon enough. David knew a whole lot more about Italian silver now. He knew they had a real treasure. Later– that would come later. Now, it was slaps on the backs, off-color jokes about sex and women, and some worse jokes about their respective parents, same mother–different fathers.

A RIGHT TO KNOW

It was so long ago. Angela looked out the window at the distant sea, then at Peter, with his expectant face. Of course, Peter had a right to know. She remembered what she had tried to forget.

David had never known about how far Michael and Angela had actually gone. Angela would never have told David. It would have hurt him too badly. Michael had so wanted to see Peter, to see if Peter had David's qualities. Angela made him keep quiet. Their indiscretion was a secret between just the two of them. Nobody else in the whole world knew. If David suspected, perhaps through the smell of Old Spice he might have also smelled on her, it was one of those things he'd probably rather not have known.

David married Angela two days later, as planned. But Angela knew that he knew he didn't love her anymore. He loved her that one day, and she put his hand there, and then, of course, he was lost in lust. But he told her the truth. He married her out of pity, and he married her to give the child a father and a name—Evans. It was silly, really. It had only happened that once; after that, they both knew he didn't love her. She was his friend and always would be, but love was another matter.

David saw Michael and his new family—Janet and Geoffrey—when he could, and he could see that Michael was unhappy. But Michael had the same sense of responsibility to Janet that David showed in marrying Angela. Perhaps Michael was even more responsible, for he'd stayed with Janet.

David returned to Italy two days after he and Angela got married and said he would send her money until the child was of age. He went back to find great antiques and to get away from his friend and her troubles. She had put his hand there. She could take the consequences. He would help her, but he would not give up his life for her and her baby.

Again, Italy was even more than David had ever hoped—the sunshine glittering on the water in Venice; the cream and orange colors reflected in the jittery water; the gondolas used as the English used their cars; museums full of ancient silver and gold and marble, and statues from ancient Greece and Rome.

David spent a month searching every corner of Venice and then Rome and Florence, wishing that he could share these experiences with Michael. But at least he could bring back some amazing souvenirs. He knew what was genuine, with an eye for the glitter that would fade and for the faded silver that was only tarnished but real.

Loneliness penetrated his excitement. He had so often shared this life with Michael, but now Michael was trapped for life. David shivered in the sunlight. He was trapped, too—at least, financially. Perhaps he would write about his travels. Maybe he would sell another article to *The Daily Mail*. It could be a travel article, and it could be an article about antiques. He bought a new pad and pen and began while sitting in his tiny rented room in Venice, overlooking a narrow canal. When he looked out of the window, he could see the water line that had risen up the side of the building across the way sometime in the past. His pen dashed across the page. He felt excited as his life began to have a larger meaning. Soon enough, he would have to return to his new office job at *The Daily Mail*.

As he wrote into the night, he watched the shimmering light against the water, listened to the sonorous singing of the gondoliers, felt the sense of history all around him, and heard the Italian language, so musical—so romantic. His writing became fluent, and he added with relish a few Italian words among his English prose.

David traveled to the small islands outside Venice to explore the old smelting workshops there. It felt as if he were back in the 1500s. He learned more about Benvenuto Cellini and started to read Cellini's autobiography in Italian with his Italian-English dictionary by lamplight.

THE TRUTH

"Peter, it was a long time ago," Angela said, wringing her hands.

Peter looked at his mother, and although he had figured it out scientifically, the anger brewing in him was like a volcano stirring in his stomach. Here she sat, looking almost pleased to tell him the truth, and he felt an urge to strangle her. His hands formed an arc that could circle her neck if he lost his English manners. The effort to hold in all this uproar inside him made him breathe out pointedly. He couldn't form the words that growled inside his head. He knew his face was contorted, but years of holding back came to his rescue, and he could only burst out verbally and clench his fists.

"Yes, but I'm here today! I'm alive! You know how much I need to know! Mum, this is my right! This isn't a small white lie about why someone is late for school!"

"Why can't you just leave it, Peter?" said Angela, shifting in her chair. "Why isn't David good enough to be your father? Why must you keep digging into the past? Leave it alone; there's a good boy."

"Mum, first off, I am *not* a 'good boy.' I'm a man. I'm not even a young man. I have children who should know the truth. I dig into the past because that is who I am. I learn about history. I learn everything I need to know to fit puzzles together. This puzzle still doesn't fit. You're getting old, Mum, sorry to say, and I don't want you dying before you tell me the truth right to my face!"

Angela looked at Peter. "All right, Peter, the truth is–there was someone else in my life at the same time as David."

Peter leaned forward, anchoring his chin in his knuckles, and studied Angela's face for twitches–lies.

"The *truth*, Mum."

"I'm getting there."

"Who was he?"

"Well…," Angela's eyes took on a pleading look, like she was giving up. This time Peter would not say, "Never mind, Mum." But he waited, and she had to talk. "His name is, he's…he's Uncle Michael."

"I knew it! I knew it!" Peter leapt up. "I'm so like him–it had to be! The DNA says it! I needed to hear it from your mouth, though, Mum, your mouth–your confession! I hope you can see what this means to me. Can you? I am free now!"

"Free from what?" Angela asked.

"Free of wondering–always wondering. Now I know. I can deal with it. I am a man, Mum. Take a look. The final words that helped make me into a total person were those you told me. I know who my father really is!"

There was a creaking sound from the floor behind the kitchen door.

"My uncle is my father! Might as well come in, Uncle Michael. We can hear you out there."

The door opened from the hallway, and there stood Michael– brogues, suit, and tie.

Peter looked at Michael, who stopped abruptly, standing almost at attention.

"Uncle Michael!" he blurted.

"No, Peter, it looks like I'm likely your father!" Michael said.

"Father?" Peter raised his voice a tone higher. "Father?" Peter took a small step backwards from Michael.

Michael stood in front of Peter as if wanting acknowledgement and closure. Peter's clenched fists turned towards Michael. Michael backed away.

"Peter, I promise you, I had no idea!"

"Rubbish! You must have known!"

"Sometimes I suspected it. Sometimes I actually hoped for it. But mostly, I felt you were David's son. My heart was always with you, Peter."

"You never said!"

"But I mean it!!"

"Well, you and Mum have been traitors to me!"

"No, Peter. Don't you think she would have told me if she'd been sure herself?"

"Mum, why didn't you tell Uncle Michael what you knew to be the truth?"

"I swear, son, I didn't know anything for sure. I wanted to let sleeping dogs lie, didn't I?"

"You lied to me, you lied to Michael, and you lied to yourself."

Angela sat in a slump, her hands folded on her lap, her head down. "Son, I'm very sorry," she said.

Michael stepped towards Peter. "Yes, I'm your father, but how did *you* know?"

"DNA proves it. It must have been your hair in Angela's hairbrush that I pulled the DNA from."

Michael looked down and blushed. "I once used it before leaving your mother's room."

There was a long silence while Peter held in his rage and pleasure, biting his lip.

"Angela and I are not landlord and tenant, Peter. I'm not your uncle," Michael paused for a moment, "but I am now, it seems, indeed, your father."

"I can't believe this, Uncle, I mean, Michael, I mean, *Father*!"

"Peter, your mother and I have loved each other all our lives, but we were committed to others. At last, we can share our lives. I have always felt very close to you, but I thought it was probably because you were the closest living being to David left to me when he died."

Peter stepped forward and offered his hand. Michael ignored it and opened his arms, pulling Peter close. Peter let the tears well up as the pink and green flowery wallpaper blurred over Michael's shoulder. He felt his father's arms about him, sinking into his bones and soul as Michael's head rested on Peter's heaving chest.

When they parted, and Peter had stuffed his handkerchief back into his pocket, Peter said, "No wonder I'm such a fish out of water. I'm crazy, just like you!"

They both laughed.

Angela watched and didn't take up her needle. As the father and son drew apart, Angela asked, as if on a cue everyone understood in their bones, "No more meeting in the graveyard in the middle of the night! Shall we have a cup of tea, then?"

"I'll put it on," Michael said, turning and grabbing the kettle and filling it up to the brim.

Peter turned to his mother, sat down, and took his mother's idle hands.

"I can't understand you, Mum–meetings in the graveyard all those years ago. Now this. Why did you hide this from me?"

"I was so ashamed," Angela began, dabbing her eyes with her handkerchief. "It was bad enough to be a single mum all those years, even if I had David's surname. People probably thought I was a bad woman. Some people shunned me. Imagine if anyone found out the real truth! Imagine then! Life was very lonely as it was. And then it was just a secret that sat there and wouldn't go away. What was the point? Why hurt more people?"

Peter dropped Angela's hands. "I was hurting all my bloody life, wondering who my father really was. I knew something was wrong–I just knew it!"

"I am so sorry, love. I was being selfish, thinking only of myself, wasn't I?"

Peter looked at Angela, growing older now. He looked at Michael, competent with the teapot–older, but still so strong. At last, Peter could see and hear and feel his father, a strange man indeed. Now Peter felt he understood his own peculiar ways of being different. Michael's presence as his father finally explained everything.

LIES

The gathering was most unusual. All other activities were cancelled at Peter's insistence and mostly Henry's protestations.

Peter had them sit by the fire in the sitting room, and he had insisted on hot chocolate and biscuits. When their patter subsided, and they looked at Peter with wide eyes, Peter began.

"Children, I have something important to tell you," he began.

"That's obvious!" Oliver said.

"After a lifetime of searching to find out who my father was–your grandfather–I have finally found out."

There was a general murmur of acknowledgement. The children leaned forward, eyes wide.

"But Grandfather David is our grandfather, right?" confirmed Henry.

"Well, Henry, that is what I was told when I was eighteen. But, in fact, your real grandfather isn't David."

The children looked up at Peter, mouths open, hanging like ripe fruit.

"No, your real grandfather isn't David."

"So, who is he then?" Cassandra asked, frowning.

"Well, it is strange, but your grandfather is, in fact, the man who I always thought was my Uncle Michael."

"Uncle Michael?" Cassandra chimed in. "He's our great uncle. He said so."

"Just because grandma called him Uncle Michael doesn't change the facts. She finally told me he was, indeed, my father."

"So, he's our grandfather now?" Oliver asked.

"He is, indeed, your grandfather."

"He lied," Cassandra pouted.

"He didn't know," Peter said.

"He lied," insisted Cassandra.

"No, I'm afraid grandma lied."

"Grandma?" Cassandra squealed.

"Yes, Grandma."

"Grandma never lies!"

"Well, this once, I'm afraid, she felt it better to keep it a secret."

"Why? What's wrong with Uncle Michael?" Cassandra asked.

"Yes, what?" Oliver echoed.

"Nothing at all. It is a long story, and I will tell it to you someday soon. For now, you have a real, live grandfather!"

"He's the same person, Uncle Michael, so nothing's changed," Henry said.

"Nothing at all," lied Peter.

THE LAST THERAPY SESSION

At the end of the last court-required psychotherapy session, Peter looked at Helen long and hard. He bit his lip, which was raw and soft from endless chomping while his mind plunged momentarily back into the depths of his memory that had unexpectedly surfaced so recently.

And there sat Helen, nodding with her serene smile. He'd never seen her teeth, really. She was so serious, and if she had ever laughed, he hadn't noticed. His brain pinched like crossed wires; he had never had a moment to relieve his torture long enough to notice her face. And now, Peter saw just the edges of her teeth, just enough to hold his gaze and see that she had truly witnessed his private agonies and had nodded with that subtle smile, like a congratulatory signal that he had passed an examination of the emotions along with the tears of recognition that no handkerchief could hold back.

Peter stood up, slightly less formally than before. He stood in the presence of a mirror. Helen stood up then and reached out both hands to him. No one had ever smiled quite that smile, nor had anyone, even Angela, reached with both hands to comfort him and acknowledge all of him.

He wanted to hug her, but he didn't dare. Instead, she threw her welcoming American arms gently around his shoulders and gave him a big, brief hug. He spluttered, "Oh, Helen, I don't know how to thank you!" His whole body warmed, and he held back a torrent of tears.

"You have done the impossible in only six months. There is a lot to do still, and you can do it. You know that now."

Peter nodded, and his throat tightened, choking the loving words that refused, even now, to squeeze from his mouth.

As he backed away, her hands momentarily grasped his own—then let them go like a boat's rope dropping into the sea, the last link with land severed.

She didn't walk after him. His eyes never left hers until he turned and stepped out of the office door.

On the high street, the cars and buses played tag, horns beeped, people crossed against the lights. They talked and laughed and walked with jaunts that proclaimed that life was moving along like a train on its tracks and that nothing much had changed.

The fresh wind bit into Peter's eyes, and he wiped them. He headed towards the police station. There was still that outstanding case that needed his complete attention. No more of this wallowing! Chin up! The past could not be changed.

"You can't change the past, but *you* can change," Helen had said. "You are the only one who can change. You can do it, Peter. It's your choice. It seems to me we only have this one life," she had said. "You can regret it or move into the present."

Peter pushed on up the chilly hill, his hair flipping from side to side as he brushed it away from his eyes. He turned into his mens' hairdresser's shop and said, "Do you have time for a short back and sides?"

"I do, Peter. Come along and sit down," said his longtime friend.

Peter sat down in the old barber's chair and said, "Much shorter this time. Spring is nearly here. It's time for a new start."

"You know what you like, Peter," said the barber, and went to work as Peter watched in the mirror the beginning of the very first change of many to come.

Peter smiled at the sky and the clouds when he left the hairdresser's. At last, he would finally be able to go for a walk with his father and get all those lifelong, burning questions answered. He walked with his head held high, the breeze tickling his bare neck. Then he chuckled to himself–those urgent questions now seemed to have melted quietly away like ice on a hot, sunny day.

IF I HAD YOU BACK AGAIN

Some days later, traveling with his children by car from Rottingdean to walk on Hampstead Heath in London, Peter sang the aria that Angela had played so often on her gramophone. They all joined in. Cassandra's voice was pure and high. Oliver's was quite mellow. Henry's was low, an alto, and with no more of those cracklings that seem to have lasted for years.

They sang in harmony, switching to *All You Need is Love*, then back to the aria. They took turns starting a new song, and the Beatles won. Once in a while, Henry would sing, *Oh, Mrs. McGrath, The sergeant said, Would you like to make a soldier out of your son, Ted*, and they all chimed in. Peter secretly remembered how fierce Jeannie had sounded when she sang it during those last days. But the children only remembered the tune and the words that had been a gift from Jeannie to their souls.

"You know...." said Peter. He drifted into silence.

"Dad, what were you saying?" Henry prompted.

"Oh, yes. Sorry. I was miles away!" But he didn't mention his former dead "father," David, and his own desperate search all his life for the truth finally pried from Angela's lips; Catherine being so long in jail; Michael being tried for David's murder; jails and police lurking in their lives over the years; his dear Jeannie going insane, and her horrible final death rattle—

and worst of all, that, perhaps, Jeannie had meant to push Peter over the cliff.

"What I was going to say was, hasn't life become serene and fun lately? It feels like a cloud has been lifted from our family."

"What cloud?" asked Cassandra, who had taken to illustrating and writing fantasy books for young children.

"Hmm, I'm not sure," Peter answered. "A cloud–so much tragedy for so long. It seems like everything evaporated at some point, and life has become normal. Even in Rottingdean, the crime levels have gone down. The whole village seems calmer. There isn't much to look into there since–since when?" Peter mumbled something to himself.

"Since you quit therapy!" Henry said.

"Since we moved into a bigger house?" tried Oliver.

"Since when?" Peter asked.

"Since Uncle Michael became my grandfather," Henry said.

"And mine," said Oliver.

"And mine, as well!" said Cassandra.

"Maybe that's when," Peter said quietly. He privately took credit for that with his limited DNA knowledge. "But since some other moment," he added.

There was a soft silence as Peter tried to put the puzzle together.

"Perhaps it was really since those silver cups were sent back to Italy," Peter said.

"Anyway, I like Grandma's porcelain cups better," Cassandra said.

Peter started their song up again, and they all joined in singing: *"Well if I had you back again, I'd never let you go to fight the king of Spain, For I'd rather have my Ted as he used to be, Then the King of France and his whole navy…with your too-ri-a, fol-di-diddle da, too-ri, oor-ri, oor-ri-a!"*

The next day Michael called Peter and said he wanted to meet up down at the pub as he had something important to tell him.

As they walked down Nevill Road, the wind over the ocean from the southwest swept their hair and their hats enough that they had to hold them down. They passed pleasantries about the cricket season coming up and where they might go together.

They entered the pub and took off their hats and scarves and hung them with their umbrellas on the hat stand by the door. There was a red glow from the fireplace, and the heat was a cozy welcome from the brisk wind outside.

The Olde Black Horse pub was dimly lit. On the left side, the workingmen laughed as they played darts and ordered pint after pint of beer. On the right side, separated by a wall and a very narrow doorway, sat men in suits, in groups of two or three in a corner, heads bowed, no raucous laughter, perhaps the odd, "Cheers!" coming forth as they quietly downed their half-pints and discussed the stock reports from the *Financial Times*. For this meeting, Michael chose the quieter venue, although he wouldn't have minded a game of darts on another occasion. This time he needed a calm, private place to tell Peter about the silver cups.

Michael wandered over to a spot as far from the other people as possible. A woman's laughter rang out between the male chuckles then died down again to a gentle murmur.

Peter bought two half-pints at the bar and brought them over to their table.

"Peter," began Michael, once Peter was seated. "The reason I asked you to come here today was not father-son bonding, as you people call it today. It's really to let you know my theory about the silver cups. As you know, I read my horoscope every day."

"I am well aware of that, Uncle…Father," said Peter.

"What I am going to say isn't a reflection of my beliefs in astrology, just to be clear. Astrology is often dismissed if I bring it up, so I need to set the story straight here."

"I understand, *Father*–calling you father still sounds strange to me. Sorry."

"I like it, Peter–feels grand to me!"

"All right, then, *Father!*"

They clinked mugs, and each took a deep swig of beer.

"Actually, I'm here to tell you that I think those silver cups must have cast some kind of spell over us all. I know that sounds bloody stupid, but think about it –bad luck came to us all ever since we got them. Look at poor David, falling dead on his knife. Look at Jeannie, plunging over the cliff she knew so well. Look at you and me, both suspected of their murders."

"You don't think there was a connection between her fall and the cups, do you?" said Peter, feeling quite crestfallen.

"I've thought and thought about it all–Catherine in jail all those years, me living with excruciating guilt about it, my wife and son so unfortunate. All that and Jeannie's fall happened once we got the cups and separated six of them from the other six. Have you noticed that since they were reunited and back in Italy, everything has turned around? I was welcomed by your mother after all those years. And I've found you, and you've found me, Peter!" Michael reached over and patted Peter on the back, and they clinked mugs once again and drank, their eyes looking towards the ceiling.

Michael said, "I feel a spell was somehow cast–perhaps by Cellini himself. We don't know how the cups got to England from Italy, but they were lost and somehow surfaced into our hands after over four hundred years when we found them on that rag-and-bone cart that day after the war. Imagine the bad luck all the previous owners must have had!"

"We'll never know, will we? David's Cellini manuscript was only fiction, wasn't it?"

Michael only smiled. "From now on, Peter, I am sure everything will go well for our family. No more tragedy. It's good that those cups are back where they always belonged. Funnily enough, the horoscopes foretold all this, but I didn't get it. I wasn't listening hard enough. But, truth to be told, I did love those silver cups!"

"Well, Father, I can't say astrology means anything to me, but I'd welcome some calm years ahead. Not too calm, however, or I would be out of a job!"

They laughed as their mugs clinked again, and they downed the rest of their drinks. They left the pub and trudged back up the hill together, through the storm and wind and into Angela's house where a bright fire was burning. Angela greeted them, then suggested they go sit by the fire to get warm and dry–and, of course, soon enough–she poured them each a nice hot cup of tea in their special porcelain teacups.

THE END

ABOUT THE AUTHOR

Wendy Bartlett currently lives in Berkeley, California. She lived in England for thirteen years and visits her family regularly where she haunts the places she writes about like the Old Bailey, the River Thames and Rottingdean. She re-published her novel *Broad Reach* in 2019 and has published four children's books recently, including the popular children's novel: *The Flood.* The new edition of *Cellini's Revenge, The Mystery of the Silver Cups,* Book 1, is the first volume of a trilogy, and this one is Book 2. Book 3 is coming out in early 2021.

Wendy has written much poetry, seven novels and one screenplay. She is excited to work on her writing every day, telling great stories.

The Elizabeth Books
Written and Illustrated by Wendy Bartlett
Available through Indiebound.org, bookshop.org, Apple Books, Nook, and Kobo as well as other print and ebook retailers worldwide

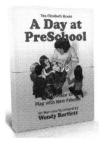

A beautifully illustrated book for children attending preschool showing all the activities children do in preschool: meeting new friends, listening to stories, swinging on the tire swing, playing table games, singing with a guitar, hammering, riding bikes, and playing in the sand. Teachers, parents, and children will love this book because they can point and say, "We go to a school like that!"

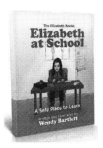

First grade is a challenge with new friends, maybe a new teacher and a feeling of advancement into the world of reading and writing. It is a time of friendship, sharing, learning and playing. It is a place where children come into their own, a secure leap into the world of math and science, and the beginning of learning to spell and sound out whole sentences. It is fun!

My mother sketches me all over Paris, whether of me eating an ice cream cone under the Eiffel Tower, or washing socks in the bidet, or going on the merry-go-round. It is lots of fun being her model! It takes many turns for me on the merry-go-round for her to finish her drawing. I don't mind a bit! Paris is amazing!

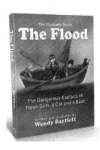

When eleven-year-old Elizabeth is left to babysit her four-year-old sister one rainy night, neither of them expect the adventure that unfolds. Their parents don't return home, and by morning there is a flood that fills the first floor of their house. Elizabeth must take initiative and make an agonizing decision: whether to stay put where her parents might find them, or to be brave and leave home to go in search of their parents. Dangers loom in either scenario.

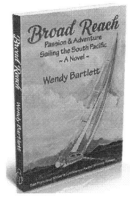

With her only child off to college, Sarah, a divorcée, is overwhelmed with emptiness. Here home overlooking San Francisco Bay is quiet, and her work with young children is routine. Most of all, her heart has become an excruciating vacuum.

When she meets a very sexy and charming Englishman tending his sailboat, Sarah makes an impulsive decision. It takes little to persuade her to join this mysterious sailor for an around-the-world cruise as his second mate, despite her amateur knowledge of sailing.

At first, warm winds, lust, and romance fill her days as they journey to the South Pacific. Soon her romantic idyll is rocked by the stormy seas as the dark side of her captain is revealed against the harsh backdrop of sailing. As life on the water becomes unforgiving, Sarah finds herself plunged into an abyss of fear and confusion, and ultimately, the greatest challenge she has ever faced.

Broad Reach *is engaging, real and powerful. While most sailing stories romanticize the experience, this gripping novel explores the hard, cold, nitty-gritty, crazy-making, dark side of small-boat ocean cruising. A must read!*
—**William McGinnis, author of** *Sailing the Greek Islands,* **Whitewater: A Thriller, Gold Bay, The Guide's Guide, Whitewater Rafting** **and more.**

COMING SOON

Cellini's Revenge

THE MYSTERY
OF THE SILVER CUPS
BOOK 3

This trilogy is about the mystery of the disappearance of the twelve silver cups that were made by the silversmith, Benvenuto Cellini, in 1527 and spans many stories of the cups for about five centuries until the early 21st Century. The cups bring bad luck to those who own them, unless and until they are returned to Italy.

Book 1: Catherine, David's wife, is blamed for David's murder and is sent to Holloway Prison for twelve years. When she gets out, she decides to find out who the real culprit is, and travels to Rottingdean to find the cups, where she finds out David's secrets.

Book 2: Peter, who wonders who his father is, meets Jeannie, a wild young woman, whom he marries. They have endless troubles, and Peter thinks it must have something to do with the cups, perhaps still in England.

Book 3: Peter, now a single father, meets Susan when the plane crashes at Heathrow and their children survive. He works through his life's tragedies, and is frustrated by his parents who are still spellbound by the Cellini cups, as he chases them to Italy and back. A mysterious man turns up from the past.

Book Club Questions

1. What was your favorite part of the book?

2. Which scene stuck with you most?

3. What surprised you about the book?

4. If you could ask the author anything, what would it be?

5. Did this book remind you of Cellini's Revenge, Book 1?

6. Did this book strike you as original?

7. Which characters did you like best?

8. How did the settings impact the story?

9. Are you looking forward to Book 3, and Peter's new adventures?

10. Could this book also be a standalone?

LETTER TO MY READERS

Thank you very much for reading my novel, *Cellini's Revenge: The Mystery of the Silver Cups, Book 2*.

I appreciate your interest and hope you found it as exciting and fun to read as it was to write.

I would so appreciate your taking a moment to please write to me at wendyberk@aol.com and let me know what you think.

If you would like, you could also write an honest review wherever you bought this book online, like Amazon. Here's a direct link to my author page on that site. amazon.com/author/wendybartlett. Just click on the blue *Cellini's Revenge* cover.

If you missed Book 1, you can find it through the above link, and do keep an eye out for Book 3 of *Cellini's Revenge*, which I will be publishing soon. If you would like to be on the advance notice list for Book 3 and any of my future writings, please go to my website and sign up.

Thank you very much again for reading my novel.

Gratefully,

Wendy Bartlett

Wendy Bartlett, author
wendybartlett.com

Printed in Great Britain
by Amazon

67771909R00197